L[illegible]

It was a w[illegible] layers—the Amerind level, the Garden o[illegible] level, the Talanac, the Atlantean—a universe of green skies and fabled beasts. It was the playground-cosmos of the Lord Jadawin, with trans-gravitational gates to the other levels and other worlds.

But now those gates were being sabotaged to permit the entry of an invading force of "Bellers"—human bodies housing the transferred minds of rebel Lords—and their minions, who were seeking two things: total domination of every lord's private cosmos, now that they had achieved immortality, and the life of Kickaha the Trickster, who knew too much. . . .

# A PRIVATE COSMOS

Other ACE Books by Philip José Farmer:

BEHIND THE WALLS OF TERRA
THE GATES OF CREATION
THE MAKER OF UNIVERSES
THE STONE GOD AWAKENS
THE WIND WHALES OF ISHMAEL

# A PRIVATE COSMOS

PHILIP JOSÉ FARMER

SF
ace books
A Division of Charter Communications Inc.
A GROSSET & DUNLAP COMPANY
51 Madison Avenue
New York, New York 10010

A PRIVATE COSMOS



All characters in this book are fictitious. Any resemblance to actual persons, living or dead, is purely coincidental.

An ACE Book

This Ace printing: June 1981

Published Simultaneously in Canada

2 4 6 8 0 9 7 5 3 1
Manufactured in the United States of America

# INTRODUCTION

IT ALL GOES BACK to my childhood of about a year ago, when I read *The Maker of Universes*. I recall it to have been a sunny Saturday in Baltimore and its morning, when I picked up Philip José Farmer's book with the green Gaughan sky and the gray Gaughan harpy (Podarge) on the front, to read a page or two before beginning work on a story of my own. I didn't do any writing that day.

I finished reading the book and immediately dashed off to my local purveyor of paperbacks, to locate the sequel which I knew existed, *The Gates of Creation*. When I'd finished reading it, the sunny morning in Saturday and its Baltimore had gone away and night filled the day all the way up to the top of the sky. The next thing that I wrote was not my story, but a fan letter to Philip José Farmer.

My intention was not to tell the man who had written *The Lovers* and *Fire and the Night* and *A Woman A Day* that I thought these two new ones were the best things he had ever done. If he'd done a painting, composed a piece of music, I couldn't compare them to his stories or even to each other. The two books I had just then finished reading were of the adventure-romance sort, and I felt they were exceedingly good examples of the type. They are different from his other stories, styles, themes, different even from each other, and hence, as always, incomparable. I had hoped there would be a third one, and I was very pleased to learn that he was working on it.

In other words, I looked forward for over a year to the book you are presently holding in your hands.

In considering my own feelings, to determine precisely what it was that caused me to be so taken by the first two books, I found that there are several reasons for the appeal they hold for me:

1) I am fascinated by the concept of physical immortality and the ills and benefits attendant thereto. This theme runs through the books like an highly polished strand of copper wire. 2) The concept of pocket universes—a thing quite distinct, as I see it, from various parallel worlds notions—the idea of such universes, specifically created to serve the ends of powerful and intelligent beings, is a neat one. Here it allows for, among other things, the fascinating structure of the World of Tiers.

To go along with these concepts, Philip Farmer assembled a cast of characters of the sort I enjoy. Kickaha is a roguish fellow; heroic, tricky and very engaging. Also, he almost steals the first book from Wolff. The second book is packed with miserable, scheming, wretched, base, lowdown, mean and nasty individuals who would cut one another's throats for the fun of it, but unfortunately have their lots cast together for a time. Being devilish fond of the Elizabethan theater, I was very happy to learn early in the story that they were all of them close relatives.

> A sacred being may be attractive or repulsive—a swan or an octopus—beautiful or ugly—a toothless hag or a fair young child—good or evil—a Beatrice or a Belle Dame Sans Merci—historical fact or fiction—a person met on the road or an image encountered in a story or a dream—it may be noble or something unmentionable in a drawing room, it may be anything it likes on condition, but this condition is absolute, that it arouse awe.
>
> —*Making, Knowing and Understanding*
>
> W. H. Auden

Philip José Farmer lives West of the Sun at the other end of the world from me in a place called California. We have never met, save in the pages of his stories. I admire his sense of humor and his facility for selecting the perfect final sentence for everything he writes. He can be stark, dark, smoky, bright, and any color of the emotional spectrum. He has a fascinating sense of the Sacred and the Profane. Put quite simply, he arouses awe. He has the talent and the skill to handle the sacred objects every writer must touch in order to convert the reader, in that timeless, spaceless place called Imagination.

Since I've invoked Auden, I must go on to agree with his observation that a writer cannot read another author's things without comparing them to his own. I do this constantly. I almost always come out feeling weak as well as awed whenever I read the works of three people who write science fiction: Sturgeon, Farmer and Bradbury. They know what's sacred, in that very special trans-subjective way where personal specifics suddenly give way and become universals and light up the human condition like a neon-lined Christmas tree. And Philip José Farmer is special in a very unusual way . . .

Everything he says is something *I* would like to say, but for some reason or other, cannot. He exercises that thing Henry James called an "angle of vision" which, while different from my own a.v., invariably jibes with the way I feel about things. But I can't do it his way. This means that somebody can do what I love most better than I can, which makes me chew my beard and think of George London as Mephistopheles, back at the old Metropolitan Opera, in Gounoud's *Faust*, when Marguerita ascended to heaven: he reached out and an iron gate descended before him; he grasped a bar, looked On High for a moment, averted his face, sank slowly to his knees, his hand sliding down the bar: curtain then: that's how I feel. *I* can't do it, but *it* can be done.

Beyond this, what can I say about a particular Philip José Farmer story?

Shakespeare said it better, in *Antony and Cleopatra*:

> *Lepidus*. What manner o' thing is your crocodile?

*Antony*. It is shaped, sir, like itself; and it is as broad as it hath breadth. It is just so high as it is, and moves with its own organs. It lives by that which nourisheth it; and the elements once out of it, it transmigrates.

*Lepidus*. What color is it of?

*Antony*. Of its own color, too.

*Lepidus*. 'Tis a strange serpent.

*Antony*. 'Tis so. And the tears of it are wet.

(Act II, Scene VII.)

Indeed, Sir, they are. It is the skill that goes with the talent that makes them so. Each of its products are different, complete, unique, and this one is no exception. I rejoice that such a man as Philip José Farmer walks among us, writes there, too. There aren't many like him. None, I'd say.

But read his story and see what I mean.

Now it is a cold, gray day in February and its Baltimore. But it doesn't matter. Philip José Farmer, out there somewhere West of the Sun, if by your writing you ever intended to give joy to another human being, know by this that you have succeeded and brightened many a cold, gray day in the seasons of my world, as well as having enhanced the lighter ones with something I'll just call splendor and let go at that.

The colors of this one are its own and the tears of it are wet. Philip José Farmer wrote it. There is nothing more to say.

ROGER ZELAZNY

*Baltimore, Md.*

# I

UNDER A GREEN SKY and a yellow sun, on a black stallion with a crimson-dyed mane and blue-dyed tail, Kickaha rode for his life.

One hundred days ago, a thousand miles ago, he had left the village of the Hrowakas, the Bear People. Weary of hunting and of the simple life, Kickaha suddenly longed for a taste—more than a taste—of civilization. Moreover, his intellectual knife needed sharpening, and there was much about the Tishquetmoac, the only civilized people on this level, that he did not know.

So he put saddles and equipment on two horses, said goodbye to the chiefs and warriors, and kissed his two wives farewell. He gave them permission to take new husbands if he didn't return in six months. They said they would wait forever, at which Kickaha smiled, because they had said the same thing to their former husbands before these rode out on the warpath and never came back.

Some of the warriors wanted to escort him through the mountains to the Great Plains. He said no and rode out alone. He took five days to get out of the mountains. One day was lost because two young warriors of the Wakangishush tribe stalked him. They may have been waiting for months in the Black Weasel Pass, knowing that some day Kickaha would ride through it. Of all the greatly desired scalps of the hundred great warriors of the fifty Nations of the Great Plains and bordering mountain ranges, the scalp of Kickaha was the most valued. At least two hundred braves had made individual efforts to waylay him, and none had returned alive. Many war parties had come up into the mountains to attack the Hrowakas' stockaded fort on the high hill, hoping to catch the Bear People unawares and lift Kickaha's scalp—or head—during the fighting. Of these, only the great raid of the Oshangstawa tribe of the Half-Horses had come near to succeeding. The story of the raid and of the destruction of the terrible Half-Horses spread through the 129 Plains tribes and was sung in their council halls and chiefs' tepees during the Blood Festivals.

The two Wakangishush kept a respectable distance behind their quarry. They were waiting for Kickaha to camp when night came. They may have succeeded where so many others had failed, so careful and quiet were they, but a red raven, eagle-sized, flew down over Kickaha at dusk and cawed loudly twice.

Then it flew above one hidden brave, circled twice, flew above the tree behind which the other crouched, and circled twice. Kickaha, glad that he had taken the trouble to train the intelligent bird, smiled while he watched it. That night, he put an arrow into the first to approach his camp and a knife into the other three minutes later.

He was tempted to go fifty miles out of his way to hurl a spear, to which the braves' scalps would be attached, into the middle of the Wakangishush encampment. Feats such as this had given him the name of Kickaha, that is, Trickster, and he liked to keep up his reputation. This time, however, it did not seem worthwhile. The image of Talanac, The City That Is A Mountain, glowed in his mind like a jewel above a fire.

And so Kickaha contented himself with hanging the two scalpless corpses upside down from a branch. He turned his stallion's head eastward and thereby saved some Wakangishush lives and, possibly, his own. Kickaha bragged a lot about his cunning and speed and strength, but he admitted to himself that he was not invincible or immortal.

Kickaha had been born Paul Janus Finnegan in Terre Haute, Indiana, U. S. A., Earth, in a universe next door to this one. (All universes were next door to each other.) He was a muscular broad-shouldered youth six feet one inch tall and weighing 190 pounds. His skin was deeply tanned with slightly copper spots, freckles, here and there, and more than three dozen scars, varying from light to deep, on parts of his body and face. His reddish-bronze hair was thick, wavy, and shoulder-length, braided into two pigtails at this time. His face was usually merry with its bright green eyes, snub nose, long upper lip, and cleft chin.

The lionskin band around his head was edged with bear teeth pointing upward, and a long black-and-red feather from the tail of a hawk stuck up from the right side of the headband. He was unclothed from the waist up; around his neck was a string of bear teeth. A belt of turquoise-beaded bearskin supported dappled fawnskin trousers, and his moccasins were lionskin. The belt held a sheath on each side. One held a large steel knife; the other, a smaller knife perfectly balanced for throwing.

The saddle was the light type which the Plains

tribes had recently adopted in place of blankets. Kickaha held a spear in one hand and the reins in the other, and his feet were in stirrups. Quivers and sheaths of leather hanging from the saddle held various weapons. A small round shield on which was painted a snarling bear's head was suspended from a wooden hook attached to the saddle. Behind the saddle was a bearskin robe rolled to contain some light cooking equipment. A bottle of water in a clay wicker basket hung from another saddle hook.

The second horse, which trotted along behind, carried a saddle, some weapons, and light equipment.

Kickaha took his time getting down out of the mountains. Though he softly whistled tunes of this world, and of his native Earth, he was not carefree. His eyes scanned everything before him, and he frequently looked backward.

Overhead, the yellow sun arced slowly in the cloudless light green sky. The air was sweet with the odors of white flowers blooming, with pine needles, and an occasional whiff of a purpleberry bush. A hawk screamed once, and twice he heard bears grunting in the woods.

The horses pricked up their ears at this but they did not become nervous. They had grown up with the tame bears that the Hrowakas kept within the village walls.

And so, alertly but pleasantly, Kickaha came down off the mountains onto the Great Plains. At this point, he could see far over the country because this was the zenith of a 160 mile gentle curve of a section. His way would be so subtly downhill for eighty miles that he would be almost unaware of it. Then there would be a river or lake to cross, and he would go almost imperceptibly up. To his left, seeming only fifty miles away, but actually a thousand, was the monolith of Abharhploonta. It towered a hundred thousand feet upward, and on its top was another land and another monolith. Up there was Dracheland, where Kickaha was known as Baron Horst von Horstmann. He had not been there for two years, and if he were to return, he would be a baron without a castle. His wife on that level had decided not to put up with his long absences and so had divorced him and married his best friend there, the Baron Siegfried von Listbat. Kickaha had given his castle to the two and had left for the Amerind level, which, of all levels, he loved the most.

His horses pulling the ground along at a canter, Kickaha watched for signs of enemies. He also watched the animal life, comprised of those still known on Earth, of those that had died off there, and of animals from other universes. All of these had been brought into this universe by the Lord, Wolff, when he was known as Jadawin. A few had been created in the biolabs of the palace on top of the highest monolith.

There were vast herds of buffalo, the small kind still known in North America, and the giants that had perished some ten thousand years ago on the American plains. The great gray bulks of curving-tusked mammoths and mastodons bulked in the distance. Some gigantic creatures, their big heads weighted down with many knobby horns and down-curving teeth projecting from horny lips, browsed on the grass. Dire wolves, tall as Kickaha's chest, trotted along the edge of a buffalo herd and waited for a calf to stray away from its mother. Further on, Kickaha saw a tan-and-black striped body slinking along behind a clump of tall grass and knew that Felis Atrox, the great maneless nine hundred pound lion that had once roamed the grassy plains of Arizona, was hoping to catch a mammoth calf away from its mother. Or perhaps it had some faint hopes of killing one of the multitude of antelope that was grazing nearby.

Above, hawks and buzzards circled. Once, a faint V of ducks passed overhead and a honking floated down. They were on their way to the rice swamps up in the mountains.

A herd of gawky long-necked creatures, looking like distant cousins of the camel, which they were, lurched by him. There were several skinny-legged foals with them, and these were what a pack of dire wolves hoped to pull down if the elders became careless.

Life and the promise of death was everywhere. The air was sweet; not a human being was in sight. A herd of wild horses galloped off in the distance, led by a magnificent roan stallion. Everywhere were the beasts of the plains. Kickaha loved it. It was dangerous, but it was exciting, and he thought of it as his world—his despite the fact that it had been created and was still owned by Wolff, the Lord, and he, Kickaha, had been an intruder. But this world was, in a sense, more his than Wolff's, since he certainly took more advantage of it than Wolff, who usually kept to the palace on top of the highest monolith.

The fiftieth day, Kickaha came to the Tishquetmoac Great Trade Path. There was no trail in the customary sense, since the grass was no less dense than the surrounding grass. But every mile of it was marked by two wooden posts the upper part of which had been carved in the likeness of

Ishquettlammu, the Tishquetmoac god of commerce and of boundaries. The trail ran for a thousand miles from the border of the empire of Tishquetmoac, curving over the Great Plains to touch various semipermanent trading places of the Plains and mountain tribes. Over the trail went huge wagons of Tishquetmoac goods to exchange for furs, skins, herbs, ivory, bones, captured animals, and human captives. The trail was treaty-immune from attack; anyone on it was safe in theory, at least, but if he went outside the narrow path marked off by the carved poles, he was fair prey for anybody.

Kickaha rode on the trail for several days because he wanted to find a trade-caravan and get news of Talanac. He did not come across any and so left the trail because it was taking him away from the direct route to Talanac. A hundred days after he had left the Hworakas village, he encountered the trail again. Since it led straight to Talanac, he decided to stay on it.

An hour after dawn, the Half-Horses appeared.

Kickaha did not know what they were doing so close to the Tishquetmoac border. Perhaps they had been making a raid, because, although they did not attack anybody on The Great TradePath, they did attack Tishquetmoac outside it.

Whatever the reason for their presence, they did not have to give Kickaha an excuse. And they would certainly do their best to catch him, since he was their greatest enemy.

Kickaha urged his two horses into a gallop. The Half-Horses, a mile away to his left, broke into a gallop the moment they saw him racing. They could run faster than a horse burdened with a man, but he had a good lead on them. Kickaha knew that an outpost was four miles ahead and that if he could get within its walls, he would be safe.

The first two miles he ran the stallion beneath him as swiftly as it would go. It gave its rider everything it had; foam blew from its mouth and wet his chest. Kickaha felt bad about this, but he certainly wasn't going to spare the animal if foundering it meant saving his own life. Besides, the Half-Horses would kill the stallion for food.

At the end of the two miles, the Half-Horses were close enough for him to determine their tribe. They were Shoyshatel, and their usual roving grounds were three hundred miles away, near the Trees of Many Shadows. They looked like the centaurs of Earth myth, except that they were larger and their faces and trappings certainly were not Grecian. Their heads were huge, twice as large as a human being's, and the faces were dark, high-cheekboned, and broad, the faces of Plains Indians. They wore feathered bonnets on their heads or bands with feathers; their hair was long and black and plaited into one or two pigtails.

The upright human body of the centaur contained a large bellows-like organ to pump air into the pneumatic system of the horse part. This swelled and shrank below the human breastbone and added to their weird and sinister appearance.

Originally, the Half-Horses were the creations of Jadawin, Lord of this universe. He had fashioned and grown the centaur bodies in his biolabs. The first centaurs had been provided with human brains from Scythian and Sarmatian nomads of Earth and from some Achaean and Pelasgian tribesmen. So it was that some Half-Horses still spoke these tongues, though most had long ago adopted the language of some Amerindian tribe of the Plains.

Now the Shoyshatel galloped hard after him, almost confident that they had their archenemy in their power. *Almost* because experience had disillusioned many of the Plains people of the belief that Kickaha could be easily caught. Or, if caught, kept.

The Shoyshatel, although they lusted to capture him alive so they could torture him, probably intended to kill him as soon as possible. Trying to take him alive would require restraint and delicacy on their part, and if they restrained themselves, they might find that he was gone.

Kickaha transferred to the other horse, a black mare with silver mane and tail, and urged it to its top speed. The stallion dropped off, its chest white with foam, shaking and blowing, and then fell when a Half-Horse speared it.

Arrows shot past him; spears fell behind him. Kickaha did not bother returning the fire. He crouched over the neck of his mare and shouted encouragement. Presently, as the Half-Horses drew closer, and the arrows and spears came nearer, Kickaha saw the outpost on top of a low hill. It was square and built of sharpened logs set upright in the ground, and had overhanging blockhouses on each side. The Tishquetmoac flag, green with a scarlet eagle swallowing a black snake, flew from a pole in the middle of the post.

Kickaha saw a sentry stare at them for a few seconds and then lift the end of a long slim bugle to his lips. Kickaha could not hear the alarm because the wind was against him and also because the pound of hooves was too loud.

Foam was pouring from the mare's mouth, but she raced on. Even so, the Half-Horses were drawing closer, and the arrows and spears were flying dangerously near. A bola, its three stones forming a triangle of death, almost struck him. And then, just as the gates to the fort opened and the Tishquetmoac cavalry rode out, the mare stumbled. She tried to recover and succeeded. Kickaha knew that the mishap was not caused by fatigue but by an arrow, which had plunged slantingly into her rump, piercing at such a shallow angle that the head of the arrow was out in the air again. She could not go much longer.

Another arrow plunged into the flesh just behind the saddle. She fell, and Kickaha threw himself out and away as she went down and then over. He tried to land running but could not because of the speed and rolled over and over. The shadow of the rolling horse passed over him; she crashed and lay still. Kickaha was up and running toward the Tishquetmoac.

Behind him, a Half-Horse shouted in triumph, and Kickaha turned his head to see a feather-bonneted chief, a spear held high, thundering in toward him. Kickaha snatched his throwing knife out, whirled, took a stance, and, as the centaur began the cast of spear at him, threw his knife. He jumped to one side immediately after the blade had left his hand. The spear passed over his shoulder, near his neck. The Half-Horse, the knife sticking out of the bellows organ below his chest, cartwheeled past Kickaha, bones of equine legs and backbone of the human upright part cracking with the impact. Then spears flew over Kickaha into the Half-Horses. One intercepted a brave who thought that he had succeeded where the chief had failed. His spear was in his hand; he was trusting to no skill in casting but meant to drive it through Kickaha with the weight of his five hundred pound body.

The brave went down. Kickaha picked up the spear and hurled it into the horse-breast of the nearest centaur. Then the cavalry, which outnumbered the Half-Horses, was past him, and there was a melee. The Half-Horses were driven off at great cost to the human beings. Kickaha got onto a horse which had lost its master to a Half-Horse tomahawk and galloped with the cavalry back to the post.

The commander of the outpost said to Kickaha, "You always bring much trouble with you. Always."

Kickaha grinned and said, "Confess now. You were glad for the excitement. You've been bored to death, right?"

The captain grinned back.

That evening, a Half-Horse, carrying a shaft of wood with a long white heron's feather at its tip, approached the fort. Honoring the symbol of the herald, the captain gave orders to withhold fire. The Half-Horse stopped outside the gates and shouted at Kickaha, "You have escaped us once again, Trickster! But you will never be able to leave Tishquetmoac, because we will be waiting for you! Don't think you can use the Great Trade Path to be safe from us! We will honor the Path; everyone on it will be untouched by the Half-Horses! Everyone except you, Kickaha! We will kill you! We have sworn not to return to our lodges, our women and children, until we have killed you!"

Kickaha shouted down to him, "Your women

will have taken other husbands and your children will grow up without remembering you! You will never catch or kill me, you half-heehaws!"

The next day a relief party rode up, and the Tishquetmoac cavalry on leave rode out with Kickaha to the city of Talanac. The Half-Horses did not appear, and after Kickaha had been in the city for a while, he forgot about the threats of the Shoyshatel. But he was to remember.

## II

THE WATCETCOL RIVER originates in a river which branches off from the Guzirit in Khamshemland, or Dracheland, on the monolith Abharhploonta. It flows through dense jungle to the edge of the monolith and then plunges through a channel which the river has cut out of hard rock. The river falls for a long distance as solid sheets of water, then, before reaching the bottom of the hundred thousand foot monolith, it becomes spray. Clouds roll out halfway down the monolith and hide the spray and foam from the eyes of men. The bottom is also hidden; those who have tried to walk into the fog have reported that it is like blackest night and, after a while, the wetness becomes solid.

A mile or two from the base the fog extends, and somewhere in there the fog becomes water again and then a river. The stream flows through a narrow channel in limestone and then broadens out later. It zigzags for about five hundred miles, straightens out for twenty miles and then splits to flow around a solid rock mountain. The river reunites on the other side of the mountain, turns sharply, and flows westward for sixty miles. There it disappears into a vast cavern, and it may be presumed that it drops through a network of caverns inside the monolith on top of which is the Amerindian level. Where it comes out, only the eagles of Podarge, Wolff, and Kickaha know.

The mountain which the river had islanded was a solid block of jade.

When Jadawin formed this universe, he poured out a three thousand foot high, roughly pyramid-shaped piece of mingled jadeite and nephrite, striated in apple-green, emerald-green, brown, mauve, yellow, blue, gray, red, and black and various shades thereof. Jadawin deposited it to cool on the edge of the Great Plains and later directed the river to flow around its base.

For thousands of years, the jade mountain was untouched except by birds that landed on it and fish that flicked against the cool greasy roots. When the Amerindians were gated through to his world, they came across the jade mountain. Some tribes made it their god, but the nomadic peoples did not settle down near it.

Then a group of civilized people from ancient Mexico were taken into this world near the jade mountain. This happened, as nearly as Jadawin (who later became Wolff) could recall, about 1,500 Earth-years ago. The involuntary immigrants may have been of that civilization which the later Mexicans called Olmec. They called themselves Tishquetmoac. They built wooden houses and wooden walls on the bank to the west and east of the mountain, and they called the mountain Talanac. Talanac was their name for the Jaguar God.

The *kotchulti* (literally, god-house) or temple of Toshkouni, deity of writing, mathematics, and music, is halfway up the stepped-pyramid city of

Talanac. It faces the Street of Mixed Blessings, and, from the outside, does not look impressively large. The front of the temple is a slight bulging of the mountainside, a representation of the bird-jaguar face of Toshkouni. Like the rest of the interior of this mountain, all hollowing out, all cleaving away, all bas- and alto-relief, have been done by rubbing or drilling. Jade cannot be chipped or flaked; it can be drilled, but most of the labor in making beauty out of the stone comes from rubbing. Friction begets loveliness and utility.

Thus, the white-and-black striated jade in this area had been worn away by a generation of slaves using crushed corundum for abrasives and steel and wooden tools. The slaves had performed the crude basic labor; then the artisans and artists had taken over. The Tishquetmoac claim that form is buried in the stone and that it is revealed seems to be true—in the case of Talanac.

"The gods hide; men discover," the Tishquetmoac say.

When a visitor to the temple enters through the doorway, which seems to press down on him with Toshkouni's cat-teeth, he steps into a great cavern. It is illuminated by sunlight pouring through holes in the ceiling and by a hundred smokeless torches. A choir of black-robed monks with shaven, scarlet-painted heads stands behind a waist-high white-and-red jade screen. The choir chants praises to the Lord of The World, Ollimaml, and to Toshkouni.

At each of the six corners of the chamber stands an altar in the shape of a beast or bird or a young woman on all fours. Cartographs bulge from the surfaces of each, and little animals and abstract symbols, all the result of years of dedicated labor and long-enduring passion. An emerald, as large as a big man's head, lies on one altar, and there is a story about this which also concerns Kickaha. Indeed, the emerald was one of the reasons Kickaha was so welcome in Talanac. The jewel had once been stolen and Kickaha had recovered it from the Khamshem thieves of the next level and returned it—though not gratis. But that is another story.

Kickaha was in the library of the temple. This was a vast room deep in the mountain, reached only by going through the public altar room and a long wide corridor. It, too, was lit by sunlight shooting through shafts in the ceiling and by torches and oil lamps. The walls had been rubbed until thousands of shallow niches were made, each of which now held a Tishquetmoac book. The books were rolls of lambskin sewn together, with the roll secured at each end to an ebony-wood cylinder. The cylinder at the beginning of the book was hung on a tall jade frame, and the roll was slowly unwound by the reader, who stood before it.

Kickaha was in one well-lit corner, just below a hole in the ceiling. A black-robed priest, Takoacol, was explaining to Kickaha the meaning of some cartographs. During his last visit, Kickaha had studied the writing, but he had memorized only five hundred of the picture-symbols, and fluency required knowing at least two thousand.

Takoacol was indicating with a long-nailed yellow-painted finger the location of the palace of the emperor, the *miklosiml*.

"Just as the palace of the Lord of this world stands on top of the highest level of the world, so the palace of the *miklosiml* stands on the uppermost level of Talanac, the greatest city in the world."

Kickaha did not contradict him. At one time, the capital city of Atlantis, the country occupying the inner part of the next-to-highest level, had been four times as large and populous as Talanac. But it had been destroyed by the Lord then in power, and now the ruins housed only bats, birds, and lizards, great and small.

"But," the priest said, "where the world has five levels, Talanac has thrice three times three levels, or streets."

The priest put the tips of the excessively long fingernails of his hands together, and, half-closing his slightly slanted eyes, intoned a sermon on the magical and theological properties of the numbers three, seven, nine, and twelve. Kickaha did not interrupt him, even though he did not understand some of the technical terms.

He had heard, just once, a strange clinking in the next room. Just once was enough for him, who had survived because he did not have to be warned twice. Moreover, the price he paid for still living was a certain uncomfortable amount of anxiety. Always, he maintained a minimum amount of tension even in moments of recreation and lovemaking. Thus, he never entered a place, not even in the supposedly safe palace of the Lord, without first finding the possible hiding places for ambushers, avenues of escape, and hiding places for himself.

He had no reason to think that there was any danger for him in this city and especially in the sacrosanct temple-library. But there had been many times when he had had no reason to fear danger and yet the danger was there.

The clinking was weakly repeated. Kickaha,

without an "Excuse me!" ran to the archway through which the unidentified, hence sinister, noise had come. Many of the black-robed priests looked up from their slant-topped desks where they were painting cartographs on skin or looked aside from the books hanging before them. Kickaha was dressed like a well-to-do Tishquetmoac, since his custom was to look as much like a native as possible wherever he was, but his skin was two shades paler than the lightest of theirs. Besides, he wore two knives, and that alone marked him off. He was the first, aside from the emperor, to enter this room armed.

Takoacol called out to him, asking if anything was wrong. Kickaha turned and put a finger to his lips, but the priest continued to call. Kickaha shrugged. The chances were that he would end up by seeming foolish or overly apprehensive to the onlookers, as had happened many times in other places. He did not care.

As he neared the archway, he heard more clinkings and then some slight creakings. These sounded to him as if men in armor were slowly—perhaps cautiously—coming down the hallway. The men could not be Tishquetmoac because their soldiers wore quilted-cloth armor. They had steel weapons, but these would not make the sounds he had heard.

Kickaha thought of retreating across the library and disappearing into one of the exits he had chosen; in the shadows of an archway, he could observe the newcomers as they entered the library.

But he could not resist the desire to know immediately who the intruders were. He risked one fast peek around the corner.

Twenty feet away walked a man in a complete suit of steel armor. Close behind him, by twos, came four knights, then at least thirty soldiers, swordsmen and archers. There might be more because the line continued on around the curve of the hall. Kickaha had been surprised, startled, and shocked many times before. This time, he reacted more slowly than ever in his life. For several seconds, he stood motionless while the ice-armor of shock thawed.

The knight in the lead, a tall man whose face was visible because of the opened visor of his helmet, was the king of Eggesheim, Erich von Turbat.

He and his men had no business being on this level! They were Drachelanders of the level above this, all natives of the inland plateau on top of the monolith which soared up from this level. Kickaha, who was known as Baron Horst von Horstmann in Dracheland, had visited the king, von Turbat, several times and once had knocked him off a horse in a joust.

To see him and his men on this level was startling enough, since they would have had to climb down a hundred thousand feet of monolith cliff to get to it. But their presence within the city was incomprehensible. Nobody had ever penetrated the peculiar defences of the city, except for Kickaha on one occasion, and he had been alone.

Unfreezing, Kickaha turned and ran. He was thinking that the Teutoniacs must have used one of the "gates" which permitted instantaneous transportation from one place to another. However, the Tishquetmoac did not know where the three "gates" were or even guessed that they existed. Only Wolff, who was the Lord of this universe, his mate Chryseis, and Kickaha had ever used them; or, theoretically, they were the only ones who knew how to use them.

Despite this, the Teutoniacs were here. How they had found the gates and why they had come through them to this palace were questions to be answered later—if ever.

Kickaha felt a surge of panic which he rammed back down. This could only mean that an alien Lord had successfully invaded this universe. That he could send men after Kickaha meant that Wolff and Chryseis were unable to prevent him. And that might mean they were dead. It did mean that, if they were alive, they were powerless and therefore needed his help. Ha! His help! He was running for his life again!

There were three hidden gates. Two were in the Temple of Ollimaml on top of the city, next to the emperor's palace. One gate was a large one and must have been used by von Turbat's men if they had entered in any force. And they must have great force, otherwise they would never have been able to overcome the large and fanatical bodyguard of the emperor and the garrison.

Unless, Kickaha thought, unless the invaders had somehow been able to capture the emperor immediately. The Tishquetmoac would obey the commands of their ruler, even if they knew they originated from his captors. This would last for a time, anyway. The people of Talanac were, after all, human beings, not ants, and they would eventually revolt. They regarded their emperor as a god incarnate, second only to the all-powerful creator Ollimaml, but they loved their jade city, too, and they had a history of twice committing deicide.

In the meantime . . . in the meantime, Kickaha

was running toward the archway opposite the one through which the invaders must be stepping just now. A shout spurred him on, then many were yelling. Some of the priests were crying out, but several of the cries were in the debased Middle High German of the Drachelanders. A clash of armors and of swords formed a base beneath the vocal uproar.

Kickaha hoped that the hallway was the only one the Drachelanders were using. If they had been able to get to all the entrances to this room—no, they couldn't. The arch ahead led to a hall which only went deeper into the mountain, as far as he knew. It could be entered by other halls, but none of these had openings to the outside. That is, he had been told so. Perhaps his informants were lying for some reason, or perhaps they hadn't understood his imperfect Tishquetmoac speech.

Lied to or not, he had to take this avenue. The only trouble with it, even if it were free of invaders, was that it would end up in the mountain.

## III

THE LIBRARY was an immense room. It had taken five hundred slaves, rubbing and drilling twenty-four hours a day, twenty years to complete the basic work. The distance from the archway he had just left to the one he desired was about 180 yards. Some of the invaders had time to enter the library and take one shot at him.

Knowing this, Kickaha began to zigzag. When he neared the arch, he threw himself down and rolled through the exit. Arrows slissed above him and kukked into the stone wall or bunged off the floor near him. Kickaha uncoiled to his feet and raced on down the hallway; he came to the inevitable curve, and then stopped. Two priests trotted past him. They looked at him but said nothing. They forgot about him when shrill cries stung their ears, and they ran toward the source of noise. He thought they would be acting more intelligently if they ran the other way, since it sounded as if the Drachelanders might be massacring the priests in the library.

However, the two would now run into the pursuers, and might delay them for a few seconds. Too bad about the priests, but it wasn't his fault if they were killed. Well, perhaps it was. But he did not intend to warn them if silence would help him keep ahead of the hunters.

He ran on. Just before he came to another forty-five degree bend, he heard screams behind him. He stopped and removed a burning torch from its fixture on the wall. Holding it high, he looked upward. Twenty feet from the top of his head was a round hole in the ceiling. It was dark, so Kickaha supposed that the shaft bent somewhere before it joined another.

The entire mountain was pierced with thousands of these shafts. All were at least three feet in diameter, since the slaves who had made the shafts and tunnels could not work in an area less than this.

Kickaha considered this shaft but gave up on it. There was nothing available to help him get up to it.

Hearing the scrape of metal against stone, he ran around the curve and then stopped. The first archer received a blazing torch in his face, screamed, staggered back, and knocked down the archer behind him. The conical steel helmets of both fell off and clanged on the floor.

Stooping, Kickaha ran forward, using the archer with the burned face, who had sat up, as a shield. He pulled the archer's long sword from his sheath. The man was holding his face with both hands and screaming that he was blind. The soldier he had knocked down stood up, thus preventing the bowmen who did see Kickaha from shooting at him. Kickaha rose and brought the sword down on the unprotected head of the soldier. Then he whirled and ran, stooping again.

Too late, some of the bowmen fired. The arrows struck the walls. He entered a large storage room.

There were many artifacts here, but those catching his attention were long extendible ladders for use in the library. He set one upright, its end propped against the lip of a shaft in the ceiling. He placed the sword at the foot of the ladder, then picked up another ladder and ran with it down the hall, went through a doorway into a branching hall, and stopped below another shaft.

Here he propped the ladder against the edge of the hole in the ceiling and climbed up. By bracing his back against one side of the shaft and his feet against the other, he could thrust-slide his body up the hollow.

He hoped that the first ladder and the sword by it would fool his pursuers, so they would waste time shooting arrows up its dark hole. When they realized he was not to be brought down like a bear in a hollow tree, they would think that he had managed to get to a branching shaft in time. Then some of them would go up the shaft after him. If they were smart, they would delay long enough to take off their heavy chain-mail shirts, skirts, leggings, and steel helmets.

If they were smart enough, though, they would also realize that he might be playing a trick. They would explore the halls deeper in. And they might soon be under this shaft and send an arrow through his body.

Inspired by this thought, he climbed more swiftly. He would back upward several inches, feet planted firmly, legs straining. Then he'd slide the feet up, then the back up, then the feet up—at least the walls were smooth and greasy-feeling jade, not rough steel, stone, or wood. After he had gone perhaps twenty feet upward—which meant a drop of forty feet to the floor—he came to a shaft which ran at right angles to his.

He had to twist around then so that he faced downward. He could see that the ladder still lay propped against the bright end of the shaft. There was no sound coming up the well. He pulled himself up and onto the horizontal floor.

At that moment, he heard a faint voice. The soldiers must have fallen for his ruse. They were either coming up that first tube after him or had already done so and were, possibly, in the same horizontal shaft in which he was.

Kickaha decided to discourage them. If he did find a way out, he might also find that they were right behind him—or worse, just below him. They could have passed bows and arrows from one to another up the shaft; if they had, they could shoot him down without danger to themselves.

Trying to figure out the direction of the shaft where he had left the first ladder, he came to a junction where three horizontal tunnels met above a vertical one. There the twilight of the place became a little brighter. He leaped across the hole in the floor and approached the brightening. On coming around a bend, he saw a Teutoniac bending over with his back to him. He was holding a torch, which a man in the vertical shaft had just handed to him. The man in the hole was muttering that the torch had scorched him. The man above was whispering fiercely that they should all be quiet.

The climbers had shed their armor and all arms except the daggers in the sheaths on their belts. However, a bow and a quiver of arrows was passed up to the soldier in the tunnel. The men in the vertical shaft were forming a chain to transport weapons. Kickaha noted that they would have been wiser to place six or seven in the tunnel first to prevent attack by their quarry.

Kickaha had thought of jumping the lone soldier at once, but he decided to wait until they had transported all the weapons they intended to use. And so bow after bow, quiver after quiver, swords, and finally even the armor was passed up and given to the man in the tunnel, who piled them neatly to one side. Kickaha was disgusted: didn't they understand that armor would only weigh them down and give their quarry an advantage? Moreover, the heavy thick mail and the heavy clothing underneath it would make them hot and sweaty. The only reason he could think of for this move was the rigidity of the military mind. If the regulations prescribed armor in every combat situation, then the armor would be worn, appropriate or not.

The soldier handling the material and those braced in the shafts bitched, though not loudly, about the heat and the strain. Kickaha could hear them plainly, but he supposed that the officers below could not.

At last, there were thirty-five bows, thirty-five quivers, and thirty-five swords, helmets, and chain mail suits piled on the floor. There were more soldiers than that in the hall when Kickaha had first seen the invaders, so it seemed that a number was going to stay below. Among them would be all the officers, who did not want to take the time and trouble to remove their steel plates and chain. From the shouted conversation between the man in the tunnel above and an officer below—which could have been done quietly if the men in the shaft had relayed the messages—the man in the tunnel was a noncom, a *shlikrum*, an aboriginal word borrowed by the medieval German conquerors from Earth to indicate a master sergeant.

Kickaha listened carefully, hoping to find out if any men were climbing up other shafts—he did not want to be trapped or jumped on from the rear. Nothing was said about other climbers, but this did not mean that there were none. Kickaha kept looking behind him, like a bird watching for cats, but he saw and heard nothing. The *shlikrum* should have been as nervously vigilant as he, but apparently he felt that he was safe.

That feeling evaporated like a glass of water in a vacuum. The *shlikrum* had bent over to help the top man out of the shaft when Kickaha plunged his knife several inches into the man's right buttock. The man screamed and then went headfirst into the hole, propelled by Kickaha's foot. He fell on the man he was trying to hoist out; the two fell on the man below; and so on until ten men, shrieking, dropped out of the hole in the ceiling. They splud-ded on top of each other, the sounds of impact weakening as the layer of bodies increased. The *shlikrum*, who had fallen further than the others, landed sprawling on the uppermost body. Although he was hurt, he was not knocked out. He leaped up, lost his footing, and fell down the pile of bodies onto the floor. There he lay moaning.

An officer in a full suit of armor strode clanking to him and bent over a little to speak to him. Kickaha could not hear the words because of the uproar in the hallway, so he aimed an arrow at the officer. The angle was awkward, but he had trained himself to shoot from many angles, and he sent the arrow true. It penetrated the juncture of shoulder and neck plates and drove deep into the flesh. The knight fell forward and on the noncom.

Kickaha was curious about the silvery casket strapped to the knight's back, because he had never seen anything like it before. Now was not the time to indulge his curiosity, however.

The soldiers who had been unpiling the bodies dropped their work and ran out of Kickaha's sight. There was a babble of voices and then silence after an officer roared for it. Kickaha recognized von Turbat's voice. It was only then that he began to realize the implications of this invasion and savage hunt for him.

Von Turbat was the king of the independent nation of Eggesheim, a mountainous country with perhaps sixty thousand citizens. At one time, as Baron Horst von Horstmann, Kickaha had had fairly amicable relations with him. After he had been defeated by Kickaha in a lancing joust and had then caught Kickaha making love to his daughter, von Turbat had been hostile. Not actively so, although he had made it plain that he would not be responsible for avenging Horstmann's death, if someone should kill Horstmann while he was under von Turbat's roof. Kickaha had taken off immediately after hearing this, and later, playing his role of robber baron, he had plundered a trade caravan on its way to Eggesheim. But circumstances had forced Kickaha to abandon his castle and identity and run for his life to this level. That had been a few years ago.

There was no reason why von Turbat should take such a terrible risk now to get revenge on Kickaha. In the first place, how had the king ever found out that Kickaha was here? How could he even know that Kickaha was von Horstmann? Why, if he had actually discovered the gates and their use, would he invade the dangerous city of

Talanac? There were too many questions.

Meanwhile, from the low voices and following sounds of leather boots running, and the sight of the end of a ladder being swung out and moved away, it was evident that the Teutoniacs would be coming up other shafts. Kickaha doubted that many of them would be armored or heavily armed, since he now had the armor and weapons of the majority. Of course, they would be sending off for reinforcements. He had better get moving.

Then one of the men in the pile crawled out, and Kickaha sent an arrow through him. He quickly shot five more bodies on the theory that if any of them were able to revive, he was eliminating a potential killer. He was busy for about five minutes, running up and down and across and back and forth through the various tunnels. Three times he was able to catch the soldiers coming up shafts and to shoot the top man. Twice he fired down through shafts at men walking in the hallway.

But he could not hope to run swiftly enough to cover all the shafts. And apparently the king was not counting casualties. The shafts originally entered were reentered, and lights and noises indicated that others were being climbed. Kickaha had to abandon all the weapons except for his knives in order to climb another vertical shaft. He intended to find a route to the openings of the shafts on the outside. There, high on the face of the mountain, above the Street of Mixed Blessings, he might be able to escape.

Von Turbat must surely know this, however; he would have archers on the streets above and below.

If he could only keep away from the soldiers in the networks of tunnels here until dark, he might be able to slip out across the jade cliffside. That is, he would if there were ornamental projections for him to use.

He became very thirsty. He had had no water all morning because he had been seized with the thirst for learning. Now the shock, the fighting and the running had dried him out. The roof of his mouth dripped a thick stalactitish saliva; his throat felt as if filled with desert pebbles dislodged from the hoof of a camel.

He might be able to go the rest of the day and the night without water if he had to, but he would be weakened. Therefore, he would get water. And since there was only one way to get it, he took that way.

He crept back toward the shaft up which he had just climbed but stopped a few feet from it. He smiled. What was the matter with him? He had been too shocked, his usual wiliness and unconventional thinking had been squeezed out of him for a while. He had passed up a chance to escape. It was a mad route to take, but its very insanity recommended it to him and, in fact, made it likely that he could succeed. If only he were not too late . . . !

The descent was easy. He came to the pile of armor. The soldiers had not yet approached this hole; they must still be coming up through shafts distant from this one. Kickaha removed his Tishquetmoac clothes and stuffed them in a mail shirt on the bottom of the pile. Hastily he put on a suit of armor, though he had to search to find a shirt and helmet big enough for him. Then he leaned over the hole and called down. He was a perfect mimic and, though it had been some years since he had heard the Eggesheimer dialect of

German, he evoked it without difficulty.

The soldiers stationed below suspected a trick. They were not so dumb after all. They did not, however, imagine what had actually happened. They thought that Kickaha might be trying to lure them into range of his bow.

"*Ikh'n d'untershlikrum Hayns Gimbat,*" he said. "I am the corporal Henry Gimbat."

Hayns was a common first name throughout Dracheland. Gimbat was an aboriginal name, as were most of the names ending in *-bat*. Gimbat was especially common in that area of Dracheland and among the lower classes, who were a mixture of aborigine and German. There were bound to be several men of that name among the invaders.

A sergeant strode out and then stopped to peer up the shaft.

"*Vo iss de trickmensh?*"

"*E n'iss hir, nettrlikh. Ikh hap durss.*" Or, "He isn't here, of course. I'm thirsty."

"*Frakk zu fyer de vass?*" the sergeant bellowed. "You ask for water? At a time like this! *Shaysskopp!*"

The request was genuine, but it was also just the thing to take suspicion away from Kickaha. While the sergeant was raving, torches from both sides of the tunnel heralded the approach of soldiers who had climbed up. Kickaha left the shaft opening to speak to the officer of the newcomers. This knight had taken off his armor, after all, apparently because von Turbat thought that an officer should be in charge of the hunt.

Kickaha recognized him; he was Baron von Diebrs, ruler of a small principality on the border of Eggesheim. He had been at court briefly while Kickaha was visiting.

Kickaha kept his head bent so the helmet would put part of his face in shadow, and he made his voice less deep. Von Diebrs listened to him but paid no attention to his features. To the baron, Kickaha was just another faceless low-class soldier. Kickaha reported that the Trickster was gone without a trace. He also hastened to say that he had asked for water, but that the sergeant seemed to think it was an unreasonable request.

The baron, licking his lips, did not think it was unreasonable. And so bottles of water were lifted on the ends of poles by men standing on the ladders, and Kickaha got to drink. He then tried to drop back out of sight, so that he could get down to the hallway and, hopefully, out of the temple. Von Diebrs frustrated him by ordering him to lead the way up the shaft to the next horizontal level. Von Diebrs also swore at him for putting the armor on, and Kickaha had to remove the mail. He was ready to strike or to run at the first sign of recognition from the baron, but von Diebrs was only interested in searching for the barbarian killer.

Kickaha wanted to ask questions. He could not, however, without making the others suspicious, so he kept quiet. He crawled up the shaft and then took the bows and quivers and long swords passed up. After that, the party split into two. One was to go one way; the other, down the opposite direction. When the party of which Kickaha was a member met another search party, they were to go upward again.

The levels they had just left became bright and noisy. More men were coming in, reinforcements to press the hunt. Von Turbat, or whoever was in charge of the entire invasion, must have affairs under excellent control, to spare so many soldiers.

Kickaha kept with the original group, since none of them knew him. And when they encountered other groups, Kickaha said nothing. He still wore the helmet, since he had not been ordered to take it off. A few others also had helmets.

The walking became more difficult, because the shafts were now so narrow that a man had to duckwalk to get through and a party must travel single file. The soldiers had thought they were in top condition, but this type of progress made their legs ache and quiver and their lower backs hurt. Although he was not suffering, Kickaha complained too, so that he did not appear different.

After what seemed like many hours but was probably no more than eighty minutes, the party of six crawled from a shaft into a little round chamber. The wall opposite had large round openings to the outside. The men leaned over the edge and looked down, where they could see troops on foot and mounted knights in the Street of Mixed Blessings. Though they were small figures, their markings were distinguishable. Kickaha recognized not only the flags and pennants and uniforms of Eggesheim but those of at least a dozen kingdoms and a few baronies.

There were bodies—predominantly those of Tishquetmoac streets and blood was spilled here and there. The fighting between the Teutoniacs and the Talanac garrisons must have taken place elsewhere, probably on top of the city.

Far below the streets was the river. The two bridges that Kickaha could see were jammed with refugees, all going outward and into the old city.

Presently, a Tishquetmoac rode down the long curving ramp from the street above and halted before von Turbat, who had just come out of the temple. The king got onto a horse before he would allow the Tishquetmoac to speak to him. This man was splendid in a headdress of long white curly feathers and a scarlet robe and green leggings. Probably, he was some functionary of the emperor. He was reporting to von Turbat, which must mean that the emperor had been captured.

There would be few hiding places for Kickaha even if he could get away. The people left in the city would obey their ruler's command, and if this was to report Kickaha's presence as soon as he was discovered, this they would do.

One of the soldiers with Kickaha spoke then of the reward offered for the capture of Kickaha or for information leading to the capture. Ten thousand *drachener* and the title, castle, lands, and citizens of the barony of Horstmann. If a commoner earned the reward, he and his family would automatically become nobles. The money was more than the king of Eggesheim got in taxes in two years.

Kickaha wanted to ask what had happened to Lisa von Horstmann, his wife, and von Listbat, his good friend who ran the barony in his absence. He dared not, but he sickened at the thought of what must have been their fate.

He leaned out of the window again to get fresh air, and he saw something that he had forgotten. Earlier, he had seen a knight just behind von Turbat, carrying a sword in one hand and a large steel casket under one arm. Now, this same knight accompanied von Turbat on the street, and when the king went back into the temple, he was followed closely by the knight with the casket.

Very strange, Kickaha thought. But this whole affair was very strange. He could explain nothing.

One thing was certain, however: Wolff couldn't be operating effectively as Lord of this world, otherwise this would not be happening. Either Wolff was dead or captive in his own palace, or he was hiding in this world or in another.

The corporal presently ordered the party to go back down. Again, all the shafts in their sector were explored. When they reached the hallway, they were tired, hot, hungry, and cross. Their ill-feelings were made worse by the verbal assaults from their officers. The knights could not believe that Kickaha had escaped them. Neither could von Turbat. He talked with his officers, made more detailed plans, and then ordered the search renewed. There was a delay while bottles of water, hard biscuits, and dried sticks of meat were passed around to the men. Kickaha hunched down against the wall with the others and spoke only when spoken to. The others of his group had served together but did not ask him what his platoon was—they were too tired and disgruntled to talk much of anything.

It was an hour after dusk before the search was called off. An officer commented that the Trickster would not get away. For one thing, the flow of refugees at all the bridges had been cut off. Every bridge was heavily guarded, and the banks of the river opposite the city were being patrolled. Moreover, a house-to-house search was being started even now.

This meant that the search parties would not get the sleep they longed for. They would stay up all night looking for Kickaha. They would stay up all the next day, and the following night, if Kickaha was not found.

The soldiers did not protest; they did not want a

whipping, ended by castration and then hanging. But among themselves, they muttered, and Kickaha paid attention to them to pick up information. They were tough, hardy men who griped but who would obey any order within reason and most senseless orders.

They marched along smartly enough though their thighs cried silently with pain. Kickaha had managed to get in the rear row of the platoon, and when they turned down onto a street with no natives and no other invaders, he disappeared into a doorway.

## IV

THE DOOR he stood by could not be opened from the outside, of course. It was barred on the inside with the big bolt that all Talanac citizens used to protect themselves from the criminals that prowled at night.

Where there is civilization, there are thieves. Kickaha was, at this moment, grateful for that fact. During the previous extended visit to Talanac, he had deliberately become intimate with some of the criminal class. These people knew many hidden routes in and out of the city, and Kickaha wanted knowledge of these in case he needed them. Moreover, he found the criminals he knew, mainly smugglers, to be interesting. One of them, Clatatol, was more than interesting. She was beautiful. She had long, straight, glossy black hair, big brown eyes, very long and thick eyelashes, a smooth bronzish skin, and a full figure, although, like most of the Tishquetmoac women, she was just a little too wide in the hips and a little too thick-calved. Kickaha seldom required perfection in others; he agreed that a little asymmetry was the foundation of genuine beauty.

So he had become Clatatol's lover at the same time he was courting the emperor's daughter. This double life had eventually tripped him up, and he was asked politely to leave Talanac by the emperor's brother and the chief of police. He could return whenever the emperor's daughter got married and so would be shut up in purdah, as was the custom among the nobility. Kickaha had left without even saying goodbye to Clatatol. He had visited one of the little dependent kingdoms to the east, a nation of civilized peoples called the Quatsl-slet. These had been conquered long ago and now paid tribute to Talanac but still spoke their own language and adhered to their own somewhat peculiar customs. While with them, Kickaha heard that the emperor's daughter had married her uncle, as was the custom. He could return, but instead he had gone back to the Hrowakas, the Bear People, in the mountains by the Great Plains.

So he would now get to Clatatol's house and find out if she could smuggle him out of the city . . . if she would have him, he thought. She had tried to kill him the last time he had seen her. And if she had forgiven him since, she would be angry again because he had returned to Talanac and had not tried to see her.

"Ah, Kickaha!" he murmured to himself. "You think you're so smart, and you're always fouling up! Fortunately, I'm the only one who knows that. And, big-mouthed as I am, I'll never tell!"

The moon rose. It was not silver, like Earth's moon, but as green as the cheese which the humorist-folklorists had said constituted lunar material. It was two and a half times as large as Earth's moon. It swelled across the starless black sky and cast a silver-green light on the white-and-brown streaked jade avenue.

Slowly, the giant orb moved across the heavens, and its light, like a team of mice pulling it along, strained ahead and presently was swarming over the lintel of the doorway in which Kickaha stood.

Kickaha looked up at the moon and wished that he were on it. He had been on its surface many times, and, if he could get to one of the small hidden gates in Talanac, he could be on it again. However, the chances were that von Turbat knew of their location, since he knew of the large gates. Even so, it would be worth finding out for sure, but one of the small gates was in the fane of a temple three streets above the lowest and the other was in the temple. The invaders were closing off all avenues out, and they had begun the house-to-house search on the lowest level. They would work upward on the theory that, if Kickaha were hiding, he would be driven upward until he would run into the soldiers stationed in the two levels just below the palace. Meanwhile, the other streets between would be patrolled, but infrequently, and by small bodies of soldiers: Von Turbat did not have enough men to spare.

Kickaha left the doorway and drifted out across the street and over the rampart and climbed down on the gods, beasts, men, abstract symbols, and cartographs which projected from the mountain face between the two streets. He went slowly because the hand and footholds were not always secure on the smooth stone and because there were troops stationed at the foot of the ramp leading from the street above to that below. They were holding torches, and several were on horseback.

Halfway down, he clung to the wall, motionless

as a fly that detects a vast shadowy hand, threatening, somewhere in the distance. A patrol of four soldiers on horseback clattered along below. They stopped to speak briefly to the guards stationed on the ramp, then moved on. Kickaha moved also, came to the street, and slid along the wall, along the fronts of houses and into and out of shadowy doorways. He still carried his bow and quiver, although he could move more smoothly and quietly while climbing without them. But he might need them desperately, and he chanced their rattling and their clumsy weight.

It took him until the moon was ready to sail around the monolith in the northwest before he reached Clatatol's street. This was the area of the poor, of slaves who had recently purchased their freedom, of lodgings and taverns for the sailors and smugglers of the riverboat trading-fleets and for the hired guards and drivers of the wagon trading-caravans of the Great Plains. There were also many thieves and murderers on whom the police had nothing tangible, and other thieves and murderers who were hiding from justice.

Normally, the Street of Suspicious Odors would have been crowded and noisy even at this late hour. But the curfew imposed by the invaders was effective. Not a person was to be seen except for several patrols, and every window and door was barred.

This level was like many of the lowest streets, rubbed into existence when the Tishquetmoac had begun their labor of making a mountain into a metropolis. There were houses and shops on the street itself. There was a secondary street on top of these houses, with other houses on that street, and a tertiary street on top of those houses, and still another street on top of these. In other words, the stepped-pyramid existed on a smaller scale within the larger.

These housetop streets were reached by narrow stairways which had been rubbed out of the jade between every fifth and sixth house on the main street. Small animals such as pigs and sheep could be driven up the steps, but a horse would go up at peril of slipping on the stone.

Kickaha scuttled across the Street of Green Birds, which was immediately above the fourth level of houses of the Street of Suspicious Odors. Clatatol's house—if she still lived there—fronted the third level. He intended to let himself over the fence, hang by his hands, and then drop to the rooftops of the fourth level and similarly to the third level street. There were no projections on which to climb down.

But as he went across the Street of Green Birds, he heard the *kulupkulik* of iron horseshoes. Out of the darkness cast by a temple-front porch, came three men on black horses. One was a knight in full armor; two were men-at-arms. The horses cracked into a gallop; the horsemen bent low over the necks of their mounts; behind them their black capes billowed, sinister smoke from fire of evil intents.

They were far enough away so that Kickaha could have escaped them by going over the fence and dropping. But they probably had bows and arrows, though he could see none, and if they got down off the horses quickly enough, they might be able to shoot him. The light from the moon was about twice as powerful as that from Earth's full moon. Moreover, even if their shafts missed him, they would call in others and start a house-to-house probing.

Well, he thought, the search would start now whatever happened, but . . . no, if he could kill them before the others heard . . . perhaps . . . it was worth trying. . . .

Under other circumstances, Kickaha would have tried for the riders. He loved horses. But when it came to saving his life, sentimentality evaporated. All creatures had to die, but Kickaha intended that his death should come as late as possible.

He aimed for the horses and in rapid succession brought two down. They both fell heavily on their right sides, and neither rider got up. The third, the knight, came unswervingly on, his lance aimed for Kickaha's belly or chest. The arrow went through the horse's neck; the animal fell front quarters first and went hooves over tail. The rider flew up and out; he held his lance most of the flight but dropped it and pulled up his legs and struck in a fetal position. His conical helmet, torn off, hit the stone, bounced, and went freewheeling down the street. The man slid on his side, his cloak ripping off and lying behind him as if his shadow had become dislodged.

Then, despite his armor, the knight was up and pulling his sword from its sheath. He opened his mouth to shout for whoever would hear and come running to his aid. An arrow drove past the teeth and through the spinal cord and he fell backward, sword *keluntking* on the jade.

A silver casket was tied to the saddle of the dead horse of the dead knight. Kickaha tried to open the casket but the key must have been on the knight someplace. He did not have time to look for it.

There were three dead horses, one dead man, possibly two other dead men. And no shouts in the distance to indicate that somebody had heard the uproar.

Carcass and corpse would not long remain unnoticed, however. Kickaha dropped his bow and quiver below and followed them. In less than sixty seconds, he was on the third level street and knocking on the thick wooden shutter over Clatatol's window. He rapped three times, counted to five, rapped twice, counted to four, and rapped once. He held a knife in his other hand.

There was no response which he could detect. He waited for sixty counts, per the code as he remembered it, and then rapped as prescribed again. Immediately thereafter, the sound of horseshoes came down to him and then an uproar. There were shouts and a bugle call. Lights began to gather on the street above and the main street below. Drums beat.

Suddenly, the shutter swung open. Kickaha had to dodge to avoid being hit in the face by it. The room within was dark, but the phantom of a woman's face and naked torso shone palely. An odor of garlic, fish, pork, and the rotten worm-infested cheese the Tishquetmoac loved puffed out past the woman. Kickaha associated the beauty of worked jade with these smells. His first visit had ruined him; he could not help it that he was a man of associations, not always desirable.

At this moment, the odor meant Clatatol, who was as beautiful as her cheese was dreadful. Or as beautiful as her language was foul and her temper hot as an Icelandic geyser.

"Shh!" Kickaha said. "The neighbors!"

Clatatol vomited another scatological and blasphemous spurt.

Kickaha clamped a hand over her mouth, twisted her head to remind her that he could easily break her neck, pushed her back so she went staggering, and climbed in through the window. He closed and locked the shutters and then turned to Clatatol. She had gotten up and found an oil lamp and lit it. By its flickering light, she advanced, swaying, to Kickaha and then embraced him and kissed him on his face, neck and chest while tears ran over these and she sobbed endearments.

Kickaha ignored her breath, thick with the resin-like wine and rotted cheese and garlic and sleep-clots, and he kissed her back. Then he said, "Are you alone?"

"Didn't I swear I would remain faithful to you?" she said.

"Yes, but I didn't ask for that. It was your idea. Besides," he said, "you couldn't be without a man for more than a week, as we both well know."

They laughed, and she took him into the back room, which was square except for the upper parts, which curved to form a dome. This was her bedroom and also her workroom since she planned smuggling operations here and dispensed various goods. Only the furniture was in evidence. This consisted mainly of the bed, a low broad wooden frame with leather straps stretched across it and mountain-lion furs and deerhides piled on the straps. Kickaha lay down on this. Clatatol exclaimed that he looked tired and hungry. She left him for the kitchen, and he called out after her to bring him only water, bread, and sticks of dried beef or some fresh fruit if she had it. Hungry as he was, he couldn't stand the cheese.

After he had eaten, he asked her what she knew of the invasion. Clatatol sat by him on the bed and handed him his food. She seemed ready to pick up their lovemaking where they had left off several years ago, but Kickaha discouraged her. The situation was too enwombed with fatality to think of love now.

Clatatol, who was practical, whatever other faults she had, agreed. She got up and put on a skirt of green, black, and white feathers and a rose-colored cotton cloak. She washed out her mouth with wine diluted with ten parts of water and dropped a bead of powerful perfume on her tongue. Then she sat down by him again and began to talk.

Even though plugged into the underworld grapevine, she could not tell him everything he wanted to know. The invaders had appeared as if out of nowhere from a back room in the great temple of Ollimaml. They had swept out and into the palace and seized the emperor and his entire family after overwhelming the bodyguard and then the garrison.

The taking of Talanac had been well planned and almost perfectly executed. While the co-leader, von Swindebarn, held the palace and began to reorganize the Talanac police and the military to aid him, von Turbat had led the ever-increasing numbers of invaders from the palace into the city itself.

"Everybody was paralyzed," Clatatol said. "It was so absolutely unexpected. These white people in armor, pouring out of the temple of Ollimaml . . . it was as if Ollimaml Himself had sent them, and this increased the paralysis."

The civilians and police who got in the way were

cut down. The rest of the population either fled into buildings or, when word reached the lowest levels, tried to get out across the river bridges. But these had been sealed off.

"The strange thing is," Clatatol said, hesitating, then continuing strongly, "the strange thing is that all this does not seem to be because of a desire to conquer Talanac. No, the seizure of our city is a, what do you call it, a byproduct? The invaders seem to be determined to take the city only because they regard it as a pond which holds a very desirable fish."

"Meaning me," Kickaha said.

Clatatol nodded. "I do not know why these people should want you so greatly. Do you?"

Kickaha said, "No. I could guess. But I won't. My speculations would only confuse you and take much time. The first thing for me is to get out and away. And that, my love, is where you come in."

"Now you love me," she said.

"If there were time . . . " he replied.

"I can hide you where we will have all the time we need," she said. "Of course, there are the others . . . "

Kickaha had been wondering if she was holding back. He wasn't in a position to get rough with her, but he did. He gripped her wrist and squeezed. She grimaced and tried to pull away.

"What others?"

"Quit hurting me, and I'll tell. Maybe. Give me a kiss, and I'll tell for sure."

It was worthwhile to spend a few seconds, so he kissed her. The perfume from her mouth filled his nostrils and seemingly filtered down to the ends of his toes. He felt heady and began wondering if perhaps she didn't deserve a reward after all this time.

He laughed then and gently released himself. "You are indeed the most beautiful and desirable woman I have ever seen and I have seen a thousand times a thousand," he said. "But death walks the streets, and he is looking for me."

"When you see this other woman . . . " she said.

She became coy again, and then he had to impress upon her that coyness automatically meant pain for her. She did not resent this, liked it, in fact, since, to her, erotic love meant a certain amount of roughness and pain.

## V

IT SEEMED THAT three strangers had fled from the inmost parts of the temple of Ollimaml a few minutes ahead of von Turbat. They were white-skinned, also. One was the black haired woman whom Clatatol, a very jealous and deprecating woman, nevertheless said was the most beautiful she had ever seen. Her companions were a huge, very fat man and a short skinny man. All three were dressed strangely and none spoke Tishquetmoac. They did speak Wishpawaml, the liturgical language of the priests. Unfortunately, the thieves who had hidden the three knew only a few words of Wishpawaml; these were from the responses of the laity during services.

Kickaha knew then that the three were Lords. The liturgical language everywhere on this world was theirs.

Their flight from von Turbat indicated that they had been dispossessed of their own universes and had taken refuge in this. But what was the minor king, von Turbat, doing in an affair that involved Lords?

Kickaha said, "Is there a reward for these three?"

"Yes. Ten thousand *kwatluml*. Apiece! For you,

thirty thousand, and a high official post in the palace of the emperor. Perhaps, though this is only hinted at, marriage into the royal family."

Kickaha was silent. Clatatol's stomach rumbled, as if ruminating the reward offers. Voices fluttered weakly through the air shafts in the ceiling. The room, which had been cool, was hot. Sweat seeped from his armpits; the woman's dark-brass skin hatched brass tadpoles. From the middle chamber, the kitchen-washroom-toilet, came gurgles of running water and little watery voices.

"You must have fainted at the thought of all that money," Kickaha said finally. "What's keeping you and your gang from collecting?"

"We are thieves and smugglers, killers even, but we are not traitors! The pinkfaces offered these . . . "

She stopped when she saw Kickaha grinning. She grinned back. "What I said is true. However, the sums *are* enormous! What made us hesitate, if you must know, you wise coyote, was what would happen after the pinkfaces left. Or if there is a revolt. We don't want to be torn to pieces by a mob or tortured because some people might think we were traitors."

"Also . . . ?"

She smiled and said, "Also, the three refugees have offered to pay us many times over what the pinkfaces offer if we get them out of the city."

"And how will they do that?" Kickaha said. "They haven't got a universe to their name."

"What?"

"Can they offer you anything tangible—right now?"

"All *were* wearing jewels worth more than the

rewards," she said. "Some—I've never seen anything like them. They're out of this world!"

Kickaha did not tell her that the cliché was literally true.

He was going to ask her if they had weapons but realized that she would not have recognized them as such if the three did have them. Certainly, the three wouldn't offer the information to their captors.

"And what of me?" he said, not asking her what the three had offered beyond their jewels.

"You, Kickaha, are beloved of the Lord, or so it is said. Besides, everybody says that you know where the treasures of the earth are hidden. Would a man who is poor have brought back the great emerald of Oshquatsmu?"

Kickaha said, "The pinkfaces will be banging on your doors soon enough. This whole area is going to be unraveled. Where do we go from here?"

Clatatol insisted that he let her blindfold him and then cover him with a hood. In no position to argue, he agreed. She made sure he could not see and then turned him swiftly around a dozen times. After that, he got down on all fours at her order.

There was a creaking sound, stone turning on stone, and she guided him through a passageway so narrow he scraped against both sides. Then he stood and, his hand in hers, stumbled up 150 steps, walked 280 paces down a slight decline, went down a ramp three hundred paces, and walked forty more on a straightway. Clatatol stopped him and removed the hood and blindfold.

He blinked. He was in a round green-and-black striated chamber with a forty foot diameter and a three foot wide air shaft above. Flames writhed at the ends of torches in wall fixtures. There were chairs of jade and wood, some chests, piles of cloth bolts and furs, barrels of spices, a barrel of water, a table with dishes, biscuits, meat, stinking cheese, and some sanitation furniture.

Six Tishquetmoac men squatted against the wall. Their glossy black bangs fell over their eyes. Some smoked little cigars. They were armed with daggers, swords, and hatchets.

Three fair-skinned people sat in chairs. One was short, gritty-skinned, large-nosed, and shark-mouthed. The second was a manatee of a man, spilling over the chair in cataracts of fat.

On seeing the third, Kickaha gasped. He said, "Podarge!"

The woman was the most beautiful he had ever seen. But he had seen her before. That is, the face was in his past. But the body did not belong to that face.

"Podarge!" he said again, speaking the debased Mycenaean she and her eagles used. "I didn't know that Wolff had taken you from your harpy's body and put you—your brain—in a woman's body. I . . ."

He stopped. She was looking at him with an unreadable expression. Perhaps she did not want him to let the others know what had happened. And he, usually silent when the situation asked for it, had been so overcome that . . .

But Podarge had discovered that Wolff was in reality the Jadawin who had originally kidnapped her from the Peloponnese of 3200 years ago and put her brain into the body of a Harpy created in his biolab. She had refused to let him rectify the wrong; she hated him so much that she had stayed in her winged bird-legged body and had sworn to get revenge upon him.

What had made her change her mind?

Her voice, however, was not Podarge's. That, of course, would be the result of the soma transfer.

"What are you gibbering about, *leblabbiy*?" she said in the speech of the Lords.

Kickaha felt like hitting her in the face. *Leblabbiy* was the Lords' perjorative for the human beings who inhabited their universes and over whom they godded it. *Leblabbiy* had been a small pet animal of the universe in which the Lords had originated. It ate the delicacies which its master offered, but it would also eat excrement at the first chance. And it often went mad.

"All right, Podarge, pretend you don't understand Mycenaean," he said. "But watch your tongue. I have no love for you."

She seemed surprised. She said, "Ah, you are a priest?"

Wolff, he had to admit, had certainly done a perfect job on her. Her body was magnificent; the skin as white and flawless as he remembered it; the hair as long, black, straight, and shining. The features, of course, were not perfectly regular; there was a slight asymmetry which resulted in a beauty that under other circumstances would have made him ache.

She was dressed in silky-looking light green robes and sandals, almost as if she had been getting ready for bed when interrupted. How in hell had Podarge come to be mixed up with these Lords? And then the answer tapped his mind's shoulder. Of course, she was in Wolff's palace when it was invaded. But what had happened then?

He said, "Where is Wolff?"

"Who, *leblabbiy*?" she said.

"Jadawin, he used to be called," he said.

She shrugged and said, "He wasn't there. Or if he was, he was killed by the Black Bellers."

Kickaha was more confused. "Black Bellers?"

Wolff had spoken of them at one time. But briefly, because their conversation had been interrupted by a subject introduced by Chryseis. Later, after Kickaha had helped Wolff recover his palace from Vannax, Kickaha had intended to ask him about the Black Bellers. He had never done so.

One of the Tishquetmoac spoke harshly to Clatatol. Kickaha understood him; she was to tell Kickaha that he must talk to these people. The Tishquetmoac could not understand the speech.

The fair-skinned woman, replying to his questions, said, "I am Anana, Jadawin's sister. This thin one is Nimstowl, called the Nooser by the Lords. This other is Fat Judubra."

Kickaha understood now. Anana, called the Bright, was one of Wolff's sisters. And he had used her face as a model when he created Podarge's face in the biolab. Rather, his memory had supplied the features, since Wolff had not then seen his sister Anana for over a thousand years. Which meant that, as of now, he had not seen her for over four thousand.

Kickaha remembered now that Wolff had said that the Black Bellers were to have been used, partly, as receptacles for memory. The Lords, knowing that even the complex human brain could not hold thousands of years of knowledge, had experimented with the transfer of memory. This could, theoretically, be transferred back to the human brain when needed or otherwise displayed exteriorly.

A rapping sounded. A round door in the wall at the other end swung out, and another smuggler entered. He beckoned to the others, and they gathered around him to whisper. Finally, Clatatol left the group to speak to Kickaha.

"The rewards have been tripled," she whispered. "Moreover, this pinkface king, von Turbat, has proclaimed that, once you're caught, he'll withdraw from Talanac. Everything will be as it was before."

"If you'd planned on turning us in, you wouldn't be telling me this," he said. But it was possible that she was being overly subtle, trying to make him at ease, before they struck. Eight against one. He did not know what the Lords could do, so he would not count on them. He still had his two knives, but in this small room . . . ah, well, when the time came, he would see.

Clatatol added, "Von Turbat has also said that if you are not delivered to him within twenty-four hours, he will kill the emperor and his family and then he will kill every human being in this city. He said this in private to his officers, but a slave overheard him. Now the entire city knows."

"If von Turbat was talking German, how could a Tishquetmoac understand him?" Kickaha said.

"Von Turbat was talking to von Swindebarn and several others in the holy speech of the Lords," she said. "The slave had served in the temple and knew the holy speech."

The Black Bellers must be the as-yet unhooded lantern to illumine the mystery. He knew the two

Teutoniac kings could follow the priest in the services, but they did not know the sacred language well enough to speak it. Thus, the two were not what they seemed.

He was given no time to ask questions. Clatatol said, "The pinkfaces have found the chamber behind the wall of my bedroom, and they will soon be breaking through it. We can't stay here."

Two men left the room but quickly returned with telescoping ladders. These were extended full-length up the air shaft. On seeing this, Kickaha felt less apprehensive. He said, "Now your patriotism demands that you hand us over to von Turbat. So . . . ?"

Two men had climbed up the ladder. The others were urging the Lords and Kickaha to go next. Clatatol said, "We have heard that the emperor is possessed by a demon. His soul had been driven out into the cold past the moon; a demon resides in his body, though not comfortably as yet. The priests have secretly transmitted this story throughout the city. They say for us to fight this most evil of evils. And we are not to surrender you, Kickaha, who is the beloved of the Lord, Ollimaml, nor should we give up the others."

Kickaha said, "Possessed? How do you know?"

Clatatol did not answer until after they had climbed the length of the shaft and were in a horizontal tunnel. One of the smugglers lit a dark lantern, and the ladder was pulled up, joint by joint, bent, folded, and carried along.

Clatatol said, "Suddenly, the emperor spoke only in the holy speech, so it was evident he did not understand Tishquetmoac. And the priests reported that von Turbat and von Swindebarn speak

Wishpawaml only, and they have their priests to translate orders for them."

Kickaha did not see why a demon was thought to possess Quotshaml, the emperor. The liturgical language was supposed to scorch the lips of demons when they tried to speak it. But he was not going to point out the illogic when it favored him.

The party hurried down a tunnel with Fat Judubra wheezing loudly and complaining. He had had to be pulled through the shaft; his robes had torn and his skin had been scraped.

Kickaha asked Clatatol if the temple of Ollimaml was well guarded. He was hoping that the smaller secret gate had not been discovered. She replied that she did not know. Kickaha asked her how they were going to get out of the city. She answered that it would be better if he did not know; if he was captured, then he could not betray the others. Kickaha did not argue with her. Although he had no idea of how they would leave the city, he could imagine what would happen after that. During his last visit, he had found out just how she and her friends got the contraband past the customs. She did not suspect that he knew.

He spoke to Anana, who was a glimmer of neck, arms, and legs ahead. "The woman Clatatol says that her emperor, and at least two of the invaders, are possessed. She means that they suddenly seem unable, or unwilling, to talk anything but the language of the Lords."

"The Black Bellers," Anana said after a pause.

At that moment, shouts cannoned down the tunnel. The party stopped; the lantern was put out. Lights appeared at both ends of the tunnel; voices flew down from the rigid mouths of shafts above and ballooned from mouths below.

Kickaha spoke to the Lords. "If you have weapons, get ready to use them."

They did not answer. The party formed into a single file, linked by holding hands, and a man led them into a cross-tunnel. They duckwalked for perhaps fifty yards, with the voices of the hunters getting louder, before they heard a distant roar of water. The lamp was lit again. Soon they were in a small chamber, exitless except for the four-foot-wide hole in the floor against the opposite wall. The roar, a wetness, and a stink funneled up from it.

"The shaft angles steeply, and the sewage tunnel to which it connects is fifty feet down. The slide, however, won't hurt," Clatatol said. "We use this way only if all others around here fail. If you went all the way down this shaft, you'd fall into the tunnel, which is full of sewage and drops almost vertically down into the river at an underwater point. If you lived to come up in the river, you would be caught by the pinkface patrol boats stationed there."

Clatatol told them what they must do. They sat down and coasted down the tube with their hands and feet braking. Two-thirds of the way down, or so it seemed, they stopped. Here they were pulled into a hole and a shaft unknown to the authorities, rubbed into existence by several generations of criminals. This led back up to a network above the level from which they had just fled.

Clatatol explained that it was necessary to get to a place where they could enter another great sewage pipe. This one, however, was dry, because it had been blocked off with great labor and some loss of life thirty years before by a large gang of criminals. The flow from above was diverted to two other sewage tunnels. The dry tunnel led directly downward to below the water level. Near its mouth was a shaft which went horizontally to an underwater port distant from the outlets being watched by the pinkfaces. It was near the wharf where the river-trade boats were. To reach the boats, they would have to swim across the mile wide river.

Three streets up, within the face of the mountain, the party came to the horizontal shaft which opened to their avenue of escape, the dry tunnel slanting at fifty-five degrees to the horizontal.

Kickaha never found out what went amiss. He did not think that the Teutoniacs could have known where they were. There must have been some search parties sent at random to various areas. And this one was in the right place and saw their quarry before the quarry saw them.

Suddenly there were lights, yells, screams, and something thudding into bodies. Several Tishquetmoac men fell, and then Clatatol was sprawled out before him. In the dim light of the lantern lying on its side before him, Kickaha saw the skin, bluish-black in the light, the hanging jaw, eyes skewered on eternity, and the crossbow bolt sticking out of her skull an inch above the right ear. Blood gushed over the blue-black hair, the ear, the neck.

He crawled over the body, his flesh numb with the shock of the attack and with the shock of the bolt to come. He scuttled down the tunnel and into one that seemed to be free of the enemy. Behind him, in the dark, was heavy breathing; Anana identified herself. She did not know what had happened to the others.

They crawled and duckwalked until their legs

and backs felt pain in the center of their bones, or so it seemed. They took left and right turns as they pleased, no pattern, and twice went up vertical shafts. The time came when they were in total darkness and quiet except for the blood punching little bags in their ears. They seemed to have outrun the hounds.

Thereafter, they went upward. It was vital to wait until night could veil their movements outside. This proved difficult to do. Though they were tired and tried to sleep, they kept awakening as if springing off the trampoline of unconsciousness into the upper air of open eyes. Their legs kicked, their hands twitched; they were aware of this but could not fully sleep to forget it nor be fully awake except when they soared out of nightmares.

Night appeared at the porthole of the shaft-end in the face of the mountain. They climbed out and up, seeing patrols below and hearing them above. After waiting until things were quiet above, they climbed over the ramparts and up the next wall and so to the next level of street. When they could not travel outside, they crawled into an air shaft.

The lower parts of the city were ablaze with torches. The soldiers and police were thoroughly probing the bottom levels. Then, as they went upward, the ring of men tightened because the area lessened. And there were spot-check search parties everywhere.

"If you're supposed to be taken alive, why did they shoot at us?" Anana said. "They couldn't see well enough to distinguish their targets."

"They got excited," Kickaha said. He was tired, hungry, thirsty, and feeling rage at the killers of Clatatol. Sorrow would come later. There would be no guilt. He never suffered guilt unless he had a realistic reason. Kickaha had some neurotic failings, and neurotic virtues—no way to escape those, being human—but inappropriate guilt was not among them. He was not responsible in any way for her death. She had entered this business of her own will and knowing that she might die.

There was even a little gladness reaped from her death. He could have been killed instead of her.

Kickaha went down a series of shafts after food and drink. Anana did not want to be left behind, since she feared that he might not be able to find her again. She went with him as far as the tube which led into the ceiling of a home, where the family snored loudly and smelled loudly of wine and beer. He came back with a rope, bread, cheese, fruit, beef, and two bottles of water.

They waited again until night sailed around the monolith and grappled the city. Then they went on up again, outside when they could, inside when they could. Anana asked him why they were going up; he replied that they had to, since the city below was swarming inside and outside.

## VI

In the middle of the night, they came out of another house, having entered by the air shaft, and stepped past the sleepers. This house was on the street just below the emperor's palace. From here on, there would be no internal shaft connections. Since all stairways and causeways were guarded, they could reach their goal only by climbing up on the outside for some distance. This would not be easy. For forty feet, the mountain face was purposely left smooth.

And then, while they were skulking in the shadows at the base of the wall, they came across two booted feet sticking out of a dark alcove. The feet belonged to a dead sentry; another man lay dead by him. One had been stabbed in the throat; the other, strangled with wire.

"Nimstowl has been here!" Anana whispered. "He is called the Nooser, you know."

The torches of an approaching patrol flared three hundred yards down the street. Kickaha cursed Nimstowl because he had left the bodies there. Actually, however, it would make little difference to the patrols if the sentries were dead or missing from their posts. There would be alarms.

The small gate set in the wall was unlocked. It

could be locked from the outside only; Kickaha and Anana, after taking the sentries' weapons, went through it, and ran up the steep stairway between towering smooth walls. They were wheezing and sobbing when they reached the top.

From below, shouts rose. Torches appeared in the tiny gateway, and soldiers began to climb the steps. Drums thoomed; a bugle bararared.

The two ran, not toward the palace to their right but toward a steep flight of steps to their left. At the top of the steps, silver roofs and gray iron bars gleamed, and the odor of animals, straw, old meat and fresh dung reached them.

"The royal zoo," Kickaha said. "I've been here."

At the far end of a long flagstone walk, something gleamed like a thread in the hem of night. It shot across the moonlight and was in shadows, out again, in again. Then it faded into the huge doorway of a colossal white building.

"Nimstowl!" Anana said. She started after him, but Kickaha pulled her back roughly. Face twisted, white as silver poured out by the moon in a hideous mold, eyes wide as an enraged owl's, she snapped herself away from him.

"You dare to touch me, *leblabbiy*?"

"Any time," he said harshly. "For one thing, don't call me *leblabbiy* again. I won't just hit you. I'll kill you. I don't have to take that arrogance, that contempt. It's totally based on empty, poisonous, sick egotism. Call me that again, and I'll kill you. You aren't superior to me in any way, you know. You *are* dependent on me."

"I? Dependent? On you?"

"Sure," he said. "Do you have a plan for escape? One that might work, even if it is wild?"

Her effort to control herself made her shudder. Then she forced a smile. And if he had not known the concealed fury, he would have thought it the most beautiful, charming, seductive, etc., smile he had seen in two universes.

"No! I have no plan. You are right. I am dependent on you."

"You're realistic, anyway," he said. "Most Lords, I've heard, are so arrogant, they'd rather die than confess dependency or weakness of any kind."

This flexibility made her more dangerous, however. He must not forget that she was Wolff's sister. Wolff had told him that his sisters Vala and Anana were probably the two most dangerous human females alive. Even allowing for pardonable family pride, and a certain exaggeration, they probably were exceedingly dangerous.

"Stay here!" he said, and he went silently and swiftly after Nimstowl. He could not understand how the two Lords had managed to go straight here. How had they learned of the small secret gate in the temple? There could be only one way: during their brief stay in Wolff's palace, they had seen the map with its location. Anana had not been with them when that had happened, or if she had, she was keeping quiet for some reason of her own.

But if the two Lords could find out about it, why hadn't the Black Bellers also located it, since they would have had more time? Within a minute, he had his answer. The Bellers had known of the gate and had stationed two guards outside it. But these two were dead, one knifed, one strangled, and the corner of the building was swung open and light streamed out from it. Kickaha cautiously slipped through the narrow opening and into the small chamber. There were four silver crescents set into the stone of the floor; the four that had been hanging on the wall-pegs were gone. The two Lords had used a gate to escape and had taken the other crescents with them to make sure that no one used the others.

Furious, Kickaha returned to Anana and told her the bad news.

"That way is out, but we're not licked yet," he said.

Kickaha walked on a curving path of diorite stones set at the edges with small jewels. He stopped before a huge cage. The two birds within stood side by side and glared at Kickaha. They were ten feet high. Their heads were pale red; their beaks, pale yellow; their wings and bodies were green as the noon sky; their legs were yellow. And their eyes were scarlet shields with black bosses.

One spoke in a giant parrot's voice. "Kickaha! What do you do here, vile trickster?"

Inside that great head was the brain of a woman abducted by Jadawin 3,200 years ago from the shores of the Aegean. That brain had been transplanted for Jadawin's amusement and use in the body created in his biolab. This eagle was one of the few human-brained left. The great green eagles, all females, reproduced parthenogenetically. Perhaps forty of the original five thousand still survived; the others, the millions now living, were their descendants.

Kickaha answered in Mycenaean Greek. "Dewiwanira! And what are you doing in this cage? I thought you were Podarge's pet, not the emperor's."

Dewiwanira screamed and bit at the bars. Kickaha, who was standing too close, jumped back, but he laughed.

"That's right, you dumb bird! Bring them running so they can keep you from escaping!"

The other eagle said, "Escape?"

Kickaha answered quickly. "Yes. Escape. Agree to help us get out of Talanac, and we will get you out of the cage. But say yea or nay now! We have little time!"

"Podarge ordered us to kill you and Jadawin-Wolff!" Dewiwanira said.

"You can try later," he said. "But if you don't give me your word to help us, you'll die in the cage. Do you want to fly again, to see your friends again?"

Torches were on the steps to the palace and the zoological gardens. Kickaha said, "Yes? No?"

"Yes!" Dewiwanira said. "By the breasts of Podarge, yes!"

Anana stepped out from the shadows to assist him. Not until then did the eagles see her face clearly. They jumped and flapped their wings and croaked, "Podarge!"

Kickaha did not tell them that she was Jadawin-Wolff's sister. He said, "Podarge's face had a model."

He ran to the storehouse, thankful that he had taken the trouble to inspect it during his tour with the emperor, and he returned with several lengths of rope. He then jumped into a pit set in stone and leaned heavily upon an iron level. Steel skreaked and the door to the cage swung open.

Anana stood guard with bow and arrow ready. Dewiwanira hunched through the door first and stood still while Kickaha tied each end of a rope to a leg. Antiope, the other eagle, left the cage and submitted to a rope being tied to her legs.

Kickaha told the others what he hoped they could do. Then, as soldiers ran into the gardens, the two huge birds hopped to the edge of the low rampart which enclosed the zoo. This was not their normal method of progress when on the ground; usually they strode. Now, only by spreading their wings to make their descent easier, could they avoid injury to their legs.

Kickaha got in between the legs of Dewiwanira, sat down with the rope under his buttocks, gripped each leg above the huge talons, and shouted, "Ready, Anana? All right, Dewiwanira! Fly!"

Both eagles bounded into the air several feet, even though weighted by the humans. Their wings beat ponderously. Kickaha felt the rope dig into his flesh. He was jerked up and forward; the rampart dropped from under him. The green-silver-spattered, torchflame-sparked, angling walls and streets of the city of Talanac were below him but rushing up frighteningly.

Far below, at least three thousand feet, the river at the foot of the mountain ran with black and tossed silver.

Then the mountain was sliding by perilously close. The eagles could support a relatively large weight, since their muscles were far stronger than those of an eagle of Earth, but they could not flap their wings swiftly enough to lift a human adult. The best they could do was to slow the rate of descent.

And so they paralleled the walls, pounding their wings frantically when they came to an outthrust of street, moved agonizingly slowly outward, or so it seemed to Kickaha, shot over the street and seemed to hurtle down again, the white or brown or red or gray or black or striped jade face of the mountain too too close, then they were rowing furiously to go outward once more.

The two humans had to draw their legs up during most of the whistling, booming, full-of-heart-stopping-crashes-just-ahead ride.

Twice they were scratched, raked, and beaten by the branches of trees as they were hauled through the upper parts. Once the eagles had to bank sharply to avoid slamming into a high framework of wood, built on top of a house for some reason. Then the eagles lost some distance between them and the mountain wall, and the two were bumped with loss of skin and some blood along brown and black jade which, fortunately, was smooth. Ornamental projections would have broken their bones or gashed them deeply.

Then the lowest level, the Street of Rejected Sacrifices, so named for some reason Kickaha had never found out, was behind them. They missed the jade fence on the outer edge of the street by a little more than an inch. Kickaha was so sure that he would be caught and torn on the points that he actually felt the pain.

They dropped toward the river at a steep angle.

The river was a mile wide at this place. On the shore opposite were docks and ships, and outside them, other ships at anchor. Most of these were long two-decked galleys with high poop decks and one or two square-rigged masts.

Kickaha saw this in two flashes, and then, as the eagles sank toward the gray and black dappled surface, he did that which he had arranged with Anana. Confident that the eagles would try to kill them as soon as they were out of danger of being caught inside the city, he had told Anana to release her hold and drop into the river at the first chance.

The river was still fifty feet below when Dewiwanira made her first attempt with her beak. Fortunately for her intended prey, she couldn't bend enough to seize or tear him. The huge yellow beak slashed eight inches above his head.

"Let go!" she screamed then. "You'll pull me into the water! I'll drown!"

Kickaha was tempted to do just that. He was afraid, however, that the obvious would occur to her. If she could sustain altitude enough while Antiope dropped so that her head was even with Kickaha, Antiope could then use her beak on him. And then the two birds could reverse position and get to Anana.

He threw himself backward, turned over, twice straightened out, and entered the water cleanly, head-down. He came up just in time to see the end of Anana's dive. They were about 250 yards from the nearest of five anchored galleys. A mile and a half down the river, torches moved toward them; beneath them, helmets threw off splinters of fire and oars rose and dipped.

The eagles were across the river now and climbing, black against the moonlight.

Kickaha called to Anana, and they swam toward the nearest boat. His clothes and the knives pulled at him, so he shed the clothes and dropped the larger knife into the depths. Anana did the same. Kickaha did not like losing the garments or the knife, but the experiences of the last forty-eight hours and the shortage of food had drained his energy.

They reached the boat finally and clung to the anchor chain while they sucked in air, unable to control the loud sobbing. No one appeared to investigate on the decks of the ship. If there was a watchman, he was sleeping.

The patrol boat was coming swiftly in their direction. Kickaha did not think, however, that he and Anana could be seen yet. He told her what they must do. Having caught up with his breathing, he dived down and under the hull. He turned when he thought he was halfway across and swam along the longitudinal axis toward the rear. Every few strokes, he felt upward. He came up under the overhanging poop with no success. Anana, who had explored the bottom of the front half, met him at the anchor chain. She reported failure, too.

He panted as he talked. "There's a good chance none of these five boats have secret chambers for the smugglers. In fact, we could go through a hundred and perhaps find nothing. Meanwhile, that patrol is getting closer."

"Perhaps we should try the land route," she said.

"Only if we can't find the hidden chambers," he said. "On land, we haven't much chance."

He swam around the boat to the next one and there repeated his search along the keel. This boat and a third proved to have solid bottoms. By then, though he could not see it, Kickaha knew that the patrol boat was getting close.

Suddenly, from the other side of the boat, something like an elephant gun seemed to explode. There was a second boom, and then the screams of eagles and men.

Though he could see nothing, he knew what had happened: the green eagles had returned to kill Kickaha. Not seeing, they had decided to take revenge on the nearest humans for their long captivity. So they had plunged out of the night sky onto the men in the boat. The booms had been their wings suddenly opening to check their fall. Now, they must be in the boat and tearing with beak and talon.

There were splashes. More screams. Then silence.

A sound of triumph, like an elephant's bugling, then a flapping of giant wings. Kickaha and Anana dived under the fourth boat, and they combined hiding from the eagles with their search.

Kickaha, coming up under the poop, heard the wings but could not see the birds. He waited in the shadow of the poop until he saw them rising out and away from the next boat. They could be giving up their hunt for him or they could be intending to plunge down out of the skies again. Anana was not in sight. She was gone so long that Kickaha knew she had either found what they were looking for or had drowned. Or had taken off by herself.

He swam along under the forepart of the boat, and presently his hand went past the lip of a well cut from the keel. He rose, opening his eyes, and saw a glimmer of darkest gray above. Then he was through the surface and in a square chamber lit by a small lamp. He blinked and saw Anana on all fours, knife in hand, staring down at him from a shelf. The shelf was two feet above the water and ran entirely around the chamber.

Beside her knife hand was the black hair of a man. Kickaha came up onto the shelf. The man was a Tishquetmoac, and he was sleeping soundly.

Anana smiled and said, "He was sleeping when I came out of the water. A good thing, too, because he could have speared me before I knew what was going on. So I hit him in the neck to make sure he continued sleeping."

The shelf went in about four feet and was bare except for some furs, blankets, a barrel with the cartograph for gin on it, and some wooden metal-bound caskets that contained food—he hoped. The bareness meant that the smuggled goods had been removed, so there wouldn't be any influx of swimmers to take the contraband.

The smoke from the lamp rose toward a number of small holes in the ceiling and upper wall. Kickaha, placing his cheek near some of them, felt a slight movement of air. He was sure that the light could not be seen, by anyone on the deck immediately above, but he would have to make sure.

He said to Anana, "There are any number of boats equipped with these chambers. Sometimes the captains know about them; sometimes they don't."

He pointed at the man. "We'll question him later." He tied the man's ankles and turned him over to bind his hands behind him. Then, though he wanted to lie down and sleep, he went back into the water. He came up near the anchor chain, which he climbed. His prowlings on the galley revealed no watchmen, and he got a good idea of the construction of the ship. Moreover, he found some sticks of dried meat and biscuits wrapped in waterproof intestines. There were no eagles in sight, and the patrol boat had drifted so far away that he could not see bodies—if there were any—in it.

When he returned to the chamber, he found the man conscious.

Petotoc said that he was hiding there because he was wanted by the police—he would not say what the charge was. He did not know about the invasion. It was evident that he did not believe Kickaha's story.

Kickaha spoke to the woman. "We must have been seen by enough people so that the search for us in the city will be off. They'll be looking for us in the old city, the farms, the countryside, and they'll be searching every boat, too. Then, when they can't find us, they may let normal life resume. And this boat may set out for wherever it's going."

Kickaha asked Petotoc where he could get enough food to last the three of them for a month. Anana's eyes opened, and she said, "Live a month in this damp, stinking hole?"

"If you want to live at all," Kickaha said. "I sincerely hope we won't be here that long, but I like to have reserves for an emergency."

"I'll go mad," she said.

"How old are you?" he said. "About ten thousand, at least, right? And you haven't learned the proper mental attitudes to get through situations like this in all that time?"

"I never expected to be in such a situation," she snarled.

Kickaha smiled. "Something new after ten millennia, huh? You should be happy to be free of boredom."

Unexpectedly, she laughed. She said, "I am tired and edgy. But you are right. It is better to be scared to death than to be bored to death. And what has happened . . . "

She spread her palms out to indicate speechlessness.

Kickaha, acting on Petotoc's information, went topside again. He lowered a small boat, rowed ashore, and broke into a small warehouse. He filled the boat with food and rowed back to the ship. Here he tied the rowboat to the anchor and then swam under to get Anana. The many dives and swims, hampered by carrying food in nets, wore them out even more. By the end of their labors, they were so tired they could barely pull themselves up onto the shelf in the chamber. Kickaha let the rowboat loose so it could drift away, and then he made his final dive.

Shaking with cold and exhaustion, he wanted desperately to sleep, but he did not dare leave the smuggler unguarded. Anana suggested that they solve that problem by killing Petotoc. The prisoner was listening, but he did not understand, since they were talking in the speech of the Lords. He did see her draw her finger across her throat though, and then he knew what they were discussing. He turned pale under his dark pigment.

"I won't do that unless it's necessary," Kickaha said. "Besides, even if he's dead, we still have to keep a guard. What if other smugglers come in? We can't be caught sleeping. Clatatol and her bunch were able to resist the temptation of the reward—although I'm not sure they could have held out much longer—but others may not be so noble."

He took first watch and only kept awake by dipping water and throwing it in his face, by talking to Petotoc, by pacing savagely back and forth on the shelf. When he thought two hours had passed, he roused her with slaps and water. After getting her promise that she would not succumb to sleep, he closed his eyes. This happened twice more, and then he was awakened the third time. But now he was not to stand guard.

She had placed her hand over his mouth and was

whispering into his ear. "Be quiet! You were snoring! There are men aboard."

He lay for a long while listening to the thumps of feet, the shouts and talking, the banging and knocking as cargo was moved about and bulkheads and decks were knocked on to check for hollow compartments.

After 1,200 seconds, each of which Kickaha had silently counted off, the search party moved on. Again, he and Anana tried to overtake their lost sleep in turns.

## VII

WHEN THE TIME came that they both felt refreshed enough to stay awake at the same time, he asked her how she had gotten into this situation.

"The Black Bellers," she said. She held up her right hand. A ring with a deep black metal band and a large dark-green jewel was on the middle finger.

"I gave the smugglers all my jewels except this," she said. "I refused to part with that; I said I'd have to be killed first. For a moment, I thought they *would* kill me for it.

"Let me see, how to begin? The Black Bellers were originally an artificial form of life created by the Lord scientists about ten thousand years ago. The scientists created the Bellers during their quest for a true immortality.

"A Beller is bell-shaped, black, of indestructible material. Even if one were attached to a hydrogen bomb, the Beller would survive the fission. Or a Beller could be shot into the heart of a star, and it would go unscathed for a billion years.

"Now, the scientists had originally constructed the Beller so that it was purely automatic. It had no mind of its own; it was a device only. When placed on a man's head, it detected the man's skin potential and automatically extruded two extremely thin but rigid needles. These bored through the skull and into the brain.

"Through the needles, the Beller could discharge the contents of a man's mind, that is, it could uncoil the chains of giant protein molecules composing memory. And it could dissociate the complex neural patterns of the conscious and unconscious mind."

"What could be the purpose of that?" Kickaha said. "Why would a Lord want his brain unscrambled, that is, discharged? Wouldn't he be a blank, a *tabula rasa*, then?"

"Yes, but you don't understand. The discharged and uncoiled mind belonged to a human subject of the Lords. A slave."

Kickaha wasn't easily shocked, but he was startled and sickened now. "What? But . . . "

Anana said earnestly, "This was necessary. The slave would die someday anyway, so what's the difference? But a Lord could live even if his body was mortally hurt."

She did not explain that the scientific techniques of the Lords enabled them to live for millennia, perhaps millions of years, if no accidents, homicide, or suicide occurred. Kickaha, of course, knew this. The agelessness was, to a slighter degree, prevalent for human beings throughout this, Wolff's universe. The waters of this world contained substances provided by Wolff which kept human beings from aging for approximately a thousand years. It also cut down on fertility, so that there was no increase in the birth rate.

"The Bellers were to provide a means whereby the mental contents of a Lord could be transferred to the brain of a host. Thus, the Lord could live on in a new body while the old one died of its wounds.

"The Beller was constructed so that the mental contents of the Lord could be stored for a very long time indeed if an emergency demanded this. The Beller contained a power-pack for operation of the stored mind if this was desired. Moreover, the Beller automatically drew on the neural energy of the host to charge the power-pack. The uncoiling and dematricising were actually the Beller's methods of scanning the mind and then recording it within the bell structure. Duplicating the mind, as it were. The duplication resulted in stripping the original brain, in leaving it blank.

"I'm repeating," she said, "but only to make sure you understand me."

"I follow you," he said. "But this stripping, dematricising, scanning, and duplication doesn't seem to me to be a true immortality. It's not like pouring the mental contents of one head into another. It's not a genuine brain transference. It consists, in reality, of recording cerebral complexes, forebrain and, I suppose, hindbrain, too, to get the entire mind—or don't Bellers have unconsciousnesses?—while destroying them. And then running off the records—tapes, if you will—to build an identical brain in a different container.

"The brain of the second party, however, is not the brain of the first party. In reality, the first party is dead. And though the second party thinks that it is the first party, because it has the brain complex of the first party, it is only a duplication."

"A baby speaks the wisdom of the ages," she said. "That would be true if there were no such thing as the psyche, or the soul, as you humans call it. But the Lords had indubitable proof that an extra-spatial, extra-temporal entity, coeval with every sentient being, exists. Even you humans have them. These duplicate the mental content of the body or soma. Rather, they reflect the psyche-soma, or perhaps it's vice versa.

"Anyway, the psyche is the other half of the 'real' person. And when the duplicate soma-brain is built up in the Beller, the psyche, or soul, transfers to the Beller. And when the Beller retransfers the mental contents to the new host, the psyche then goes to the new host."

Kickaha said, "You have proof of this psyche? Photographs? Sensual indications? And so on?"

"I've never seen any," she said. "Or known anyone who had seen the proofs. But we have been assured that the proofs existed at one time."

"Fine," he said with a sarcasm that she may or may not have detected. "So then?"

"The experiment took over fifty years, I believe, before the Bellers were one hundred percent safe and perfectly operational. Most of the research was done on human slaves, who often died or became idiots."

"In the name of science!"

"In the name of the Lords," she said. "In the name of immortality for the Lords. But the human subjects, and later the Lords who became subjects, reported an almost unendurable feeling of detachment from reality, an agony of separation, while their brains were housed in the Bellers. You see, the brains did have some perception of the world outside if the needle-antennae were extruded. But this perception was very limited.

"To overcome the isolation and panic, the perceptive powers of the antennae were improved. Sound, odor, and a limited sense of vision were made available through the antennae."

Kickaha said, "These Black Bellers are former Lords?"

"No! The scientists accidentally discovered that an unused bell had the potentialities for developing into an entity. That is, an unused bell was a baby Beller. And if it were talked to, played with, taught to speak, to identify, to develop its embryonic personality—well, it became, not a thing, a mechanical device, but a person. A rather alien, peculiar person, but still a person."

"In other words," he said, "The framework for housing a human brain could become a brain in its own right?"

"Yes. The scientists became fascinated. They made a separate project out of raising Bellers. They found that a Beller could become as complex and as intelligent as an adult Lord. Meanwhile, the original project was abandoned, although undeveloped Bellers were to be used as receptacles for storing excess memories of Lords."

Kickaha said, "I think I know what happened."

She continued, "No one knows what really happened. There were ten thousand fully adult Bellers in the project and a number of baby Bellers. Somehow, a Beller managed to get its needle-antennae into the skull of a Lord. It uncoiled and dematricised the Lord's brain and then transferred itself into the host's brain. Thereafter, one by one, the other Lords in the project were taken over."

Kickaha had guessed correctly. The Lords had created their own Frankensteins.

"At that time, my ancestors were creating their private custom-made universes," she said. "They were indeed Lords—gods if there ever were any.

The home universe, of course, continued to be the base for the stock population.

"Many of the Bellers in the hosts' bodies managed to get out of the home universe and into the private universes. By the time that the truth was discovered, it was impossible to know who had or had not been taken over, there had been so many transfers. Almost ten thousand Lords had been, as it was termed, 'belled.'

"The War of the Black Bellers lasted two hundred years. I was born during this time. By then, most of the Lord scientists and technicians had been killed. Over half the laymen population was also dead. The home universe was ravaged. This was the beginning of the end of science and progress and the beginning of the solipsism of the Lords. The survivors had much power and the devices and machines in their control. But the understanding of the principles behind the power and the machines was lost.

"Of the ten thousand Bellers, all but fifty were accounted for. The 9,950 were placed inside a universe specially created for them. This was triple-walled so that nobody could ever get in or out."

"And the missing fifty?"

"Never found. From then on, the Lords lived in suspicion, on the verge of panic. Yet, there was no evidence that any Lords were belled. In time, though the panic faded, the missing fifty were not forgotten."

She held up her right hand. "See this ring? It can detect the bell-housing of a Black Beller when it comes within twenty feet. It can't detect a Beller who's housed in a host-body, of course. But the Bellers don't like to be too far from the bells. If anything should happen to the host-body, a Beller wants to be able to transfer his mind back into the bell before the body dies.

"The ring, detecting the bell, triggers an alarm device implanted in the brain of the Lord. This alarm stimulates certain areas of the neural system so that the Lord hears the tolling of a bell. Now, to my knowledge, the tolling of the alarm bell has not sounded for a little less than ten thousand years. But it sounded for three of us not two weeks ago. And we knew that the ancient horror was loose."

"The fifty are now accounted for?" he said.

"Not all fifty. At least, I've seen only a few," she replied. "I think what happened is that all fifty must have been cached together in some universe. They lay in suspended animation for ten millennia. Then some human, some *leb*–" She stopped on seeing his expression and then continued, "Some human stumbled across the cache. He was curious and put one of the bell shapes on his head. And the Beller automatically extruded the needle-antennae. At the same time, the Beller awoke from his ten thousand year sleep. It anesthetized the human through his skin so that he wouldn't struggle, bored into the skull and brain, discharged the human neural configuration and memories, and then transferred itself into the brain. After that, the human-Beller found hosts for the remaining forty-nine. Then the fifty set out on their swift and silent campaign."

There was no telling how many universes the Bellers had taken nor how many Lords they had slain or possessed. They had been unlucky with three: Nimstowl, Judubra, and Anana. She and Nimstowl had managed to inform Judubra of the situation, and he had permitted them to take refuge in his universe. Only the Black Bellers could have made a Lord forget his perpetual war against every other Lord. Judubra was resetting his defenses when the enemy burst through. All three Lords had been forced to gate through to Wolff's palace in this universe.

They had chosen his palace because they had heard that he was now soft and weak; he would not try to kill them if they were friendly. But the palace seemed to be vacant except for the taloses, the half-metal, half-protein machines that were servants and guards for Wolff and Chryseis.

"Wolff gone?" Kickaha said. "Chryseis, too? Where?"

"I do not know," Anana said. "We had little time to investigate. We were forced to gate out of the control room without knowing where we were going. We came out in the Temple of Ollimaml, from which we fled into the city of Talanac. We were fortunate to run into Clatatol and her gang. Not four days later, the Drachelanders invaded Talanac. I don't know how the Black Bellers managed to possess von Turbat, von Swindebarn, and the others."

"They gated through to Dracheland," he said, "and they took over the two kings without the kings' subjects knowing it, of course. They probably didn't know that I was in Talanac, but they must have known about me, I suppose, from films and recordings in the palace. They came here after you Lords, but heard that I was here also and so came after me."

"Why would they want you?"

"Because I know a lot about the secret gates and traps in the palace. For one thing, they won't be able to get into the armory unless they know the pattern of code-breaking. That's why they wanted me alive. For the information I had."

She asked, "Are there any aircraft in the palace?"

"Wolff never had any."

"I think the Bellers will be bringing in some from my world. But they'll have to dismantle them to get them through the narrow gates in the palace. Then they'll have to put them together again. But when the humans see the aircraft, the Bellers will have to do some explaining."

"They can tell the people they're magical vessels," Kickaha said.

Kickaha wished he had the Horn of Shambarimen, or of Ilmarwolkin, as it was sometimes called. When the proper sequence of notes was blown from it at a resonant point in any universe, that point became a gate between two universes. The Horn could also be used to gate between various points on this planet. All that business of matching crescents of gates could be bypassed. But she had not seen the Horn. Probably Wolff had taken it with him, wherever he had gone.

The days and nights that followed were uncomfortable. They paced back and forth to exercise and also let Petotoc stretch his muscles while Kickaha held a rope tied around Petotoc's neck. They slept jerkily. Though they had agreed not to burn the lamp much, because they wanted to save fuel, they kept it lit a good part of the time.

The third day, many men came aboard. The anchor was hauled and the boat was, apparently, rowed into dock. Sounds of cargo being loaded filtered through the wooden bulkheads and decks.

These lasted for forty-eight hours without ceasing. Then the boat left the dock, and the oarsmen went to work. The hammer of the pacer, the creak of locks, the dip and whish of oars went on for a long time.

# VIII

THE JOURNEY took about six days. Then the boat stopped, the anchor was run out, and sounds of unloading beat at the walls of the chamber. Kickaha was sure that they had traveled westward to the edge of the Great Plains.

When all seemed quiet, he swam out. Coming up on the landward side, he saw docks, other boats, a fire in front of a large log building, and a low, heavily wooded hill to the east.

It was the terminus frontier town for the river boats. Here the trade goods were transferred to the giant wagons, which would then set out in caravans toward the Great Trade Path.

Kickaha had no intention of letting Petotoc go, but he asked him if he wished to stay with them or would he rather take his chance on joining the Tishquetmoac. Petotoc replied that he was wanted for the murder of a policeman—he would take his chances with them.

They sneaked onto a farm near the edge of town and stole clothes, three horses, and weapons. To do this, it was necessary to knock out the farmer, his wife, and the two sons while they slept. Then the three rode out past the stockaded town and the fort. They came to the edge of the Great Plains an hour before dawn. They decided to follow the trade path for a while. Kickaha's goal was the village of the Hrowakas in the mountains a thousand miles away. There they could plan a campaign which involved some secret gates on this level.

Kickaha had tried to keep up Anana's morale during their imprisonment in the hidden chamber in the boat, joking and laughing, though softly so that he would not be heard by the sailors. But now he seemed to explode, he talked and laughed so much. Anana commented on this, saying that he was now the happiest man she had ever seen; he shone with joy.

"Why not?" he said, waving his hand to indicate the Great Plains. "The air is drunk with sun and green and life. There are vast rolling prairies before us, much like the plains of North America before the white man came. But far more exotic or romantic or colorful, or whatever adjective you choose. There are buffalo by the millions, wild horses, deer, antelope, and the great beasts of prey, the striped Plains lion or Felis Atrox, the running lion, which is a cheetah-like evolution of the puma, the dire wolf and the Plains wolf, the coyote, the prairie dog! The Plains teem with life! Not only pre-Columbian animals but many which Wolff gated through from Earth and which have become extinct there. Such as the mastodon, the mammoth, the uintathere, the plains camel, and many others.

"And there are the nomadic tribes of Amerinds; a fusion of American Indian and Scythian and Sarmatian white nomads of ancient Russia and Siberia. And the Half-Horses, the centaurs created by Jadawin, whose speech and customs are those of the Plains tribes.

"Oh, there is much to talk about here! And much which I do not know yet but will some day! Do you realize that this level has a land area larger than that of the North and South Americas of my native Earth combined?

"This fabulous world! My world! I believe that I was born for it and that it was more than a coincidence that I happened to find the means to get to it! It's a dangerous world, but then what world, including Earth, isn't? I have been the luckiest of men to be able to come here, and I would not go back to Earth for any price. This is my world!"

Anana smiled slightly and said, "You can be enthusiastic because you are young. Wait until you are ten thousand years old. Then you will find little to enjoy."

"I'll wait," he said. "I am fifty years old, I think, but I look and feel a vibrant twenty-five, if you will pardon the slick-prose adjective."

Anana did not know what slick-prose meant, and so Kickaha explained as best he could. He found out that Anana knew something about Earth, since she had been there several times, the latest visit being in the Earth year 1888 A.D. She had gone there on "vacation" as she put it.

They came to a woods, and Kickaha said they should camp here for the night. He went hunting and came back with a pygmy deer. He butchered it and then cooked it over a small fire. Afterwards, all three chopped branches and made a platform in the fork of two large branches of a tree. They agreed to take one-hour watches. Anana was doubtful about sleeping while Petotoc remained awake, but Kickaha said that they did not have to worry. The fellow was too frightened at the idea of being alone in this wild area to think of killing them or trying to escape on his own. It was then that Anana confessed that she was glad Kickaha was with her.

He was surprised, but agreeably. He said, "You're human after all. Maybe there's some hope for you."

She became angry and turned her back on him and pretended to go to sleep. He grinned and took his watch. The moon bulged greenly in the sky. There were many sounds but all faraway, an occasional trumpet from a mammoth or mastodon, the thunder of a lion, once the whicker of a wild horse, and once the whistle of a giant weasel. This made him freeze, and it caused his horses to whinny. The beast he feared most on the Plains, aside from man and Half-Horse, was the giant weasel. But an hour passed without sound or sight of one, and the horses seemed to relax. He told Petotoc about the animal, warned him to strain all shadows for the great long slippery bulk of the weasel, and not to hesitate to shoot with his bow if he thought he saw one. He wanted to make sure that Petotoc would not fall asleep on guard-duty.

Kickaha was on watch at dawn. He saw the flash of light on something white in the sky. Then he could see nothing, but a minute later the sun gleamed on an object in the sky again. It was far away but it was dropping down swiftly, and it was long and needle-shaped. When it came closer, he could see a bulge on its back, something like an enclosed cockpit; briefly, he saw silhouettes of four men.

Then the craft was dwindling across the prairie.

Kickaha woke Anana and told her what he'd seen. She said, "The Bellers must have brought in aircraft from my palace. That is bad. Not only can the craft cover a lot of territory swiftly, it is armed with two long-range beamers. And the Bellers must have hand-beamers, too."

"We could travel at night," Kickaha said. "But even so, we'd sometimes have to sleep in the open during the day. There are plenty of small wooded areas on the Great Plains, but they are not always available on our route."

"They could have more than one craft," she said. "And one could be out at night. They have means for seeing at night and also for detecting bodies at some distance by radiated heat."

There was nothing to do but ride on out into the open and hope that chance would not bring the Bellers near them. The following day, as Kickaha topped the crest of a slight hill, he saw men on horseback far off. These were not Plains nomads as he would have expected, nor Tishquetmoac. Their armory gleamed in the sun: helmets and cuirasses. He turned to warn the others.

"They must be Teutoniacs from Dracheland," he said. "I don't know how they got out here so fast . . . wait a minute! Yes! They must have come through a gate about ten miles from here. Its crescents are embedded in the tops of two buried boulders near a waterhole. I was thinking about swinging over that way to investigate, though there wasn't much sense in that. It's a one-way gate."

The Teutoniacs must have been sent to search for and cut off Kickaha if he were trying for the mountains of the Hrowakas.

"They'd need a million men to look for me on the Great Plains, and even then I could give them the slip," Kickaha said. "But that aircraft. That's something else."

Three days passed without incident except once, when they came upon a family of Felis Atrox in a little hollow. The adult male and female sprang up and rumbled warnings. The male weighed at least nine hundred pounds and had pale stripes on a tawny body. He had a very small mane; the hairs were thick but not more than an inch long. The female was smaller, weighing probably only seven hundred pounds. The two cubs were about the size of half-grown ocelots.

Kickaha softly told the others to rein in behind him and then he turned his trembling stallion away from the lions, slowly, slowly, and made him walk away. The lions surged forward a few steps but stopped to glare and to roar. They made no move to attack, however; behind them the half-eaten body of a wild striped ass told why they were not so eager to jump the intruders.

The fourth day, they saw the wagon caravan of Tishquetmoac traders. Kickaha rode to within a half mile of it. He could not be recognized at that distance, and he wanted to learn as much as he could about the caravan. He could not answer Anana's questions about the exact goal of his curiosity—he just liked to know things so he would not be ignorant if the situation should change. That was all.

Anana was afraid that Petotoc would take advantage of this to run for the caravan. But Kickaha had his bow ready, and Petotoc had seen enough of his ability to handle the bow to respect it.

There were forty great wagons in the caravan. They were the double-decked, ten wheeled type favored by the Tishquetmoac for heavy-duty Plains transportation. A team of forty mules, larger than Percherons, drew each wagon. There were also a number of smaller wagons which furnished sleeping quarters and food for the cavalry protecting the caravan. The guards numbered about fifty. And there were strings of extra horses for the cavalry and mules for the wagons. There were about three hundred and fifty men, women, and children.

Kickaha rode along to one side and studied the caravan. Finally, Anana said, "What are you thinking?"

He grinned and said, "That caravan will go within two hundred miles of the mountains of the Hrowakas. It'll take a hell of a long time to get there, so what I have to mind wouldn't be very practical. It's too daring. Besides, Petotoc has to be considered."

After he had listened to her plead for some time, he told her what he'd been thinking. She thought he was crazy. Yet, after some consideration, she admitted that the very unconventionality and riskiness of it, its unexpectedness, might actually make it work . . . if they were lucky. But, as he had said, there was Petotoc to consider.

For some time, whenever the Tishquetmoac had not been close enough to hear, she had been urging that they kill him. She argued that he would stab them in the back if he felt he would be safe afterward. Kickaha agreed with her, but he could not kill him without more justification. He thought of abandoning him on the prairie, but he was afraid that Petotoc would be picked up by the searchers.

They swung away from the caravan but rode parallel with it for several days at a distance of a few miles. At night, they retreated even further, since Kickaha did not want to be surprised by them. The third day he was thinking about leaving the caravan entirely and traveling in a southerly direction. Then he saw the flash of white on an object in the sky, and he rode toward a group of widely separated trees, which provided some cover. After tying the horses to bushes, the three crawled up a hill through the tall grass and spied on the caravan.

They were far enough so that they could just distinguish the figures of men. The craft dropped down ahead of the lead wagon and hovered about a foot off the ground. The caravan stopped.

For a long time, a group of men stood by the craft. Even at this distance, Kickaha could see the violent arm-wavings. The traders were protesting, but after a while, they turned and walked back to the lead wagon. And there a process began which took all day, even though the Tishquetmoac worked furiously. Every wagon was unloaded, and the wagons were then searched.

Kickaha said to Anana, "It's a good thing we didn't put my plan into action. We'd have been found for sure! Those guys"—meaning the Bellers—"are thorough!"

That night, the three went deeper into the woods and built no fire. In the morning, Kickaha, after sneaking close, saw that the aircraft was gone. The Tishquetmoac, who must have gotten up very early, were almost finished reloading. He went back to the camping place and spoke to Anana.

"Now that the Bellers have inspected that caravan, they're not very likely to do so again. Now we could do what I proposed—if it weren't for Petotoc."

He did, however, revise his original plan to cut to the south. Instead, he decided to keep close to the caravan. It seemed to him that the Bellers would not be coming back this way again for some time.

The fifth day, he went out hunting alone. He returned with a small deer over his saddle. He had left Anana and Petotoc beneath two trees on the south slope of a hill. They were still there, but Petotoc was sprawled on his back, mouth open, eyes rigid. A knife was stuck in his solar plexus.

"He tried to attack me, the *leblabbiy*!" Anana said. "He wanted me to lie down for him! I refused, and he tried to force me!"

It was true that Petotoc had often stared with obvious lust at Anana, but this was something any man would do. He had never tried to put his hand on her or made any suggestive remarks. This did not mean that he hadn't been planning to do so at the first chance, but Kickaha did not believe that Petotoc would dare make an advance to her. He was, in fact, in awe of Anana, and much too scared of being left alone.

On the other hand, Kickaha could not prove any accusation of murder or of lying. The deed was done, and it could not be undone, so he merely said, "Pull your knife out and clean it. I've wondered what you'd do if I said I wanted to lie with you. Now I know."

She surprised him by saying, "You aren't that one. But you'll never know unless you try, will you?"

"No," he said harshly. He looked at her curiously. The Lords were, according to Wolff, thoroughly amoral. That is, most of them were. Anana was an exceedingly beautiful woman who might or might not be frigid. But ten thousand years seemed like a long time for a woman to remain frigid. Surely techniques or devices existed in the great science of the Lords to overcome frigidity. On the other hand, would a thoroughly passionate woman be able to remain passionate after ten thousand years?

But Wolff had said that even the long-lived Lords lived from day to day. Like mortals, they were caught in the stream of time. And their memories were far from perfect, fortunately for them. So that, though they were subject to much greater boredom and ennui than the so-called mortals, they still weren't overwhelmed. Their rate of suicide was, actually, lower than a comparable group of humans, but this could be attributed to the fact that those with suicidal tendencies had long ago done away with themselves.

Whatever her feelings, she was not revealing them to him. If she was suffering from sexual frustration, as he was at this time, she was not showing any signs. Perhaps the idea of lying with him, a lowly, even repulsive, mortal, was unthinkable to her. Yet he had heard stories of the sexual interest Lords took in their more attractive human subjects. Wolff himself had said that, when he was Jadawin, he had rioted among the lovely females of this world, had used his irresistible powers to get what he wanted.

Kickaha shrugged. There were more important matters to think about at this moment. Survival outweighed everything.

# IX

FOR THE next two days they had to ride far away from the caravan because the hunting parties from it foraged wide in their quest for buffalo, deer, and antelope meat. And then, while dodging the Tishquetmoac, the two almost ran into a small band of Satwikilap hunters. These Amerinds, painted in white and black stripes from head to foot, their long black hair coiled on top of their heads, bones stuck through their septums, strings of lion teeth around their necks, wearing lionskin pantaloons and deer moccasins, rode within a hundred yards of Anana and Kickaha. But they were intent on shooting the buffalo in the rear of a running herd and did not see them.

Moreover, the Tishquetmoac hunters were after the same bison, but they were on the other side of the herd, separated from the Satwikilap by a mile of almost solid flesh.

Kickaha suddenly made up his mind. He told Anana that tonight was the time. She hesitated, then said they might as well try. Certainly, anything that would take them out of the sight of the Bellers should be tried.

They waited until the eating of roast meat and the drinking of gin and vodka was finished and the caravaneers had staggered off to bed. There were non-drinking sentries posted at intervals along the sides of the wagon train, but the caravan was within the borders of the Great Trade Path marked by the carved wooden images of the god of trade and business so the Tishquetmoac did not really worry about attack from men or Half-Horses. Some animal might blunder into the camp or a giant weasel or lion try for a horse or even for a Tishquetmoac, but this wasn't likely, so the atmosphere was relaxed.

Kickaha removed all harness from the horses and slapped them on the rumps so they would take off. He felt a little sorry for them, since they were domesticated beasts and not likely to flourish on the wild Great Plains. But they would have to take their chances, as he was taking his.

Then he and Anana, a pack of bottled water and dried meat and vegetables tied to their backs, knives in their teeth, crawled in the moon-spattered darkness toward the caravan. They got by two guards, stationed forty yards apart, without being seen. They headed for a huge ten-wheeler wagon that was twentieth in line. They crept past small wagons holding snoring men, women, and children. Fortunately, there were no dogs with the caravan and for a good reason. The cheetah-like puma and the weasel were especially fond of dogs, so much so that the Tishquetmoac had long ago given up taking these pets along on the Plains voyage.

Arranging living quarters inside the tightly packed cargo in the lower deck of a wagon was not easy. They had to pull out a number of wooden boxes and bolts of cloth and rugs and then remass them over the hole in which they would spend their daylight hours. The dislodged cargo was jammed in with some effort wherever it would go. Kickaha hoped that nobody would notice that the arrangements were not what they were when the wagon left the terminus.

They had two empty bottles for sanitary purposes; blankets provided a fairly comfortable bed for them—until the wagon started rolling in the morning. The wagon had no springs; and though the prairie seemed smooth enough to a man walking, the roughnesses became exaggerated in the wagon.

Anana complained that she had felt shut-in in the boat chamber, but now she felt as if she were buried in a landslide. The temperature outside seldom got above seventy-five degrees Fahrenheit at noon, but the lack of ventilation and the closeness of their bodies threatened to stifle them. They had to sit up and stick their noses into the openings to get enough oxygen.

Kickaha widened the openings. He hated to do so because it made discovery by the caravaneers more likely; while the wagon was traveling however, no one was going to peep into the lower deck.

They got little sleep the first day. At night, while the Tishquetmoac slept, they crept out and crawled past the sentries into the open. Here they bathed in a waterhole, refilled their bottles, and discharged natural functions which had been impossible, or highly inconvenient, inside the wagon. They exercised to take the stiffness out of muscles caused by cramped conditions and the jostling and bouncing. Kickaha wondered if he was so clever after all. It had seemed the most impudent thing in the world, hiding out literally under the noses, not to mention the buttocks, of the Tishquetmoac. Alone, he might have been more comfortable, more at ease. But though Anana did not really complain much, her not-quite-suppressed groans and moans and invectives irked him. It was impossible in those closely walled quarters not to touch each other frequently, but she reacted overviolently every time. She told him to stay to his own half of the "coffin," not to make his body so evident, and so on.

Kickaha began to think seriously about telling her to take off on her own. Or, if she refused, knocking her out and dragging her away some place and leaving her behind. Or, at times, he fantasized about slitting her throat or tying her to a tree so the lions or wolves could get her.

It was, he told himself, a hell of a way for a love affair to start.

And then he caught himself. Yes, he had said that: *love affair*. Now, how could he be in love with such a vicious, arrogant, murderous bitch?

He was. Much as he hated, loathed, and despised her, he was beginning to love her.

Love was nothing new to Kickaha in this or that other world . . . but never under these circumstances.

Undoubtedly, except for Podarge, who looked just like Anana as far as the face was concerned, and the strange, really unearthly Chryseis, Anana was the most beautiful woman he had ever seen.

To Kickaha, this would not automatically bring love. He appreciated beauty in a woman, of course, but he was more liable to fall in love with a woman with an agreeable personality and a quick brain and humor than with a disagreeable and/or dumb woman. If the woman was only reasonably attractive or perhaps even plain, he could fall in love with her if he found certain affinities in her.

And Anana was certainly disagreeable.

So why this feeling of love side by side with the hostility he felt toward her?

*Who knows*? Kickaha thought. *Evidently, I don't. And that in itself is pleasing, since I would not like to become bored and predictable about myself.*

The bad thing about this affair was that it would probably be one-sided. She might take a sensual interest in him, but it would be ephemeral and there would be contempt accompanying it. Certainly, she could never love a *leblabbiy*. For that matter, he doubted that she could love anyone. The Lords were beyond love. Or at least that was what Wolff had told him.

The second day passed more quickly than the first; both were able to sleep more. That night, they were treed by a pride of lions that had come down to drink at a stream shortly after the two humans arrived. Finally, as the hours had gone by and the lions showed no desire to wander on, Kickaha became desperate. Dawn would soon lighten this area. It would be impossible to sneak back into the wagon. He told Anana that they would have to climb down and try to bluff the big cats.

Kickaha, as usual, had another motive than the obvious. He hoped that, if she had any weapons concealed or implanted in her body, she would reveal them now. But either she had none or she did not think the situation desperate enough to use them. She said that he could attempt to scare the monsters, if he wished, but she intended to stay in the tree until they went away.

"Under ordinary circumstances, I'd agree with you," he said. "But we have to get back inside the wagon within the next half hour."

"I don't have to," she said. "Besides, you didn't kill anything for us to eat before we went back. I don't want to spend another hungry day inside that coffin."

"You had plenty of dried meat and vegetables to eat," he said.

"I was hungry all day," she replied.

Kickaha started to climb down. Most of the lions seemed to be paying no attention to him. But a male sprang into the air and a long-clawed paw came within six inches of his foot. He went back up the tree.

"They don't seem to be in a mood to be bluffed," he said. "Some days they are. Today, well . . . "

From his height in the tree he could see part of the wagon train, even in the moonlight. Presently the moon went around the monolith and the sun followed it from the east. The caravaneers began to wake. Campfires were built, and the bustle of getting ready for breakfast and then breaking camp began. Presently, a number of soldiers, colorful in long-feathered wooden casques, scarlet quilt-cuirasses, green feathered kilts, and yellow-dyed leggings, mounted their horses. They formed a crescent within which men and women, carrying pots, kettles, jugs, and other utensils, marched. They headed toward the waterhole.

Kickaha groaned. Occasionally he outfoxed himself, and this could be one of the occasions.

There was not the slightest doubt about his choice. It would be far better to face the lions than to be captured by the Tishquetmoac. While he might be able to talk them out of turning him over to the Teutoniacs, he doubted it very much. Anyway, he could not afford to risk their mercy.

He said, "Anana, I'm going north, and I'm going fast. Coming along?"

She looked down at the big male lion, crouched at the foot of the tree and staring up with huge green eyes. His mouth also stared. Four canines, two up, two down, seemed as long as daggers.

"You must be crazy," she said.

"You stay here if you want to. So long, if ever!"

He began to climb down but on the other side of the tree, away from the lion. The great beast arose and roared, and then the others were on their feet and pointing toward the approaching humans. The wind had brought their scent.

For a moment, the cats did not seem to know what to do. Then the male under the tree roared and slunk off and the others followed him. Kickaha dropped the rest of the way and ran in the same direction as the lions. He did not look back, but he hoped that Anana would have enough presence of mind to follow him. If the soldiers caught her, or even saw her, they would search the area on the premise that other fugitives might be nearby.

He heard her feet thudding on the earth, and then she was close behind him. He looked back then, not at her but for signs of the cavalry. He saw the head of one soldier appear over a slight rise, and he grabbed Anana and pulled her down into the high grass.

There was a shout—the rider had seen them. It was to be expected. And now . . . ?

Kickaha stood up and looked. The first rider was in full view. He was standing up in the stirrups and pointing in their direction. Others were coming up behind him. Then the lead man was riding toward them, his lance couched.

Kickaha looked behind him. Plains and tall grass and a few trees here and there. Far off, a gray many-humped mass that was a herd of mammoths. The lions were somewhere in the grass.

The big cats would have to be his joker. If he could spring them at the right time, and not get caught himself, then he might get away.

He said, "Follow me!" and began to run as swiftly as he had ever run in his life. Behind him, the soldiers yelled and the horses' hooves krok-krok-krokked.

The lions failed him. They scattered away, bounding easily, not panicked but just not wanting to turn to fight at this moment. They did not give him the opportunity he sought to flee while horse and rider were being clawed down by lions at bay.

Some of the cavalry passed him and then they had turned and were facing him, their lances forming a crescent. Behind him, other lances made a half ring. He and Anana were between the crescents with no place to go unless they hurled themselves on the lance-points.

"This is what I get for being too smart," he said to Anana.

She did not laugh. He did not feel much like laughing himself.

He felt even less like it when they were brought back, bound and helpless, to the caravan. The chief, Clishquat, informed them that the rewards had been tripled. And though he had heard of Kickaha, and of course admired and respected him as the beloved of the Lord, well, things had changed, hadn't they?

Kickaha had to admit that they had. He asked

Clishquat if the emperor was still alive. Clishquat was surprised at the question. Of course the *miklosiml* was alive. He was the one offering the rewards. He was the one who had proclaimed the alliance with the pinkface sorcerers who flew in a wheelless wagon. And so on.

Kickaha's intention to talk the caravaneers out of keeping him captive by telling them the true situation in Talanac did not work. The empire-wide system of signal drums and of pony express had acquainted the frontier towns with conditions in the capital city. It was true that some of the news was false, but Clishquat would not believe Kickaha concerning it. Kickaha could not blame him.

The two captives were given a full meal; and women bathed them, oiled their bodies and hair, combed their hair and put fresh clothes on them. During this, the chiefs, the underchiefs, and the soldiers who had captured the two, argued. The chief thought that the soldiers should split the reward with him. The underchiefs believed they should get in on the money. And then some representatives of the rest of the caravaneers marched up. They demanded that the reward be split evenly throughout the caravan.

At this, the chiefs and the soldiers began screaming at the newcomers. Finally, the chief quieted them down. He said that there was only one way to settle the matter. That would be to submit the case to the emperor. In effect, this meant the high court of judges of Talanac.

The soldiers objected. The case would limp along for years before being settled. By then, the legal fees would have devoured much of the reward money.

Clishquat, having scared everybody with this threat, then offered a compromise which he hoped would be satisfactory. One-third should go to the soldiers; one-third to the civilian leaders of the caravan, the chief and chieflings; one-third to be divided equally among the remaining men.

There was a dispute that lasted through lunch and supper. The train did not move during this.

Then, when everybody had agreed, more or less amicably, on the splitting of the reward, a new argument started. Should the caravan move on, taking the prisoners with them, in the hope that the magic airboat would come by again, as the pinkface sorcerers had promised? The prisoners could then be turned over to the sorcerers. Or should a number of soldiers take the prisoners back to Talanac while the caravan moved on to its business?

Some objectors said that the sorcerers might not return. Even if they did, they would not have room in the boat for the fugitives.

Others said that those picked to escort the prisoners home might claim the entire reward for themselves. By the time the caravan returned to civilization, it might find that the escort had spent the money. And suit in court would be useless.

And so on and so on.

Kickaha asked a woman how the pinkfaces had communicated with the caravan chief.

"There were four pinkfaces and each had a seat in the magic car," she replied. "But a priest talked for them. He sat by the feet of the one who was in a chair in front and to the right. The pinkfaces talked in the language of the Lords—I know it at least when I hear it, though I do not speak it as the priests do—and the priests listened and then spoke to the chief in our language.''

Late at night, when the moon was halfway across the bridge of sky, the argument was still going on. Kickaha and Anana went to sleep in their beds of furs and blankets in the upper deck of a wagon. They awoke in the morning to find camp being broken. It had been decided to take the prisoners along with the hope that the magic flying car would return as its occupants had promised.

The two captives were permitted to walk behind the wagon during the day. Six soldiers kept guard throughout the day, and another six stood watch over the wagon at night.

# X

THE THIRD NIGHT, events developed as Kickaha had been hoping they would. The six guards had been very critical of the decision to split the reward throughout the caravan. They spent a good part of the night muttering among themselves, and Kickaha, awake part of the time, testing his bonds, overheard much of what they said.

He had warned Anana to make no outcry or struggle if she should be awakened by the sentries. The two were rousted out with warnings to keep silent or die with slit throats. They were marched off between two unconscious sentries and into a small group of trees. Here were horses, saddled, packed, ready to be mounted by the six soldiers and two prisoners, and extra pack horses. The party rode out slowly for several miles, then began to canter. Their flight lasted the night and half the next day. They did not stop to make camp until they were sure that they were not pursued. Since they had left the trade trail and swung far north, they did not expect to be followed.

The next day, they continued parallel with the trade trail. On the third day, they began to angle back toward it. Being so long outside the safety of the trade path made them nervous.

Kickaha and Anana rode in the center of the party. Their hands were tied with ropes but loosely, so they could handle the reins. They stopped at noon. They were just finishing their cooked rabbit and greens boiled in little pots, when a lookout on a hill nearby called out. He came galloping toward them, and, when he was closer, he could be heard.

"Half-Horses!"

The pots were emptied on top of the fire, and dirt was kicked over the wet ashes. In a panic, the soldiers packed away most of their utensils. The two captives were made to remount, and the party started off southward, toward the trade trail, many miles away.

It was then that the soldiers saw the wave of buffalo moving across the plains. It was a tremendous herd several miles across and of a seemingly interminable length. The right flank was three miles from them, but the earth quivered under the impact of perhaps a quarter of a million hooves.

For some reason known only to the buffalo, they were in flight. They were stampeding westward, and they were going so swiftly that the Tishquetmoac party might not be able to get across the trade path in time. They had a chance, but they would not know how good it was until they got much closer to the herd.

The Half-Horses had seen the humans, and they had bent into full gallop. There were about thirty of them: a chief with a full-feathered and long-tailed bonnet, a number of blooded warriors with feathered headbands, and three or four unblooded juveniles.

Kickaha groaned; it seemed to him that they

were of the Shoyshatel tribe. They were so far away that the markings were not quite distinct. But he thought that the bearing of the chief was that of the Half-Horse who had shouted threats at him when Kickaha had taken refuge at the Tishquetmoac fort.

Then he laughed, because it did not matter which tribe it was. All Half-Horse tribes hated Kickaha and all would treat him as cruelly as possible if they caught him.

He yelled at the leader of the soldiers, Takwoc, "Cut the ropes from our wrists! They're handicapping us! We can't get away from you, don't worry!"

Takwoc looked for a moment as if he might actually cut the ropes. The danger involved in riding so close to Kickaha, the danger of the horses knocking each other down or Kickaha knocking him off the saddle, probably made him change his mind. He shook his head.

Kickaha cursed and then crouched over the neck of the stallion and tried to evoke from him every muscle-stretching-contracting quota of energy in his magnificent body. The stallion did not respond because he was already running as swiftly as he could.

Kickaha's horse, though fleet, was half a body-length behind the stallion which Anana rode. Perhaps they were about equal in running ability, but Anana's lighter weight made the difference. The others were not too far behind and were spread out in a rough crescent, with horns curving away from him, three on each side. The Half-Horses were just coming over the rise; they slowed down a moment, probably in amazement at the sight of the tremendous herd. Then they waved their weapons and charged on down the hill.

The herd was rumbling westward. The Tishquetmoac and prisoners were coming on the buffalos' right at an angle of forty-five degrees. The Half-Horses had swung a little to the west before coming over the hill and their greater speed had enabled them to squeeze the distance down between them and their intended victims.

Kickaha, watching the corner formed by the flank of the great column of beasts and the front part—almost square—saw that the party could get across in front of the herd. From then on, speed and luck meant safety to the other side or being overwhelmed by the racing buffalo. The party could not directly cut across the advance; it would have to run ahead of the beasts and at an angle at the time time.

Whether or not the horses could keep up their present thrust of speed, whether or not a horse or all horses might slip, that would be known in a very short time.

He shouted encouragement at Anana as she looked briefly behind, but the rumble of the hooves, shaking the earth and sounding like a volcano ready to blow its crust, tore his voice to shreds.

The roar, the odor of the beasts, the dust, frightened Kickaha. At the same time, he was exhilarated. This wasn't the first time that he had been raised by his fright out of fright and into near-ecstasy. Events seemed to be on such a grand scale all of a sudden, and the race was such a fine one, with the prize sudden safety or sudden death, that he felt as if he were kin to the gods, if not a god. That moment when mortality was so near, and so probable, was the moment he felt immortal.

It was quickly gone, but while it lasted he knew that he was experiencing a mystical state.

Then he was seemingly heading for a collision with the angle formed by the flank and front of the herd.

Now he could see the towering shaggy brown sides of the giant buffalo, the humps heaving up and down like the bodies of porpoises soaring from wave to wave, the dark brown foreheads, massive and lowering, the dripping black snouts, the red eyes, the black eyes, the red-shot white eyes, the legs working so swiftly they were almost a blur, foam curving from the open foam-toothed mouths onto thick shaggy chests and the upper parts of the legs.

He could hear nothing at first but that rumbling as of the earth splitting open, so powerful that he expected, for a second, to see the plain open beneath the hooves and fire and smoke spurt out.

He could smell a million buffalo, beasts extinct for ten thousand years on Earth, monsters with horns ten feet across, sweating with panic and the heart-shredding labor of their flight, excrement of fear befouling them and their companions, and something that smelled to him like a mixture of foam from mouth and blood from lungs, but that, of course, was his imagination.

There was also the stink of his horse, sweat of panic and labor of flight and of foam from its mouth.

"Haiyeeee!" Kickaha shouted, turning to scream at the Half-Horses, wishing his hands were not tied and he had a weapon to shake at them. He could not hear his own defiance, but he hoped that the Half-Horses would see his open mouth and his grin and know that he was mocking them.

By now, the centaurs were within a hundred and fifty yards of their quarry. They were frenzied in their efforts to catch up; their great dark broad-cheekboned faces were twisted in agony.

They could not close swiftly enough, and they knew it. By the time their quarry had shot across the right shoulder of the herd at an angle, they would still be fifty or so yards behind. And by the time they reached the front of the herd, their quarry would be too far ahead. And after that, they would slowly lose ground before the buffalo, and before they could get to the other side, they would go down under the shelving brows and curving horns and cutting hooves.

Despite this, the Half-Horses galloped on. An unblooded, a juvenile whose headband was innocent of scalp or feather, had managed to get ahead of the others. He left the others behind at such a rate that Kickaha's eyes widened. He had never seen so swift a Half-Horse before, and he had seen many. The unblooded came on and on, his face twisted with an effort so intense that Kickaha would not have been surprised to see the muscles of the face tear loose.

The Half-Horse's arm came back, and then forward, and the lance flew ahead of him, arcing down, and suddenly Kickaha saw that what he had thought would be impossible was happening.

The lance was going to strike the hind quarters or the legs of his stallion. It was coming down in a curve that would fly over the Tishquetmoac riders behind him and would plunge into some part of his horse.

He pulled the reins to direct the stallion to the left, but the stallion pulled its head to one side and slowed down just a trifle. Then he felt a slight shock, and he knew that the lance had sunk into its flesh.

Then the horse was going over, its front legs crumpling, the back still driving and sending the rump into the air. The neck shot away from before him, and he was soaring through the air.

Kickaha did not know how he did it. Something took over in him as it had done before, and he did not fall or slide into the ground. He landed running on his feet with the black-and-brown wall of the herd to his left. Behind him, so close that he could hear it even above the rumble-roar of the herd, was the thunk of horses' hooves. Then the sound was all around him, and he could no longer stay upright because of his momentum, and he went into the grass on his face and slid.

A shadow swooped over him; it was that of a horse and rider as the horse jumped him. Then all seven were past him; he saw Anana looking back over her shoulder just before the advancing herd cut her—cut all the Tishquetmoac, too—from his sight.

There was nothing they could do for him. To delay even a second meant death for them under the hooves of the buffalo or the spears of the Half-Horses. He would have done the same if he had been on his horse and she had fallen off hers.

Surely the Half-Horses must have been yelling in triumph now. The stallion of Kickaha was dead, a lance projecting from its rump and its neck broken. Their greatest enemy, the trickster who had so often given them the slip when they knew they had him, even he could not now escape. Not unless he were to throw himself under the hooves of the titans thundering not ten feet away!

This thought may have struck them, because they swept toward him with the unblooded who had thrown the lance trying to cut him off. The others had thrown their lances and tomahawks and clubs and knives away and were charging with bare hands. They wanted to take him alive.

Kickaha did not hesitate. He had gotten up as soon as he was able and now he ran toward the herd. The flanks of the beasts swelled before him; they were six feet high at the shoulder and running as if time itself were behind them and threatening to make them extinct like their brothers on Earth.

Kickaha ran toward them, seeing out of the corner of his eyes the young unblooded galloping in. Kickaha gave a savage yell and leaped upward, his hands held before him. His foot struck a massive shoulder and he grabbed a shag of fur. He kicked upward and slipped and fell forward and was on his stomach on the back of a bull!

He was looking down the steep valley formed by the right and left sides of two buffalo. He was going up and down swiftly, was getting sick, and also was slowly sliding backward.

After loosing his hold on the tuft of hair, he grabbed another one to his right and managed to work himself around so that his legs straddled the back of the beast. The hump was in front of him; he was hanging onto the hair of it.

If Kickaha believed only a little in what had happened, the Half-Horse youth who had thought he had Kickaha in his hands believed it not at all.

He raced alongside the bull on which Kickaha was seated, and his eyes were wide and his mouth worked. His arms were extended in front of him as if he still thought he would scoop Kickaha up in them.

Kickaha did not want to let loose of his hold, insecure though it was, but he knew that the Half-Horse would recover in a moment. Then he would pull a knife or tomahawk from the belt around the lower part of his human torso, and he would throw it at Kickaha. If he missed, he had weapons in reserve.

Kickaha brought his legs up so that he was squatting on top of the spine of the great bull, his feet together, one hand clenching buffalo hair. He turned slowly, managing to balance himself despite the up-and-down jarring movement. Then he launched himself outward and onto the back of the next buffalo, which was running shoulder to shoulder with the animal he had just left.

Something dark rotated over his right shoulder. It struck the hump of a buffalo nearby and bounced up and fell between two animals. It was a tomahawk.

Kickaha pulled himself up again, this time more swiftly, and he got his feet under him and jumped. One foot slipped as he left the back, but he was so close to the other that he grabbed fur with both hands. He hung there while his toes just touched the ground whenever the beast came down in its galloping motion. Then he let himself slide down a little, pushed against the ground, and swung himself upward. He got one leg over the back and came up and was astride it.

The young Half-Horse was still keeping pace with him. The others had dropped back a little; perhaps they thought he had fallen down between the buffalo and so was ground into shreds. If so, they must have been shocked to see him rise from the supposed dead, the Trickster, slippery, cunning, many-turning, the enemy who mocked them from within death's mouth.

The unblooded must have been driven a little crazy when he saw Kickaha. Suddenly, his great body, four hooves flying, soared up and he was momentarily standing on the back of a buffalo at the edge of the herd. He sprang forward to the next one, onto its hump, like a mountain goat skipping on moving mountains.

Now it was Kickaha's turn to be amazed and dismayed. The Half-Horse held a knife in his hand, and he grinned at Kickaha as if to say, "At last, you are going to die, Kickaha! And I, I will be sung of throughout the halls and tepees of the Nations of the prairies and the mountains, by men and Half-Horses everywhere!"

Some such thoughts must have been in that huge head. And he would have become the most famous of all dwellers on and about the Plains, if he had succeeded. Trickster-killer he would have been named.

He Who Skipped Over Mad Buffalo To Cut Kickaha's Throat.

But on the third hump, a hoof slipped and he plunged on over the hump and fell down between two buffalo, his back legs flying and tail straight up. And that was the end of him, though Kickaha could not see what the buffalo hooves were doing.

Still, the attempt had been magnificent and had

almost succeeded, and Kickaha honored him even if he was a Half-Horse. Then he began to think again about surviving.

## XI

SOME OF the centaurs had drawn up even with him and began loosing arrows at Kickaha.

Before the first shaft was released, he had slipped over to one side of the buffalo on which he was mounted, hanging on with both hands to fur, one leg bent as a hook over the back. His position was insecure, because the rough gallop loosened his grip a little with every jolt, and the beast next to him was so close that he was in danger of being smashed.

Shafts passed over him; something touched the foot sticking up in the air. A tomahawk bounced off the top of the buffalo's head. Suddenly, the bull began coughing, and Kickaha wondered if his lungs had been penetrated by an arrow. The bull began to slow down, stumbled a little, recovered, and went on again.

Kickaha reached out for the next beast, grabbed a fistful of fur, released the other hand, clutched more fur, let loose with the right leg, and his body swung down. Like a trick horse rider, he struck the ground with both feet; his legs and body swung up, and he hooked his left leg over the back just behind the hump.

Behind him, the buffalo he had just left fell, slid,

stopped, on its side, kicking, two arrows sticking from it. Then the beasts behind it jumped, but the third one tripped, and there was a pile-up of at least ten mammoth bodies kicking, struggling, goring, and then dying as even more crashed into them and over them and on them.

Something was happening ahead. He could not see what it was because he was hanging on the side of the buffalo, his view blocked by tails, rumps, and legs. But the beasts were slowing down and were also turning to the left.

The buffalo on the right bellowed as if mortally hurt. And so it was. It staggered off, fortunately away from Kickaha, otherwise it would have smashed him if it had fallen against him. It collapsed, blood running from a large hole in its hump.

Kickaha became aware of two things: one, the thunder of the stampede had lessened so much that he could hear individual animals nearby as they cried out or bellowed; two, in addition to the other odors, there was now that of burned flesh and hair.

The beast on the other side fell away, and then that carrying Kickaha was alone. It charged on, passing the carcasses of just-killed buffalo. It bounded over a cow with its great head half cut off. And when it came down, the shock tore Kickaha's grip loose. He fell off and rolled over and over and came up on his feet, ready for he knew not what.

The world seesawed about him, then straightened out. He was gasping for breath, shaking, sweaty, bloody, filthy with buffalo dung and foam and dirt. But he was ready to jump this way or that, depending upon the situation.

There were dead buffalo everywhere. There were also dead Half-Horses here and there. The living in the herd were racing off to the left now; the torrent of millions of tons of flesh and hooves roared by and away.

A crash sounded, so unexpectedly and loudly that he jumped. It was as if a thousand large ships had simultaneously smashed into a reef. Something had killed all of the beasts in a line a mile across, killed them one after the other within six or seven seconds. And those behind the line stumbled over these, and those behind rammed them and went hoof-over-hoof.

Abruptly, the stampede had stopped. Those animals fortunate enough to stop in time stood stupidly about, wheezing for air. Those buried in the huge mounds of carcasses, but still living, bellowed; they were the only ones with enough motive to voice any emotion. The others were laboring to run their breaths down.

Kickaha saw the cause of the dead and of the halted stampede. To his left, a quarter of a mile away and about twenty feet up, was an aircraft. It was needle-shaped, wingless; its lower part was white with black arabesques, its upper part was transparent coaming. Five silhouettes were within the covering.

It was chasing after a Tishquetmoac who was trying to escape on his horse. Chasing was the wrong word. The craft moved swiftly enough but leisurely and made no effort to get immediately behind the horse. A bright white beam shot out from the cylinder mounted on the nose of the craft. Its end touched the rump of the horse which fell. The Tishquetmoac man threw himself out and, though he rolled heavily, he came up and onto his feet.

Kickaha looked around on all sides. Anana was a quarter of a mile away in the other direction. Several Tishquetmoac stood near her. A couple lay on the ground as if dead; one was caught beneath his horse. All the horses were dead, apparently rayed down by the craft.

Also dead were all the Half-Horses.

The Bellers had killed the horses to keep the party from escaping. They might not even know that the man and woman they were looking for were in this group. They might have spotted the chase and swung over for a look and decided to save the chased because they might have some information. On the other hand, both Anana and Kickaha were lighter skinned than the Tishquetmoac in the party. The Tishquetmoac did, however, vary somewhat in darkness; a small minority were not so heavily pigmented. So the Bellers would have decided to check them out. Or . . . there were many possibilities. None mattered now. The important thing was that he and Anana were, seemingly, helpless. They could not get away. And the weapons of the Bellers were overwhelming.

Kickaha did not just give up, although he was so tired that he almost felt like it. He thought, and while he was thinking, he heard a pound of hooves and a harsh rasping breathing. He launched himself forward and at an angle on the theory that he might evade whatever was attacking him—if he were being attacked.

A lance shot by him and then slid along the ground. A bellow sounded behind him; he whirled to see a Half-Horse advancing on him. The centaur was badly wounded; his hindquarters were burned, his tail was half charred off, and his back legs could scarcely move. But he was determined to get Kickaha before he died. He held a long heavy knife in his left hand.

Kickaha ran to the lance, picked it up, and threw it. The Half-Horse yelled with frustration and despair and tried to evade the spear. Handicapped by his crippled legs, he did not move fast enough. He took the lance in his human chest—Kickaha had aimed for the protruding bellows organ below the chest—and fell down. Up he came, struggling to his front legs while the rear refused to move again. He tore the lance out with his right hand, turned it, and, ignoring the spurt of blood from the wound, again cast it. This surprised Kickaha, who was running to push in on the lance and so finish him off.

The arm of the dying centaur was weak. The lance left his hand to fly a few feet and then plunged into the earth before Kickaha's feet. The Half-Horse gave a cry of deep desolation—perhaps he had hoped for glory in song here and a high place in the councils of the dead. But now he knew that if a Half-Horse ever slew Kickaha, he would not be the one.

He fell on his side, dropping the knife as he went down. His front legs kicked several times, his huge fierce face became slack, and the black eyes stared at his enemy.

Kickaha glanced quickly around him, saw that the aircraft was flying a foot above the ground about a quarter of a mile away. Apparently it was corraling several Tishquetmoac who were fleeing on foot. Anana was down. He did not know what had happened to her. Perhaps she was playing possum, which was what he intended to do.

He rubbed some of the centaur's blood over him, lay down in front of him, placed the knife so it was partly hidden under his hip, and then placed the lance point between his chest and arm. Its shaft rose straight up, looking from a distance as if the lance were in his chest, he hoped.

It was a trick born out of desperation and not likely to succeed. But it was the only one he had now, and there was the chance that the Bellers, being nonhuman, might not be on to certain human ruses. In any event, he would try it, and if it didn't work, well, he didn't really expect to live forever.

Which was a lie, he told himself, because he, in common with most men, did expect to live forever. And he had managed to survive so far because he had fought more energetically and cunningly than most.

For what seemed a long time afterward, nothing happened. The wind blew coolly on the blood and sweat. The sweat dried off and the blood dried up. The sun was sinking in the last quarter of the green sky. Kickaha wished that it were dusk, which would increase his chances, but if wishes were horses, he would ride out of here.

A shadow flitted over his eyes. He tensed, thinking it might be that of the aircraft. A harsh cry told him that it was a crow or raven, coming to feed. Soon the carrion eaters would be flying in thicker than pepper on a pot roast: crows, ravens, buzzards, giant vultures, even larger condors, hawks, and eagles, some of which would be the mammoth green eagles, Podarge's pets.

And the coyote, the Plains fox, the common wolf, and the dire wolf would be following their noses and running in to the toothsome feast.

And the greater predators, not too proud to eat meat which they had not brought down, would pad in from the tall grass and then roar to frighten away the lesser beasts. The nine hundred pound palely striped Plains lions would attend with much roaring and snarling and scrapping among themselves and slashes and dashes at the smaller beasts and birds.

Kickaha thought of this and began to sweat again. He shooed a crow away by hissing and cursing out of the corner of his mouth. Far away, a wolf howled. A condor sailed overhead and banked slowly as it glided in for a landing, probably on some fallen buffalo.

Then another shadow passed. Through his half-closed eyelids, he saw the aircraft slide silently over him. It dipped its nose and began to sink, but he could not follow it without turning his head. It had been about fifty feet up, which he hoped would be far enough away so that they might still believe the lance had gone into his chest or armpit.

Somebody shouted in the language of the Lords. The voice was downwind, so he could not distinguish many words.

After a silence, several voices came to him, this time from upwind. If the Bellers were still in the craft, then it had moved between him and Anana. He hoped that a Beller would get out and walk over to examine him; he hoped that the craft would not first fly to a point just above him, where the occupants could lean out and look at him. He knew that the Bellers probably had hand-beamers and that these would be in readiness. In addition, the Bellers left in the craft would be using the larger projectors to cover those outside.

He did not hear the footsteps of the approaching Beller. The fellow had undoubtedly had his beamer on Kickaha, ready to shoot if he thought Kickaha was pretending to be dead or unconscious. Kickaha would not have had a chance.

But luck was with him again. This time it was a bull buffalo. It rose behind the Beller and, bellowing, tried to charge him. The Beller whirled. Kickaha rolled over, using the dead Half-Horse as a shield, and looked over it. The buffalo was badly hurt and fell on its side again before it had taken three steps. The Beller did not even use his beamer. But his back was momentarily turned to Kickaha, and the attention of those in the craft seemed to be on the other Beller on the ground. He was walking toward Anana's pile of buffalo.

At the bellow, one of the men in the craft turned. He swung the projector on its pivot. The Beller on the ground waved reassuringly at him and pointed to the carcass. The fellow in the craft resumed watching the other Beller. Kickaha rose and rushed the man, knife in hand. The Beller turned slowly and he was completely taken by surprise. He swung his beamer up, and Kickaha hurled the knife even if it was unfamiliar and probably unsuited for such work.

He had spent literally thousands of hours in practicing knife-throwing. He had cast knives of many kinds at many distances from many angles, even while standing on his head. He had forced himself to engage in severe discipline; he had thrown knives until he began to think he was breathing knives and the sight of one made him lose his appetite.

The unending hours, the sweat, frustration, and discipline paid off. The knife went into the Beller's throat, and the Beller fell over backward. The beamer lay on the ground.

Kickaha threw himself at the weapon, picked it up, saw that, though not of a familiar make, it was operated like the others. A little catch on the side of the butt had to be depressed to activate the weapon. The trigger could then be pulled; this was a slightly protruding plate on the inner side of the butt.

The Beller in the rear of the craft was swinging the big projector around toward Kickaha. Its ray sprang out whitely and dug a smoking swath in the ground; it struck a mound of buffalo, which burst into flames. The projector was not yet on full-power.

Kickaha did not have to shoot the Beller. A ray struck the Beller from the side, and he slumped over. Then the ray rose and fell, and the craft was cut in half. The others in the cockpit had already been struck down.

Kickaha rose cautiously and shouted, "Anana! It's me! Kickaha! Don't shoot!"

Presently Anana's white face came around the hillock of shaggy, horned carcasses. She smiled at him and shouted back, "It's all right! I got all of them!"

He could see the outflung hand of the Beller who had been approaching her. Kickaha walked toward her, but he felt apprehensive.

Now that she had a beamer and a craft—part of

a craft, anyway—would she need him?

Before he had taken four more steps, he knew that she still needed him. He increased his pace and smiled. She did not know this world as he did, and the forces against her were extremely powerful. She wasn't going to turn on such a valuable ally.

Anana said, "How in Shambarimen's name did you manage to live through all that? I would have sworn that you had been cut off by the herd and that the Half-Horses would get you."

"The Half-Horses were even more confident," he said, and he grinned. He told her what had happened. She was silent for a moment, then she asked, "Are you sure you're not a Lord?"

"No, I'm human and a mere Hoosier, though not so mere at that, come to think of it."

"You're shaking," she said.

"I'm naturally high-strung," he said, still grinning. "You look like you're related to an aspen leaf, yourself."

She glanced at the beamer, quivering in her hand, and smiled grimly. "We've both been through a lot."

"There's nothing to apologize for, for chrissakes," he said. "Okay, let's see what we have here."

The Tishquetmoac men were small figures in the distance. They had begun running when Anana had started beaming, and they evidently did not plan on returning. Kickaha was glad. He had no plans for them and did not want to be appealed to for help.

Anana said, "I played dead, and I threw a spear at him and killed him. The Bellers in the craft were so surprised that they froze. I picked up the beamer and killed them."

It was a nice, clean, simple story. Kickaha did not believe it. She had not been helped by a disturbance, as he had, and he could not see how she could have gotten up and thrown a spear before the beamer went into action. The Beller was pierced in the hollow of the throat with the spear, but there was little blood from the wound, and there was no wound that could have been made by a beamer. Kickaha was certain that a close investigation would find a small hole bored through the corpse somewhere. Probably through the armor too, because the Beller wore chain mail shirt and skirt and a conical helmet.

It wouldn't do to poke around the body and let her know his suspicions, though. He followed her to the craft, the two sections of which still hung two feet from the ground. A dead Beller sprawled in each part, and in the front section, huddled in a charred mass, was a Tishquetmoac priest, the Bellers' interpreter. Kickaha pulled the bodies out and examined the aircraft. There were four rows of two seats each with a narrow aisle running down between them. The front row was where the pilot and copilot or navigator sat. There were many instruments and indicators of various sorts on a panel. These were marked with hieroglyphs, which Anana told him were from the Lords' classic writing and used rarely.

"This craft is from my palace," she said. "I had four. I suppose the Bellers dismantled all four and brought them through."

She told him that the two parts did not fall because the keel-plate had been charged with gravitons in stasis when the craft halted. The operating equipment was in the front section, which could still be flown as if it were a whole craft. The rear part would continue to hover above the ground for some time. Then, as the graviton field decayed, it would slowly sink.

"It'd be a shame to waste the rear projector or let it fall into the hands of somebody else," Kickaha said. "And we've only got two good hand-beamers; the others were ruined when you rayed the ship. Let's take it with us."

"And where are we going?" she said.

"To Podarge, the Harpy-queen of the green eagles," he said. "She's the only useful ally I can think of at this moment. If I can stop her from trying to kill us long enough to talk to us, she may agree to help."

He climbed into the rear section and took some tools out of the storage compartment. He began to disconnect the big projector from the pivot, but suddenly stopped. He grinned and said to Anana, "I can't wait to see the expressions on your face and Podarge's! You will be looking at yourselves!"

She did not answer. She was using the beamer and the knife to cut off parts of a buffalo calf. Later, they would fly the meat to a spring and cook it. Both were so hungry, they felt as if their bellies were ravening animals eating up their own bodies. They had to feed them swiftly or lose their flesh to their flesh.

Though they were so tired they had trouble moving their arms and legs, Kickaha insisted that they fly on after eating. He wanted to get to the nearest mountain range. There they could hide the craft in a cave or ledge and sleep. It was too dangerous to remain on the prairie. If the Bellers had other craft around, they might detect them and investigate. Or try to communicate with them.

Anana agreed that he was right, and she fell asleep. Kickaha had learned from her how to operate the craft, so he took it toward the mountains as swiftly as it would go. The wind did not strike him directly, since the cowling protected him, but it did curve in through the open rear part, and it howled and beat at him—at least it kept him awake.

# XII

THEY GOT TO the mountains just as the sun went around the monolith, and he flew around for fifteen minutes before finding exactly what he wanted. This was a shallow cave with an opening about twenty feet high; it was located two thousand feet up on the face of a sheer cliff. Kickaha backed the craft into the cave, turned off the controls, lay down on the floor of the aisle, and passed out.

Even in his exhaustion and in the safety of the cave, he did not sleep deeply; he swam just below the surface of unconsciousness. He dreamed much and awoke with a start at least a dozen times. Nevertheless, he slept better than he had thought, because the sun was quartering the sky before he fully awoke.

He breakfasted on buffalo steak and some round biscuits he had found in a compartment under one of the seats. Since this was the only food in the craft, he deduced that the fliers had been operating out of a camp not too far away from the scene of the stampede. Or else the craft had been out for a long time and rations were short. Or there might be another explanation.

If there was one thing certain in both worlds, it was uncertainty.

By the time Anana awoke, she found that her companion had eaten, exercised vigorously to remove the stiffness from his muscles, and had dabbed water on his face and hands. He had bathed in the spring the evening before and so was presentable enough. He did not worry about shaving, since he had applied a chemical which retarded beard growth for months, just before he left the Hrowakas' village. It was a gift from Wolff. It could be neutralized at any time by another chemical if he wished to have a beard, but this chemical was not available; it was in a cabin in the Hrowakas' village.

Anana had the ability to wake up looking as if she were getting ready to go to a party. She did complain, however, about a bad taste in her mouth. She also voiced dislike for the lack of privacy in excretion.

Kickaha shrugged and said that a ten thousand year old woman ought to be above such human inhibitions. She did not respond angrily, but merely said, "Do we take off now? Or could we rest today?"

He was surprised that she seemed to give him authority. It was not what he would have expected from a Lord. But apparently she had a certain resiliency and flexibility, a realistic attitude. She recognized that this was his world and that he knew it far better than she did. Also, it must be evident that he had a tremendous capacity for survival. Her true feelings about him were not apparent. She was probably going along with him for her own sake and would drop him if he became a liability rather than an asset—which was an attitude he approved, in some respects. At least, they were operating together smoothly enough.

Not too smoothly, since she had made it obvious that she would never think of letting him make love to her.

"I'm all for resting," he said. "But I think we'll be better off if we rest among the Hrowakas. We can hide this boat in a cave near their village. And while we're living there, we can talk to my people. I'm planning on using them against the Bellers, if they're willing. And they will be. They love a fight."

Shortly afterward, Anana noticed a light flashing on the instrument panel. She said, "Another craft is trying to call this one or perhaps the headquarters in Jadawin's palace. They must be alarmed because it hasn't reported in."

"I'd bluff by talking to them, but I'm not fluent enough in Lord-speech to fool them," Kickaha said. "And you could try, but I don't think they'd accept a woman's voice either. Let it flash. But one thing does bother me: do the Bellers have any means for tracking down this craft?"

"Only if we transmit a message for several minutes," she said. "Or if the craft is in a line-of-sight position. These are my machines and I had them equipped with some protection devices. But not many."

"Yes, but they have the devices of four palaces to draw on," he said. "Wolff's, yours, Nimstowl's, and Judubra's. They may have removed devices from these to equip their crafts."

She pointed out that, if they had, they had not equipped this one. She yawned and got ready to take a catnap. Kickaha shouted that she had slept over twelve hours already, and she should get up off her beautiful rump. If they were to survive, they had better get in gear, stir their stumps, and so on with a number of earthier and more personal clichés.

She admitted he was right. This surprised him but did not put him off guard. She got into the pilot's seat, put on the stasis harness, and said that she was ready.

The machine slid parallel to the face of the mountain and then headed for the edge of the level, keeping a few feet above the surface of the jagged terrain. It took two hours to get out of the range, by which time they were on the lip of the monolith on which rested the Amerind level. The stone cliff dropped vertically—more or less—for over a hundred thousand feet. At its base was Okeanos, which was not an ocean but a sea shaped like a ring, girdling the monolith and never more than three hundred miles wide.

On the other side of Okeanos, entirely visible from this height, was the strip of land which ran around the bottom of this planet. The strip was actually fifty miles across, but from the edge of the monolith, it looked thread-thin. On its comparatively smooth, well-treed surface lived human beings and half-human creatures and fabulous beasts. Many of them were the products of Jadawin's biolab; all owed their longevity and unfading youth to him. There were mermen and mermaids, goat-hoofed and goat-horned satyrs, hairy-legged and horned fauns, small centaurs, and other creatures which Jadawin had made to resemble the beings of Greek mythology. The strip was a type of Paradeisos and Garden of Eden with, in addition, a number of extra-terrestrial, extra-universal touches.

On the other side of the Garden strip was the edge of the bottom of the world. Kickaha had been down there several times on what he called "vacations" and once when he had been pursued by the horrible *gworl*, who wanted to kill him for the Horn of Shambarimen.* He had looked over the edge and been thrilled and scared. The green abyss below—nothing beneath the planet—nothing but green sky and a sense that he would fall forever if he lost his hold.

Kickaha told her of this and said, "We could hide down there for a long time. It's a great place—no wars, no bloodshed beyond an occasional bloody nose or two. It's strickly for sensual pleasure, no intellectualism, and it gets wearisome after a few weeks, unless you want to be an alcoholic or drug addict. But the Bellers'll be down there eventually. And by that time, they may be much stronger."

"You can be sure of that," she said. "They have started making new Bellers. I suppose that one of the palaces has facilities for doing this. Mine hasn't, but . . . "

"Wolff's has," he replied. "Even so, it'll take ten years for a Beller to mature and be educated enough to take its place in Beller society, right? Meantime, the Bellers are restricted to the original fifty. Forty-four, I mean."

"Forty-four or four, they won't stop until we three Lords, and you, are captured or killed. I doubt they'll invade any more universes until then. They've got all of us cornered in this world, and they'll keep hunting until they've got us."

"Or we've got them," Kickaha said.

She smiled and said, "That's what I like about

**The Maker of Universes*, Philip José Farmer, ACE.

you. I wish that you were a Lord. Then . . . "

He did not ask her to elaborate. He directed her to fly the machine down the monolith. As they descended, they saw that its seemingly smooth surface was broken, gnarled, and flattened in many places. There were ledges and projections which furnished roads for many familiar and many strange creatures. There were fissures which sometimes widened to become comparatively large valleys. There were streams in the valleys and cataracts hurled out of holes in the steep side and there was a half mile wide river which roared out of a large cave at the end of a valley-fissure and then fell over the edge and onto the sea seventy-five thousand feet below.

Kickaha explained that the surface area on all the levels of this planet, that is, the horizontal area on the tops of the monoliths, equaled the surface area of the watery bodies of Earth. This made the land area more than that of Earth's. In addition, the habitable areas on the verticalities of the monoliths were considerable. These alone probably equaled the land area of Earth's Africa. Moreover, there were immense subterranean territories, great caverns in vast networks that ran under the earth everywhere. And in these were various peoples and beasts and plants adapted to underground life.

"And when you consider all this, plus the fact that there are no arid deserts or ice- and snow-covered areas, you can see that the inhabitable land of this planet is about four times that of Earth."

Anana said that she had been on Earth briefly only and that she didn't remember its exact size. The planet in her own universe, however, was, if she remembered correctly, about the size of Earth.

Kickaha said, "Take my word for it, this is a hell of a big place. I've traveled a lot in the twenty-three years I've been here, but I've seen only a small part. I have a lot ahead of me to see. If I live, of course."

The machine had descended swiftly and now hovered about ten feet above the rolling waves of Okeanos. The surf shattered with a white bellow against the reefs or directly against the butt of the monolith. Kickaha wanted to make sure that the water was deep enough. He had Anana fly the craft two miles further out. Here he dumped the four caskets and bell-shaped contents into the sea. The water was pure and the angle of sunlight just right. He could see the caskets a long way before the darkness swallowed them. They fell through schools of fish that glowed all hues of all colors and by a Brobdingnagian octopus, striped purple and white, that reached out a tentacle to touch a casket as it went by.

Dumping the bells here was not really necessary, since they were empty. But Anana would not feel easy until they were sunk out of reach of any sentients.

"Six down. Forty-four to go," Kickaha said. "Now to the village of the Hrowakas, the Bear People. My people."

The craft followed the curve of the monolith base for about seven hundred miles. Then Kickaha took over the controls. He flew the craft up and in ten minutes had climbed a little over twelve miles of precipitousness to the edge of the Amerind level. Another hour of cautious threading through the valleys and passes of the mountain ranges and half an hour of reconnoitering brought them to the little hill on top of which was the village of the Hrowakas.

Kickaha felt as if a warlance had driven into his skull. The tall sharp-pointed logs that formed the wall around the village were gone. Here and there, a blackened stump poked through the ashes.

The great V-roofed council hall, the lodge for bachelor warriors, the bear pens, the horse barns, the granary storage, the smokehouses, and the log-cabin family dwellings—all were gone. Burned into gray mounds.

It had rained the night before, but smoke rose weakly from a few piles.

On the hillside were a dozen widely scattered charred corpses of women and children and the burned carcasses of a few bears and dogs. These had been fleeing when rayed down.

He had no doubt that the Black Bellers had done this. But how had they connected him with the Hrowakas?

His thoughts, wounded, moved slowly. Finally, he remembered that the Tishquetmoac knew that he came from the Hrowakas. However, they did not know even the approximate location of the village. The Hrowaka men always traveled at least two hundred miles from the village before stopping along the Great Trade Path. Here they waited for the Tishquetmoac caravan. And though the Bear People were talkers, they would not reveal the place of their village.

Of course, there were old enemies of the Bear People, and perhaps the Bellers had been informed by these. And there were also films of the village and of Kickaha, taken by Wolff and stored in his palace. The Bellers could have run these off and so found the Hrowakas, since the location was shown on a map in the film.

Why had they burned down the village and all in it? What could serve the Bellers by this act?

With a heavy halting voice, he asked Anana the same question. She replied in a sympathetic tone, and if he had not been so stunned, he would have been agreeably surprised at her reaction.

"The Bellers did not do this out of vindictiveness," she said. "They are cold and alien to our way of thinking. You must remember that while they are products of human beings"—Kickaha was not so stunned that he did not notice her identification of Lords with human beings at this time—"and were raised and educated by human beings, they are, in essence, mechanical life. They have self-consciousness, to be sure, which makes them *not* mere machines. But they were born of metal and in metal. They are as cruel as any human. But the cruelty is cold and mechanical. Cruelty is used only when they can get something desired through it. They can know passion, that is, sexual desire, when they are in the brain of a man or woman, just as they get hungry because their host-body is hungry.

"But they don't take illogical vengeance as a human would. That is, they wouldn't destroy a tribe just because it happened to be loved by you. No, they must have had a good reason—to them, anyway—for doing this."

"Perhaps they wanted to make sure I didn't take refuge here," he said. "They would have been smarter to have waited until I did and then move in."

They could be hiding someplace up on the mountains where they could observe everything.

However, Kickaha insisted on scouting the area before he approached the village. If Bellers were spying on them, they were well concealed indeed. In fact, since the heat-and-mass detector on the craft indicated nothing except some small animals and birds, the Bellers would have to be behind something large. In which case, they couldn't see their quarry either.

It was more probably that the Beller machine, after destroying the village, had searched this area. Failing to find him, it had gone elsewhere.

"I'll take over the controls," Anana said softly. "You tell me how to get to Podarge."

He was still too sluggish to react to her unusual solicitude. Later, he would think about it.

Now he told her to go to the edge of the level again and to descend about fifty thousand feet. Then she was to take the craft westward at 150 MPH until he told her to stop.

The trip was silent except for the howling of the wind at the open rear end. Not until the machine stopped below an enormous overhang of shiny black rock did he speak.

"I could have buried the bodies," he said, "but it would have taken too long. The Bellers might have checked back."

"You're still thinking about them," she said with a trace of incredulity. "I mean, you're worrying because you couldn't keep the carrion eaters off them? Don't! They're dead; you can do nothing for them."

"You don't understand," he said. "When I called them my people, I meant it. I loved them, and they loved me. They were a strange people when I first met them, strange to me. I was a young, mid-twentieth century, Midwestern

American citizen, from another universe, in fact. And they were descendants of Amerinds who had been brought to this universe some twenty thousand years ago. Even the ways of an Indian of America are alien and near-incomprehensible to a white American. But I'm very adaptable and flexible. I learned their ways and came to think something like them. I was at ease with them and they with me. And I was Kickaha, the Trickster, the man of many turns. Their Kickaha, the scourge of the enemy of the Bear People.

"This village was my home, and they were my friends, the best I've ever had, and I also had two beautiful and loving wives. No children, though Awiwisha thought she might be pregnant. It's true that I'd established other identities on two other levels, especially that of the outlaw Baron Horst von Horstmann. But that was fading away. I'd been gone so long from Dracheland.

"The Hrowakas were my people, dammit! I loved them, and they loved me!"

And then he began to sob loudly. The cries tore the flesh as they mounted upward with spurs toward his throat. And even after he had quit crying, he hurt from deep within him. He did not want to move for fear he would hurt even more. But Anana finally cleared her throat and moved uneasily.

Then he said, "All right. I'm better. Set her down on that ledge there. The entrance to Podarge's cave is about ten miles westward. It'll be dangerous to get near it any time, but especially at night. The only time I was there was two or three years ago when Wolff and I talked Podarge into letting us out of her cage."

He grinned and said, "The price was that I should make love to her. Other captives had been required to do this, too, but a lot of them couldn't because they were too frightened, or too repulsed or both. When this happened, she'd shred them as if they were paper with her great sharp talons.

"And so, Anana," he continued, "in a way I've already made love to you. At least to a woman—a thing with a woman's face—with your face."

"You must be feeling better," she said, "if you can talk like that."

"I have to joke a little, to talk about things far removed from death," he said. "Can't you understand that?"

She nodded but did not say anything. He was silent, too, for a long while. They ate cold meat and biscuits—it would be wise not to make a fire. Lights might attract the Bellers or the green eagles. Or other things that would be crawling around the cliffs.

# XIII

THE NIGHT passed without incident, although they were awakened from time to time by roars, screams, whoops, bellows, trumpetings, and whistlings, all at a distance.

After breakfast, they set out slowly in the craft along the cliffside. Kickaha saw an eagle out above the sea. He piloted the craft toward her, hoping she would not try to escape or attack. Her curiosity won over whatever other emotions she had. She circled the machine, which remained motionless. Suddenly, she swept past them, crying, "Kickaha-a-a!" and plunged down. He expected her to wing full speed toward Podarge's cave. Instead, behaving unexpectedly, as might be expected from a female—so he said to Anana—she climbed back up. Kickaha indicated that he was going to land on a ledge, where he would like to talk to her.

Perhaps she thought that this would give her a chance to attack him. She settled down beside the machine with a small blast of closing wings. She towered over him, her yellow hooked beak and glaring black red-rimmed eyes above his head. The cowling was open, but he held the beamer, and on seeing it, she stepped back. She squawked,

"Podarge?" but said nothing more about Anana's face.

One eagle looked like another to Kickaha. She, however, remembered when he had been in the cage with Wolff and when the eagles had stormed the palace on top of the highest monolith, the pinnacle of the planet.

"I am Thyweste," she said in the great parrot's voice of the green eagle. "What are you doing here, Trickster? Don't you know that Podarge sentenced you to death? And torture before death, if possible?"

"If that's so, why don't you try to kill me," he said.

"Because Podarge has learned from Dewiwanira that you released her and Antiope from the Tishquetmoac cage. And she knows that something is gravely amiss in Talanac, but she hasn't been able to find out what yet. She has temporarily suspended the sentence on you—though not on Jadawin-Wolff—until she discovers the truth. The orders are that you shall be escorted to her if you show up begging for an audience. Although I will be fair, Kickaha, and warn you that you may never leave the cave, once you've entered it."

"I'm not *begging* for an audience," he said. "And if I go in, I go inside this craft and fully armed. Will you tell Podarge that? But also tell her that if she wants revenge on the Tishquetmoac for having killed and imprisoned many of her pets, then I will be able to help her. Also, tell her there is a great evil abroad. The evil does not threaten her—yet. But it will. It will close its cold fingers upon her and her eagles and their nestlings. I will tell her of this when—or if—I get to see her.

Thyweste promised to repeat what he had told

her, and she flapped off. Several hours passed. Kickaha got increasingly nervous. He told Anana that Podarge was so insane that she was liable to act against her own interests. He wouldn't be surprised to see a horde of the giant eagles plunging down out of the camouflaging green sky.

But it was a single eagle who appeared. Thyweste said that he should come in the flying machine and bring the human female with him. He could bring all the weapons he wished; much good they would do him if he tried to lie or trick Podarge. Kickaha translated for Anana, since they spoke the degenerate descendant of Mycenaean Greek, the speech used by Odysseus and Agamemnon and Helen of Troy.

Anana was startled and then scornful. "*Human* female! Doesn't this stinking bird know a Lord when she sees one?"

"Evidently not," he replied. "After all, you look exactly like a human. In fact, you can breed with humans, so I would say that you are human, even if you do have a different origin. Or do you? Wolff has some interesting theories about that."

She muttered some invective or pejorative in Lord-speech. Kickaha sent the craft up and followed Thyweste to the entrance of the cave, where Podarge had kept house and court for five hundred years or so. She had chosen the site well. The cliff above the entrance slanted gently outward for several thousand feet and was almost as smooth as a mirror. There was a broad ledge in front of the cave, and the cave could be approached on the ledge from only one side. But this path was always guarded by forty giant eagles. Below the ledge, the cliff slanted inward. No creature could climb up to or down from the cave. An army of determined men could have dropped ropes from above to let themselves down to the cave, but they would have been open to attack.

The entrance was a round hole about ten feet in diameter. It opened to a long curving corridor of rock polished from five centuries of rubbing by feathered bodies.

The craft had to be driven through the tunnel with much grating and squealing. After fifty yards of such progress, it came out into an immense cavern. This was lit by torches and by huge plants resembling feathers, which glowed whitely. There were thousands of them hanging down from the ceiling and sticking out from the walls, their roots driven into the rock.

From somewhere, air brushed Kickaha's cheek softly.

The great chamber was much as he remembered it except that there was more order. Apparently, Podarge had done some housecleaning. The garbage on the floor had been removed, and the hundreds of large chests and caskets containing jewels, *objets d'art*, and gold and silver coins and other treasures had been stacked alongside the walls or carried elsewhere.

Two columns of eagles formed an aisle for the craft, the aisle crossed fifty yards of smooth granite floor to end at a platform of stone. This was ten feet high and attained by a flight of steps made from blocks of quartz. The old rock-carved chair was gone. In its place was a great chair of gold set with diamonds, formed in the shape of a phoenix with outstretched wings that was placed in the middle of the platform. The chair had been that of the Rhadamanthus of Atlantis, ruler of the next-to-highest level of this planet. Podarge had taken the chair in a raid on the capital city some four hundred years ago. Now there was no Rhadamanthus, almost no Atlanteans left alive, and the great city was shattered. And the plans of Wolff for recolonizing the land were interrupted by the appearance of the Black Bellers and by his disappearance.

Podarge sat upon the edge of the throne. Her body was that of a Harpy's as conceived by Wolff-as-Jadawin 3,200 years ago. The legs were long and avian, thicker than an ostrich's, so they could bear the weight of her body. The lower part of the body was also avian, green-feathered and long-tailed. The upper part was that of a woman with magnificent white breasts, long white neck, and the archingly beautiful face. Her hair was long and black; her eyes were mad. She had no arms—she had wings, very long and broad wings with green and crimson feathers.

Podarge called to Kickaha in a rich husky voice, "Stop your aerial car there! It may approach no closer!"

Kickaha asked for permission to get out of the machine and come to the foot of the steps. She said that would be granted. He told Anana to follow him and then walked with just a hint of a swagger to the steps. Podarge's eyes were wide on seeing Anana's face. She said, "Two-legged female, are you a creation of Jadawin's? He has given you a face that is modeled on mine!"

Anana knew that the situation was just the reverse, and her pride must have been pierced deeply. But she was not stupid in her arrogance. She replied, "I believe so. I do not know my origin. I have just been, that's all. For some fifty years, I think."

"Poor infant! Then you were the plaything of that monster Jadawin! How did you get away from him! Did he tire of you and let you loose on this evil world, to live or die as events determined?"

"I do not know," Anana said. "It may be. Kickaha thinks that Jadawin was merciful in that he removed part of my memory, so that I do not remember him or my life in his palace, if indeed I had one."

Kickaha approved of her story. She was as adept at lying as he. And then he thought, *Oh! Oh! She tripped up!* Fifty years ago, Jadawin wasn't even in the palace or in this universe. He was living in America as a young amnesiac who had been adopted by a man named Wolff. The Lord in the palace was Arwoor then.

But, he reassured himself, this made no difference. If Anana pretended to have no memory of her origin or palace, then she wouldn't know who had been Lord.

Podarge apparently wasn't thinking about this. She said to Kickaha, "Dewiwanira has told me of how you freed her and Antiope from the cage in Talanac."

"Did she also tell you that she tried to kill me in payment for having given her her freedom?" he said.

She raised her wings a little and glared. "She had her orders! Gratitude had nothing to do with it! You were the right-hand man of Jadawin, who now calls himself Wolff!"

She folded her wings and seemed to relax, but Kickaha was not deceived. "By the way, where is Jadawin? What is happening in Talanac? Who are these Drachelanders?" she asked.

Kickaha told her. He left out the two Lords,

Nimstowl and Judubra, and made it appear that Anana had been gated through a long time ago to the Amerind level and had been a slave in Talanac. Podarge was insanely hostile to the Lords. If she found out that Anana was one, and especially if she suspected that Anana might be Wolff's sister, she would have ordered her killed. This would have put Kickaha into a predicament which he would have to settle within one or two seconds. He would either chose to live and so be able to fight the Bellers but have to let Anana die, or he could back Anana and so die himself. That the two of them could slaughter many eagles before they were overwhelmed was no consolation.

*Or perhaps,* he thought, *just perhaps, we might be able to escape. If I were to shoot Podarge quickly enough and so create confusion among the eagles and then get into the craft quickly enough and bring the big projectors to bear, maybe we could fight our way out.*

Kickaha knew in that moment that he had chosen for Anana.

Podarge said, "Then Jadawin may be dead? I would not like that, because I have planned for a long time on capturing him. I want him to live for a long long time while he suffers! While he pays! And pays! And pays!"

Podarge was standing up on her bird legs, her talons outspread, and she was screeching at Kickaha. He spoke from the corner of his mouth to Anana. "Oh, oh! I think she's cracked! Get ready to start shooting!"

But Podarge stopped yelling and began striding back and forth, like a great nightmare bird in a cage. Finally, she stopped and said, "Trickster! Why should I help you in your war against the enemies of Jadawin! Aside from the fact that they may have cheated me of my revenge?"

"Because they are your enemies, too," he said. "It is true that, so far, they have used only human bodies as hosts. But do you think that the Bellers won't be thinking of eagles as hosts? Men are earthbound creatures. What could compare with being housed in the body of a green eagle, of flying far above the planet, into the house of the sun, of hovering godlike above all beasts of earth and the houses and cities of man, of being unreachable, yet seeing and knowing all, taking in a thousand miles with one sweep of the eye?

"Do you think that the Black Bellers won't realize this? And that when they do, they won't capture your eagles, perhaps you, Podarge, and will place the bell shape over your heads, and empty your brains of your thoughts and memory, uncoil you into death, and then possess your brains and bodies for their use?

"The Black Bellers use the bodies of flesh and blood creatures as we humans wear garments. When the garments are worn out, they are discarded. And so will you be discarded, thrown onto the trash heap, though of course it won't matter to you, since *you* will have died long before your body dies."

He stopped speaking for a moment. The eagles, ten foot high green towers, shifted uneasily and made tearing sounds in their throats. Podarge's expression was undecipherable, but Kickaha was sure she was thinking hard.

"There are only forty-four Black Bellers now in existence," he said. "They have great power, yes, but they are few. Now is the time to make sure they do not become a far greater threat. Because they will be making more infant Bellers in the laboratories of the Lords' palaces—you may be sure of that. The time will come when the Black Bellers will number thousands, millions perhaps, because they will want to ensure survival of their kind. And in numbers is survival of kind.

"The time will come when the Bellers will be so numerous and powerful that they will be irresistible. They can then do as they please. And if they want to enjoy the bodies of the green eagles, they will do so without a by-your-leave."

After a long silence, Podarge said, "You have spoken well, Trickster. I know a little about what is happening in Talanac because some of my pets have seized Tishquetmoacs and forced them to talk. They did not reveal much. For instance, they have never heard of the Black Bellers. But they say that the Talanac priests claim that their ruler is possessed by a demon. And the presence of this flying machine and of others which my pets have seen substantiates your story. It is too bad that you did not bring the captured bells here so that we could see them, instead of dumping them into the sea as you did."

"I am not always as clever as I think I am," Kickaha said.

"There is another thing to consider, even if your story is only half true or entirely a lie," Podarge said. "That is, I have long been planning revenge against the Tishquetmoac because they have killed some of my pets and caged others as if they were common beasts. They began to do that when the present ruler, Quotshaml, inherited the throne. That was only three years ago, and since then he has ignored the ancient understanding between his people and mine. In his crazed zeal to add specimens to that zoo of his and to mount stuffed creatures in that museum, he has waged war against us. I sent word that he should stop immediately, and he imprisoned my messengers. He is mad, and he is doomed!"

Podarge talked on. Apparently she tired of the eagles' conversation and longed for strangers with interesting news. Now that Kickaha had brought probably the most exciting news she had ever heard, aside from the call to storm the palaces of the Lords three years before, she wanted to talk and talk. And she did so with a disregard for the feelings of her guests which only an absolute monarch could display. She had food and drink brought in and joined them at a great table. They were glad for the nourishment, but after a while Anana became sleepy. Kickaha just became more exhilarated. He suggested to Anana that it would be wise if she did sleep. She guessed what he meant but did not comment. She rose and went to the craft and stretched out on the floor on a rug provided by Podarge.

## XIV

WHEN SHE awoke, she saw Kickaha sleeping beside her. His short-nosed, long-upper-lipped face looked like a baby's, but his breath stank of wine and he smelled of some exotic perfume. Suddenly, he stopped snoring and opened one eye. Its leaf-green iris shot out fine red lightning veins. He grinned and said, "Good morning! Although I think it's closer to afternoon!"

Then he sat up and patted her shoulder. She jerked herself away from his touch. He smiled more broadly. "Could it be that the arrogant superwoman Lord, Anana the Bright, could be a trifle jealous? Unthinkable!"

"Unthinkable is correct," she said. "How could I possibly care? How? Why?"

He stretched and yawned. "That's up to you to figure out. After all, you are a woman, even if you deny being human, and we've been in close, almost too-intimate, contact, if I do say so myself. I'm a handsome fellow and a daredevil and a mighty warrior—if I do say so myself and I do, though I'm just repeating what thousands have said. You couldn't help being attracted, even if you had some self-contempt for thinking of a *leblabbiy* as attractive in any way."

"Have any women ever tried to kill you?" she snarled.

"At least a dozen. In fact, I've come closer to death from wounds inflicted by women than by all the great warriors put together."

He fingered two scars over his ribs. "Twice, they came very close to doing what my most determined enemies could not do. And both claimed they loved me. Give me your honest, open hate anytime!"

"I neither hate nor love you, of course," she said loftily. "I am a Lord, and . . . "

She was interrupted by an eagle, who said that Podarge wanted to talk to them while they breakfasted. The eagle was upset when Anana said that she wanted to bathe first and were any cosmetics, perfumes, etc., available in all these treasures? Kickaha smiled slightly and said he would go ahead to Podarge and would take the responsibility for her not showing up immediately. The eagle strode stiff-legged ahead of Anana to a corner of the cave where an ornately filigreed dresser held what she wanted.

Podarge was not displeased at Anana's coming late because she had other things to consider. She greeted Kickaha as if she held him in high regard and then said that she had some interesting news. An eagle had flown in at dawn with a tale of a great fleet of warriors on the river which the Tishquetmoac called Petchotakl. It was the broad and winding stream that ran along the edge of the Trees of Many Shadows.

There were one hundred longboats with about fifty men each. So the fleet would total about five thousand of the Red Beards, who called themselves the Thyuda, that is, People. Kickaha said that he had heard of them from the Tishquetmoac, who complained of increasing raids by the Red Beards on the frontier posts and towns. But what was a fleet this size intending to do? Surely, it must mean a raid on, perhaps a siege of, Talanac itself?

She said that the Thyuda came from a great sea to the west, beyond the Glittering Mountains. Kickaha said that he had not yet crossed the Glittering Mountains, though he had long intended to. But he did know that the sea was about a thousand miles long and three hundred wide. He had always thought that Amerinds, people like those on the Plains, lived on its shore.

No, Podarge said, self-satisfied because of the extent of her knowledge and power. No, her eagles reported that a long, long time ago there were feather-caps (Amerinds) there. But then Jadawin let in from Earth a tribe of tall light-skinned people with long beards. These settled down on the eastern shore and built fort-towns and ships. In time, they conquered and absorbed the dark-skins into the population. The dark-skins were slaves at first but eventually they became equals and they blended with the Thyuda, became Thyuda, in fact. The language became a simplified one, basically Thyuda but pidiginized and with many aboriginal loan-words.

The eastern end of the sea had been a federation under the joint kingship of Brakya, which meant Strife, and of Saurga, which meant Sorrow. But there had been a long hard civil war, and Brakya had been forced to flee with a loyal band of warriors and women. They had come over the Glittering Mountains and settled along the upper river. During the years they had increased in numbers and strength and begun their raiding of Tishquetmoac posts and riverboats and sometimes even caravans. They often encountered the Half-Horses and did not always win against them, as they did against all other enemies, but, for the most part, they thrived.

The Tishquetmoac had sent out several punitive expeditions, one of which had destroyed a river-town; the others had been cut to pieces. And now it looked as if the Red Beards were making a big move against the people of Talanac. They were a well-disciplined body of tall, fierce warriors, but they apparently did not realize the size or the defenses of the nation against which they were marching.

"Perhaps," Kickaha said, "but by the time they get to Talanac, they will find the defenses greatly weakened. We will have attacked and perhaps conquered the City of Jade by then."

Podarge lost her good humor. "We will attack the Red Beards first and scatter them like sparrows before a hawk! I will not make their way easy for them!"

"Why not make them our allies?" Kickaha said. "The battle against Bellers, Tishquetmoac, and Drachelanders will not be easy, especially when you consider the aircraft and the beamers they have. We need all the help we can get. I suggest we get them on our side. There will be plenty of killing and loot for all, more than enough."

Podarge stood up from her chair and with a sweep of a wing dashed the tableware onto the floor. Her magnificent breasts rose and fell with fury. She glared at him with eyes from which reason had flown. Kickaha could not help shrinking inwardly, though he faced her boldly enough and spoke up.

"Let the Red Beards kill our enemies and die for us," he said. "You claim to love your eagles; you call them your pets. Why not save many of their lives by strengthening ourselves with the Red Beards?"

Podarge screamed at him, and then she began to rave. He knew he had made a serious mistake by not agreeing with her in every particular, but it was too late to undo the harm. Moreover, he felt his own reason slipping away in a suddenly unleashed hatred of her and her arrogant, inhumanly cruel ways.

He shoved away his anger before it could bring him down into the dust from which no man gets up. He said, "I bow to your superior wisdom, not to mention strength and power, O Podarge! Have it your way, as it should be!"

But he was thoughtful afterward and determined to talk to Podarge again when she seemed more reasonable.

The first thing he did after breakfast was to take the craft outside and up fifty thousand feet to the top of the monolith. Then he flew to the top of a mountain peak in a high range near the edge of the monolith. Here he and Anana sat in the craft while they talked loudly of what had happened recently and also slipped in descriptions of the entrance to Podarge's cave. He had turned on the radio so that their conversation was being broadcast. She had set the various detecting apparatus. After several hours had passed, Anana suddenly pretended to notice that the radio was on. She rebuked Kickaha savagely for being so awkward and stupid, and she snapped it off. An indicator was showing the blips of two aircraft approaching from the edge of the monolith, which rose from the center of the Amerind level. Both had come from the palace of the Lord on top of the apical monolith of the planet.

Since the two vessels had undoubtedly located them with their instruments, they would be able to locate the area into which their quarry would disappear. Kickaha took the vessel at top speed back over the edge of the level and on down. He hovered before the cave entrance until the first of the two pursuers shot over the edge. Then he snapped the craft into the cave and through the tunnel without heeding the scraping noises.

After that, they could only wait. The big projectors and hand-beamers were in the claws of the eagles gliding back and forth some distance above the cave. When they saw the two vessels before the cave entrance, they were to drop out of the green of the sky. The Bellers would detect the eagles above them, of course, but they would pay no attention to them. After identifying them, they would concentrate on sending their rays into the cave.

Those in the cave did not have long to wait. An eagle, carrying a beamer in her beak, entered to report. The Bellers, three in each vessel, had been completely surprised. They were fried, and the crafts were floating where they had stopped, undamaged except for some burned seats and slightly melted metal here and there.

Kickaha suggested to Podarge that the two vessels be brought into the cave. There should be at least one craft yet in the Bellers' possession, and they might send that one down to investigate the disappearance of these. Also, there might be more than one, because Nimstowl and Judubra could have had such vessels.

"Twelve Bellers down. Thirty-eight to go," Kickaha said. "And we now have some power and transportation."

He and Anana went out in the half-craft. He transferred into a vessel, brought it into the cave, then came out again to bring in the second. When all three vessels were side by side in the huge cavern, Podarge insisted that the two instruct her and some chosen eagles in the operation of the vessels. Kickaha asked, first, for the return of their handbeamers and the projectors that went with the half-craft. Podarge hesitated so long that Kickaha thought she was going to turn against him then and there. He and Anana were helpless because they had loaned their weapons out to ensure the success of the plan. He did have his knife, which he was determined to throw into the Harpy's solar plexus if she showed any sign of ordering the eagles to seize them. This would not save him and Anana, but he at least would have taken Podarge along with him.

The Harpy, however, finally gave the desired order to her subjects. The beamers were returned; the projectors were put back into the half-craft. Still, he felt uneasy. Podarge was not going to forgive him for being Wolff's friend, no matter what services he rendered her. As soon as his usefulness ended, so would his life. That could be thirty minutes or thirty days from now.

When he had a chance to speak to Anana alone, he told her what to expect.

"It's what I thought would happen," she said. "Even if you weren't Jadawin's friend, you would be in danger because you have been her lover. She must know that, despite her beautiful face and beautiful breasts, she is a hybrid monster and therefore disgusting to the human males she forces to make love to her. She cannot forgive that; she must eliminate the man who secretly despises her. And I am in danger because, one, I have a woman's body, and she must hate all women because she is condemned to her half-bird body. Two, I have her face, and she's not going to let a woman with my body and her face live long to enjoy it. Three, she is insane! She frightens me!"

"You, a Lord, admit you're scared!" he said.

"Even after ten thousand years, I'm scared of some things. Torture is one of them, and I'm sure that she will torture me horribly—if she gets a chance. Moreover, I worry about you."

He was startled. "About me? A *leblabbiy*?"

"You aren't an ordinary human," she said. "Are you sure you're not at least half-Lord? Perhaps Wolff's son?"

"I'm sure I'm not," he said, grinning. "You wouldn't be feeling the emotions of a human woman, would you? Perhaps you're just a little bit fond of me? Maybe a trifle attracted to me? Possibly, perish the thought, you even desire me? Possibly, O most hideous idea, even love me a little? That is, if a Lord is capable of love?"

"You're as mad as the Harpy!" she said, glaring. "Because I admire your abilities and courage doesn't mean that I would possibly consider you as a mate, my equal!"

"Of course not," he said. "If it weren't for me, you'd have been dead a dozen times or would now be screaming in a torture chamber. I'll tell you what. When you're ready to confess you're wrong. I'll save you embarrassment. Just call me lover, that's all. No need for apologies or tears of contrition. Just call me lover. I can't promise I'll be in love with you, but I will consider, just consider, mind you, the prospect of being your lover. You're damnably attractive, physically, anyway. And I wouldn't want to offend Wolff by turning his sister down, although, come to think of it, he didn't speak very fondly of you."

He had expected fury. Instead, she laughed. But he wasn't sure that the laughter wasn't a cover-up.

They had little time to talk thereafter. Podarge kept them busy teaching the eagles about the crafts and weapons. She also questioned both about the layout of Talanac, where she could expect the more resistance, the weak points of the city, etc. She herself was interrupted by the need to give orders and receive information. Hundreds of messengers had been sent out to bring in other eagles for the campaign. The early-arriving recruits, however, were to assemble at the confluence of the Petchotakl river and the small Kwakoyoml river. Here the eagles were to marshal to await the Red Beard fleet. There were many problems for her to solve. The feeding of the army that would gather required logistical reorganization. At one time, the eagles had been an army as thoroughtly disciplined and hierarchical as any human organization. But the onslaught on the palace several years before had killed so many of her officers that she had never bothered to reorganize it. Now, she was faced with this immediate, almost overwhelmingly large, problem.

She appointed a certain number of hunters. Since the river areas of the Great Plains were full of large game, they should afford all the food needed for the army. The result, however, was that two eagles out of ten would be absent hunting most of the time.

The fourth morning, Kickaha dared to argue again. He told her that it was not intelligent to waste the weapons on the Red Beards, that she should save them for the place where they were absolutely required—that is, at Talanac, where the Bellers had weapons which could only be put out of commission by similar weapons.

Moreover, she had enough eagles at her command now to launch an attack on the Tishquetmoac. Feeding them was a big enough headache without waiting to add more. Also . . .

He got no farther. The Harpy screamed at him to keep quiet, unless he wanted his eyes torn out. She was tired of his arrogance and presumptuousness. He had lived too long, bragged too much of his trickster ways. Moreover, she could not stand Anana, assuredly a most repulsive creature. Let him trick his way out of the cave now, if he could; let the woman go jump off the cliff into the sea. Let them both try.

Kickaha kept quiet, but she was not pacified. She continued to scream at him for at least half an hour. Suddenly, she stopped. She smiled at him. Cold thrummed a chord deep in him; his skin seemed to fold, as if one ridge were trying to cover itself with another.

There was a time to await developments, and there was a time to anticipate them. He reared up from his chair, heaving up his end of the table, heavy though it was, so that it turned over on Podarge. The Harpy shrieked as she was pressed between chair and table. Her head stuck out from above the edge, and her wings flapped.

He would have burned her head off then, but she was no immediate danger personally. The two attendant eagles were, since they carried beamers in their beaks. But they had to drop these to catch them with one foot, and in the interim, Kickaha shot one. His beamer, on half-power, set the green feathers ablaze.

Anana had pulled out her beamer, and her ray intersected with his on the second eagle.

He yelled at her and ran toward the nearest craft. She was close behind him in his dive into it, and, without a word from him, she seized the big projector. He sat down before the control panel and activated the motors. The craft rose a foot and shot toward the entrance to the tunnel. Three eagles tried to stop it with their bodies. The vessel went thump . . . thump . . . thump, jarring Kickaha each time. Then he was thrown forward and banged his chest on the panel—no time to strap himself in—as the vessel jammed into the narrow bore of stone. He increased the power. Metal squealed against granite as the vessel rammed through like a rod cleaning out a cannon.

For a second, the bright round of the cave exit was partially blocked by a great bird; there was a thump and then a bump and the vessel was out in the bright yellow sun and bright green sky with the blue-white surf-edge sea fifty thousand feet below.

Kickaha restrained his desire to run away. He brought the craft up and back and down, hovering over the top of the entrance. And, as he had expected, a craft slid out. This was the one captured by the eagles; it was followed by the half-craft. Anana split both along the longitudinal axis with the projector on at full-power. Each side of the craft broke away and fell, the sliced eagles with them, and the halves and green bodies were visible for a long time before being swallowed up in the blue of the distance.

Kickaha lowered the craft and shot the nose-projector at full-power into the tunnel. Screams from within told him that he might have killed some eagles and at least panicked them for a long time. He thought then of cutting out rocks above the entrance and blocking it off but decided that it would take too much power. By then the eagle patrols outside the monolith face and the new-comers were swarming through the air. He rammed the craft through their midst, knocking many to one side while Anana burned others. Soon they were through the flock and going at full speed over the mountain range which blocked off the edge of the level from the Great Plains.

## XV

THEN HE WAS swooping over the prairie, hedgehopping because, the closer he stayed to the surface, the less chance there was of being detected by a Beller craft. Kickaha flew just above the grass and the swelling hills and the trees and the great gray mammoths and mastodons and the giant shaggy black buffalo and the wild horses and the gawky, skinny, scared-faced Plains camels; the nine hundred pound tawny Felis Atrox, the atrocious lion, the long-legged, dogfaced cheetah-lions, the saber-toothed smilodons and the shaggy dumb-looking, megatherium; a sloth as large as an elephant, the dire wolf, six feet high at the shoulder, and the twenty-one foot high archaic ass-headed baluchitherium; the megaceros, deer with an antler spread of twelve feet, and thousands of species of antelopes including one queer species that had a long forked horn sticking up from its snout; the "terrible hog" which stood six feet at the shoulder, and the dread-making earth-shaking brontotherium, recreated in the biolabs of Wolff and released on the Great Plains, gray, fifteen feet long and eight feet high at the shoulder, with a large flat bone horn at the end of its nose; and the coyote, the fox, an ostrich-like bird, the ducks, geese, swans, herons, storks, pigeons, vultures, buzzards, hawks—many thousands of species of beasts and birds and millions, millions of proliferations of life, all these Kickaha shot over and past, seeing within three hours what he could not have seen in five years of travel on the ground.

He passed near several camps of the Nations of the Plains. The tepees and round lodges of the Wingashutah, the Khaikhowa, the Takotita and once over a cavalcade of Half-Horses, the fierce warriors guarding all sides and the females dragging on poles the tribal property and the young gamboling, frisking like colts.

Kickaha thrilled at these sights. He alone of all Earthmen had been favored with living in this world. He had been very lucky so far and if he were to die at this moment, he could not say that he had wasted his life. On the contrary, he had been granted what very few men had been granted, and he was grateful. Despite this, he intended to keep on living. There was much yet to visit and explore and wonder at and great talk and lovely loving women. And enemies to fight to the death.

This last thought had no sooner passed than he saw a strange band on the prairie. He slowed down and ascended to about fifty feet. They were mounted Drachelanders with a small troop of Tishquetmoac cavalry. And three Bellers. He could see the silver caskets attached to the saddles of their horses.

They reined in, doubtless thinking that the craft contained other Bellers. Kickaha did not give them much time to remain in error. He dropped down and Anana cut all three in half. The others took off in panic. Kickaha picked up the caskets, and later dropped them into the broad Petchotakl river. He could not figure out how the party had gotten so far from Talanac even if they had ridden night and day. Moreover, they were coming from the opposite direction.

It struck him then that they must have been gated through to this area. He remembered a gate hidden in a cave in a group of low but steep-sided hills and rocky hills about fifty miles inland. He took the craft there and found what he had expected. The Bellers had left a heavy guard to make sure that Kickaha did not use it. He took them by surprise, burned them all down, and rammed the craft into the cave. A Beller was a few feet from the large single-unit gate-ring toward which he was running. Kickaha bored a hole through him before he reached the gate.

"Sixteen down. Thirty-four to go," Kickaha said. "And maybe a lot more down in the next few minutes."

"You're not thinking about going through the gate?" she said.

"It must be connected to the temple-gate in Talanac," he said. "But maybe we should save it for later, when we have some reserve force." He did not explain but instead told her to help him get rid of the bodies. "We're going to be gone a while. If any more Bellers gate through here, they won't know what's happened—if anything."

Kickaha's plan had a good chance of being successful, but only if he could talk effectively in its next phase. The two flew up the river until they saw a fleet of many boats, two abreast, being rowed down the river. These reminded him of

Viking ships with their carved dragon heads, and the sailors also looked from a distance like Norsemen. They were big and broad-shouldered and wore horned or winged helmets and shaggy breeches and carried double-axes and broad-swords and heavy spears and round shields. Most of them had long red-dyed beards, but there were a number clean-shaven.

A glut of arrows greeted him as he dropped down. He persisted in getting close to the lead boat on which a man in the long white and red-collared robes of a priest stood. This boat had used up all its arrows, and the craft stayed just out of axe range. Spears flashed by or even struck the craft, but Kickaha maneuvered the vessel to avoid any coming into the open cockpit. He called to the priest in Lord-speech and presently the king, Brakya, agreed through the priest to talk to Kickaha. He met him on the banks of the river.

There was a good reason for the Red Beards' hostility. Only a week ago, a craft had set fire to several of their towns and had killed a number of young men. All of the marauders had a superficial resemblance to Kickaha. He explained what was happening, although it took him two days to complete this. He was slowed by the necessity of speaking through the *alkhsguma*, as the priest was called in Thyuda. Kickaha gained in the estimation of Brakya when Withrus, the priest, explained that Kickaha was the righthand man of *Allwaldands*, The Almighty.

The progress of the entire fleet down the river was held up for another day while the chiefs and Withrus were taken via air-car to the cave of the gate. Here Kickaha restated his plan. Brakya wanted a practical demonstration of gating, but Kickaha said that this would warn the Bellers in Talanac that the gate was open to invaders.

Several more days went by while Kickaha outlined and then detailed how five thousand warriors could be marched through the gate. It would take exact timing to get so many men into the gate at a time, because mistiming would result in men in the rear being cut in half when the gate activated. But he pointed out that the Bellers and Drachelanders had come out in a large body, so the Thyuda could go in.

Meantime, he was very exasperated and impatient and uneasy, but he dared not show it. Podarge must have taken her huge winged armada to attack Talanac. If she meant to destroy the Red Beards first, she would have descended upon the fleet before this.

Brakya and the chiefs were by this time eager to get going. Kickaha's colorful and enthusiastic descriptions of the Talanac treasures had converted them to zealots.

Kickaha had a mock-up of the big gate in the cave built outside it and he and the chiefs put the men through a training which took three days and a good part of the nights. By the time that the men seemed to be skilled in the necessities, everybody was exhausted and hot-tempered.

Brakya decided they needed a day of rest. Rest meant rolling out great barrels of beer and a flame-threaded liquor from the boats into the camp and drinking these while deer and buffalo and wild horses and bear were roasted. There was much singing, yelling, laughing, boasting, and quite a few fights which ended in severe wounds or deaths.

Kickaha made Anana stay in her tent, mostly because Brakya had made little effort to hide his lust for her. And while he had never offered anything but compliments that bordered on the obscene (perfectly acceptable in Thyuda society, the priest said), he might take action if alcohol uninhibited him. That meant that Kickaha would have to fight him, since everybody had taken it for granted that she was his woman. In fact, they had had to share the same tent to keep up the pretense. Kickaha engaged Brakya that night in a drinking duel, since he would lose face if he refused the king's challenge. Brakya intended, of course, to drink him into unconsciousness and then go to Anana's tent. He weighed perhaps forty pounds more than Kickaha and should have been able to outdrink him. However, Brakya fell asleep about dawn—to the great amusement of those few Red Beards who had not passed out before then.

In the afternoon, Kickaha crawled out of his tent with a head which felt as if he had tried to outbutt a bull bison. Brakya woke up later and almost tore some muscles in his sides laughing at himself. He was not angry at Kickaha and when Anana appeared he greeted her in a subdued manner. Kickaha was glad that was settled, but he did not want to launch the attack that day, as originally planned. The army was in no shape to battle women, let alone the enemies that awaited them in Talanac.

Brakya ordered more barrels rolled out, and the drinking began all over again. At this time, a raven, a bird the size of a bald eagle of Earth, one of Wolff's Eyes, lit on a branch above Kickaha. It spoke in a harsh croaking voice. "Hail, Kickaha! Long have I looked for you! Wolff, the Lord, sent me out to tell you that he has to leave the palace for another universe. Someone has stolen his Chryseis from him, and he is going to find the thief and kill him and then bring his woman back."

The raven Eye proceeded to describe what traps had been left active, what gates were open, and how he could get into and out of the palace safely if he wished. Kickaha informed the Eye that all had changed, and he told him of the Bellers' occupancy of the palace. The raven was not too startled by this. He had just been to Talanac, because he had heard that Kickaha was there. He had seen the Bellers, though he did not know, of course, who they were then. He also had seen the green eagles and Podarge on their way to attack Talanac. They cast a mighty shadow that inked the ground with a signature of doom and the beat of their wings was like the drums of the day of last judgment. Kickaha, questioning him, judged that the armada had fallen upon Talanac the preceding day.

He went after Brakya and told him the news. By then the whole camp was yelling-laughing drunk. Brakya gave the orders; the great horns were blown; the war drums were beaten; the warriors arranged themselves in ragged but recognizable ranks. Brakya and the chiefs were to go first with Kickaha and Anana, who carried a big projector from the craft. Next was a band of the great warriors, two of whom handled the second projector. After them, the clean-shaven youths, who could not grow a beard and dye it red until they had killed a man in battle. Then the rest of the army.

Kickaha, Anana, Brakya, and six chiefs quick-stepped into the circle of gray metal. The chief of the band behind them had started counting to check that the activation time was correct. Abruptly, the group was in a room which was not the vast chamber in the temple which Kickaha had expected. It was a smaller room, though still large by most standards. He recognized it instantly as the gate-chamber near the middle of the city, the one which he had not been able to get to when being pursued by the Bellers. He shoved the Thyuda on out of the circle; they had frozen at the seemingly magical passage.

Thereafter, events happened swiftly, though they consumed many hours and much energy and many lives. The old city seemed to be aflame; fires raged everywhere. These came from torches which the eagles had dropped. There was little material in the jade city burning, but there were thousands of eagles sputtering or smoldering. These had been caught by the Bellers' projectors. The bodies of the big birds, of Tishquetmoac warriors, and Drachelanders lay in the streets and on the housetops. Most of the fighting was now taking place near the top of the city, around the temple and palace.

The defenders and the eagles were so occupied with the struggle, they did not notice the Red Beards until there were three thousand gated into Talanac. By then, it was too late to stop the remaining two thousand from coming through. Hundreds of eagles turned from the city-top battle to attack the Thyuda, and from then on, Kickaha remembered only firing the projector and advancing up each bloody, smoky, burning level. The time came when the power packs of the projector had been used up, and from then on the hand-beamers were used. Before the summit was gained, these were useless, and it was swords then.

In the temple, he came across a group of charred bodies recognizable as Bellers only because of the silver caskets strapped to their backs. There were six of them, and they had been caught in a cross fire from eagles with handbeamers. This must have been at the very beginning, perhaps the first few moments of the surprise attack. The eagles with the beamers had been killed by projectors, but they had taken a toll catastrophic to the Bellers.

He counted four more dead Bellers before he and Anana and Brakya and other Thyuda burst into the immense room in which the Bellers had installed a large permanent gate. Podarge and her eagles, those left to fight, had cornered a number of Drachelanders, Tishquetmoac and two, no, three, Bellers. There were von Turbat, von Swindebarn, and the emperor of the Tishquetmoac, Quotshaml. They were surrounded by their warriors, who were rapidly dwindling in numbers under the fury of the Harpy and the big birds.

Kickaha, with Anana behind him, and the Red Beards to one side, attacked. He slashed at the eagles from the rear; blood and feathers and flesh flew. He shouted with exultation; the end was near for his enemies.

And then, in the meleee that followed, he saw the three Bellers desert their fellows and run for the big circle of metal, the gate, in one corner. Podarge and some eagles raced after them. Kickaha ran after the eagles. The Bellers disappeared; Podarge followed them; the eagles close behind her flashed out of existence.

He was so disappointed he wanted to weep, but he did not intend to go after them. No doubt the Bellers had set a trap for any pursuers, and the Harpy and eagles should be in it. He was not going to get caught, no matter how much he wanted to get hold of the Bellers.

He started to turn away but had to defend himself against two of the great birds. He managed to wound them enough to make them uneager to close with him, but they persisted and slowly backed him toward the big gate in the corner of the room. One advanced and chopped at him with her beak; he slashed out to make the beak draw short. The other eagle would then move up a little and feint at him, and he would have to slash at her to be sure that it was only a feint.

He could not call for help, since the others were similarly occupied. Suddenly, he knew he was going to be forced to take the gate. If he did not, he would be struck by one of those huge sharp-hooked beaks. The two birds were now separating; one was circling to a position behind him, or perhaps they would both attack from his flanks, so, even if he got one, he would go down under the beak of the other.

Despairingly, he glanced about the room, saw that Anana and the Red Beards were still busy, and so he did what he must. He whirled, leaped onto the plate, whirled around to defend himself for the few seconds needed before the gate would activate, and then something—a wing perhaps—struck his head and knocked him half-unconscious.

## XVI

HE OPENED his eyes upon a strange and weird landscape.

He was in a broad and shallow valley. The ground on which he sat and the hills roundabout were covered with a yellow moss-like vegetation.

The sky was not the green on the world he had just left. It was a blue so dark that it trembled on the edge of blackness. He would have thought it was late dusk if the sun were not just past its zenith. To his left, a colossal tower shape hung in the sky. It was predominantly green with dark blue and light blue patched here and there and white woolly masses over large areas. It leaned as the Tower of Pisa leans.

The sight of this brought Kickaha out of his daze. He had been here before, and only the blow on his head had delayed recognition. He was on the moon, the round satellite of the stepped planet of this universe.

Forgetting his previous experiences, he jumped to his feet and soared into the air, sprawling, and landed on his face and then his elbows and knees. The impact was softened by the cushiony ocher moss-stuff, but he was still jarred.

Cautiously, he got to his hands and knees and

shook his head. It was then that he saw von Turbat, von Swindebarn, and Quotshaml running with Podarge and the four eagles after them. Running defined the intent, however, not the performance. The three men were going in incredibly long leaps which ended frequently in their feet sliding out from under them when they landed on the vegetation, or a loss of balance while going through the high arcs. Their desperation added to their awkwardness, and under other circumstances, their situation would have been comical to them.

It was comical to Kickaha, who was in no immediate danger. He laughed for a few seconds, then sobered up as he realized that his own situation was likely to be as dangerous. Perhaps more so, because the three seemed to be striving for a goal that might take them away from their pursuers.

He could just see the edge of a thin round stone set in the moss. This, he suddenly knew, must be a gate of some kind. The three had known they would be gated from the temple-room in Talanac to this gate on the moon. They must have deliberately set it up for this purpose, so that they could maroon any pursuers on the moon, while they gated back to Talanac or, more likely, to the Lord's palace.

Undoubtedly, that gate toward which they were racing was a one-time unit. It would receive and transmit the first to step into it. After that, it would be shut off until reactivated. And the means for reactivation, of course, were not at hand.

The trap was one that Kickaha appreciated, since he liked to set such himself and quite often had. But the trapper might become the trapped. Podarge and the eagles were a type of pursuer not reckoned on. Although handicapped also by their unfamiliarity with the low gravity and the shock of finding themselves here, they were using their wings to aid themselves in control and in braking on landing. Moreover, they were covering ground much more swiftly than the men because they were gliding.

Von Turbat and von Swindebarn, jumping simultaneously and holding hands, came down exactly upon the rock. And they disappeared.

Quotshaml was five seconds behind them, and when he landed on the rock, he remained in sight. His cry of desperation sounded in the quiet and lifeless air.

Podarge, wings spread out to check her descent, came down upon his back, and he fell under her weight. Podarge screamed long and loudly, like a great bird in agony instead of triumph, as she tore gobbets of flesh from the man's back. Then the eagles landed and strode forward and circled Podarge and the writhing victim, and they bent down and slashed with their beaks whenever they got a chance.

The casket which Quotshaml had been carrying on his back had been torn off and now lay to one side near the rock.

Twenty-three Bellers to go.

Kickaha rose slowly to his feet. As soon as Podarge and her pets had finished their work, they would look around. And they would see him unless he quickly got out of sight. The prospects for this were not excellent. The ruins of the city of Korad lay a mile away. The great white buildings gleamed in the sun like a distant hope. But even if he did get to it in time, he would find it to be not a hope but a prison. The only gate nearby which he could use was not in the city but hidden in a cave in the hills. Podarge and the eagles were between him and the cave.

Kickaha took advantage of their concentration on their fun to relearn how to run. He had been here many times for some lengthy periods. Thus, the adaptation was almost like swimming after years of desert living. Once learned, the ability does not go away. However, the analogy was only that, an analogy. A man thrown into the water immediately begins to swim. Kickaha took several minutes to teach himself the proper coordination again.

During this time, he gained a quarter of a mile. Then he heard screams which contained a different emotion than that of bloodletting and revenge gratified. He looked behind him. Podarge and the four birds had seen him and were speeding after him. They were launching themselves upward and covering long stretches in glides, like flying fish. Apparently, they did not trust themselves to try flying yet.

As if they were reading his mind, they quit their hopgliding and took completely to the air. They rose upward far more swiftly than they would have on the planet, and again they screamed. This time, the cries were of frustration. Their flying had actually lost them ground.

Kickaha knew this only because he risked swift glances behind him as he soared through the air. Then he lost ground as his feet slipped on landing and he shot forward and up again and turned over twice. He tried to land on his feet or feet and hands but slammed into the ground hard. His breath was knocked out and he whooshed for air, writhed, and forced himself to get up before he was completely recovered.

During his next leap, he pulled his sword from the sheath. It looked now as if he might need it before he got to the city. Podarge and one eagle were ahead of him, though still very high. They were banking, and then they were coming in toward him in a long flat glide. The other eagles were above him and were now plunging toward him, their wings almost completely folded.

Undoubtedly, the falling birds and the Harpy had automatically computed the ends of their descents to coincide with his forward leap. Kickaha continued forward. A glance upward showed him the bodies of the eagles swelling as they shot toward him. Their yellow claws were spread out, the legs stiff, like great shock absorbers set for the impact of his body. Podarge and friend were coming in now almost parallel to the ground; they had flapped their wings a few times to straighten out the dive. They were about six feet above the moss and expected to clutch him as he rose in the first leg of the arc of a jump.

Podarge was showing almost all her teeth in triumph and anticipation. Her claws dripped blood, and her mouth and teeth were red with blood. Her chin was wet with red.

"Kickaha-a-a-a!" she screamed. "At la-a-a-ast!"

Kickaha wondered if she did not see the sword in his hand or if she was so crazed that she just did not care.

It did not matter. He came down and then went up again in a leap that should have continued on and so brought him into the range of Podarge's claws. But this time he leaped straight upward as hard as he could. It was a prodigious bound, and it carried him up past a very surprised Podarge and eagle. Their screams of fury wailed off like a train whistle.

Then, there were more screams. Panic and fright. Thuds. Wings clapping thunder as the falling eagles tried to check their hurtling.

Kickaha came down and continued his forward movement. On the second bound, he risked a look over his shoulder. Podarge and eagles were on the ground. Green feathers, dislodged by the collision of the Harpy and four mammoth eagle bodies, flew here and there. Podarge was on her back, her legs sticking up. One eagle was unconscious; two were up and staggering around in a daze. The fourth was trying to get onto his talons, but he kept falling over and fluttering and shrieking.

Despite the accident and the new headstart he gained, he still got into the safety of an entrance only a few feet ahead of Podarge. Then he turned and struck her with his sword, and she danced backward, wings flapping, and screamed at him. Her mouth was bloodied and her eyes were pulled wide by insane anger. She was losing blood from a big gash in her side just below her right breast. During the collision or the melee afterward, she had been wounded by a talon.

Kickaha, seeing that only three eagles were following her, and these still at a distance, ran out from the doorway, his sword raised. Podarge was so startled by this that some reason came back to her. She whirled and leaped up and beat her wings. He was close to her and his sword swished out and cut off several long tail feathers. Then he fell to the ground and had to take refuge in the doorway again. The eagles were trying to get to him now.

He wounded two slightly, and they withdrew. Podarge turned to glide back beside them. Kickaha fled through a large hall and across a tremendous room with many ornately carved desks and chairs. He got across the room, down another hall, across a big courtyard and into another building just in time. An eagle came through the doorway of the building he had just left, and the Harpy and another eagle came around the corner of the building. As he had expected, he would have been rushed from the rear if he had stayed in the original doorway.

He came to a room which he knew had only one entrance and hesitated. Should he take a stand here or try for the underground pits? He might get away from them in the dark labyrinths. On the other hand, the eagles would be able to smell him out wherever he hid. And there were things down in the pits that were as deadly as the eagles and far more loathsome. Their existence had been his idea, and Wolff had created them and set them there.

A scream. He jumped through the door and turned to defend it. His mind was made up for him. He had no choice to get to the pits. Now that he had no choice, he wished he had not paused but had kept on going. As long as he was free to move, he felt that he could outwit his pursuers and somehow win out. But now he was trapped, and he could not see, at this moment, how he could win. Not that that meant he had given up. And Podarge was as trapped as he. She had no idea of how to get off the moon and back to the planet, and he did. There could be a trade, if he were forced to deal with her. Meantime, he would see what developed.

The room was large and was of marble. It had a bed of intricately worked silver and gold swinging from a large gold chain which hung down from the center of the ceiling. The walls were decorated with brightly colored paintings of a light-skinned, well-built, and handsomely featured people with graceful robes and many ornaments of metal and gems. The men were beardless, and both sexes had beautiful long yellow or bronze hair. They were playing at various games. Through the windows of some of the painted buildings a painted blue sea was visible.

The murals had been done by Wolff himself, who had talent, perhaps genius. They were inspired, however, by Kickaha, who had, in fact, inspired everything about the moon except the ball of the moon itself.

Shortly after the palace had been retaken, and Wolff had established himself as the Lord, he had mentioned to Kickaha that it had been a long time since he had been on the moon. Kickaha was intrigued, and he had insisted that they visit it. Wolff said that there was nothing to see except grassy plains and a few hills and small mountains. Nevertheless, they had picnicked there, going via one of the gates. Chryseis, the huge-eyed, tiger-haired dryad wife of Wolff, had prepared a basket full of goodies and liquors, just as if she had been a terrestrial American housewife preparing for a jaunt into the park on the edge of town. However, they did take weapons and several taloses, the half-protein robots which looked like knights in armor. Even there, a Lord could not relax absolutely. He must always be on guard against attack from another Lord.

They had a good time. Kickaha pointed out that there was more to see than Wolff had said. There was the glorious, and scary, spectacle of the planet hanging in the sky; this alone was worth making the trip. And then there was the fun of leaping like a grasshopper.

Toward the end of the day, while he was half-drunk on wine that Earth had never been fortunate enough to know, he got the idea for what he called *Project Barsoom*. He and Wolff had been talking about Earth and some of the books they had loved to read. Kickaha said that when he was young Paul Janus Finnegan and living on a farm outside Terre Haute, Indiana, he had loved the works of Edgar Rice Burroughs. He loved especially Tarzan and David Innes and John Carter and couldn't say that he had favored one over the others. Perhaps he had just a bit more love for John Carter.

It was then he had sat up so suddenly that he had spilled his glass of wine. He had said, "I have it! Barsoom! You said this moon is about the size of Mars, right? And you still have tremendous potentialities for biological 'miracles' in your labs, don't you? What about creating Barsoom?"

He had been so exhilarated he had leaped high up into the air but had been unable to pilot himself accurately and so had come down on the picnic lunch. Fortunately, they had eaten most of it. Kickaha was streaked with food and wine, but he was so full of glee he did not notice it.

Wolff listened patiently and smiled often, but his reply sobered Kickaha.

"I could make a reasonable facsimile of Barsoom," he said. "And I find your desire to be John

Carter amusing. But I refuse to play God any more with sentient beings."

Kickaha pleaded with him, though not for very long. Wolff was as strong-minded a man as he had ever known. Kickaha was stubborn, too, but arguing with Wolff when his mind was made up was like trying to erode granite by flicking water off one's finger-ends against the stone.

Wolff did say, however, that he would plant a quick-growing yellow moss-like vegetation on the moon. It would soon kill the green grass and cover the moon from ice-capped north pole to ice-capped south pole.

He would do more, since he did not want to disappoint Kickaha just to be arbitrary. And the project did interest him. He would fashion *thoats*, *banths*, and other Barsoomian animals in his biolabs. Kickaha must realize, however, that this would take a long time and the results might differ from his specifications.

He would even try to create a Tree of Life, and he would build several ruined cities. He would dig canals.

But he would *not* create green *Tharks* or red, black, yellow, and white *Barsoomians*. As Jadawin, he would not have hesitated. As Wolff, he could not.

Aside from his refusal to play God, the scientific and technical problems and the work involved in creating whole peoples and cultures from scratch was staggering. The project would take over a hundred Earth years just to get started.

Did Kickaha realize, for instance, the complexities of the Martian eggs? These were small when laid, of course, probably no bigger than a football at the largest and possibly smaller, since

Burroughs had not described the size when they were first ejected by the female. These were supposed to be placed in incubators in the light of the sun. After five years, the egg hatched. But in the meantime they had grown to be about two and a half feet long. At least, the green-Martian eggs were, although these could be supposed to be larger than those of the normal-sized human-type Martians.

Where did the eggs get the energy to grow? If the energy derived from the yolk, the embryo would never develop. The egg was a self-contained system; it did not get food for a long period of time from the mother as an embryo did through the umbilical cord. The implication was that the eggs picked up energy by absorbing the sun's rays. They could do so, theoretically, but the energy gained by this would be very minute, considering the small receptive area of the egg.

Wolff could not, at this moment, imagine what biological mechanisms could bring about this phenomenal rate of growth. There had to be an input of energy from someplace, and since Burroughs did not say what it was, it would be up to Wolff and the giant protein computers in his palace to find out.

"Fortunately," Wolff said, smiling, "I don't have to solve that problem, since there aren't going to be any sentient Martians, green or otherwise. But I might tackle it just to see if it could be solved."

There were other matters which required compromises in the effort to make the moon like Mars. The air was as thick as that on the planet, and though Wolff could make it thinner, he didn't think Kickaha would like to live in it. Presumably, the atmospheric density of Barsoom was equivalent to that found about ten thousand feet above Earth's surface. Moreover, there was the specification of Mars' two moons, Deimos and Phobos. If two bodies of comparable size were set in orbits similar to the two moonlets, they would burn up in a short time. The atmosphere of the moon extended out to the gravitational warp which existed between the moon and planet. Wolff did, however, orbit two energy configurations which shone as brightly as Deimos and Phobos and circled the moon with the same speed and in the same directions.

Later, after sober reflection, Kickaha realized that Wolff was right. Even if it would have been possible to set biolab creations down here and educate them in cultures based on the hints in Burroughs' Martian books, it would not have been a good thing to do. You shouldn't try to play God. Wolff had done that as Jadawin and had caused much misery and suffering.

Or could you do this? After all, Kickaha had thought, the Martians would be given life and they would have as much chance as sentients anywhere else in this world or the next to love, to hope, and so on. It was true that they would suffer and know pain and madness and spiritual agony, but wasn't it better to be given a chance at life than to be sealed in unrealization forever? Just because somebody thought they would be better off if they didn't chance suffering? Wouldn't Wolff himself say that it had been better to have lived, no matter what he had endured and might endure, than never to have existed?

Wolff admitted that this was true. But he said the Kickaha was rationalizing. Kickaha wanted to play John Carter just as he had when he was a kid on a Hoosier farm. Well, Wolff wasn't going to all the labor and pains and time of making a living, breathing, thinking green Martian or red *Zodangan* just so Kickaha could run him through with a sword. Or vice versa.

Kickaha had sighed and then grinned and thanked Wolff for what he had done and gated on up to the moon and had a fine time for a week. He had hunted *banth* and roped a small *thoat* and broken it in and prowled through the ruins of Korad and Thark, as he called the cities which Wolff's taloses had built. Then he became lonely and went back to the planet. Several times he came back for "vacations," once with his Drachelander wife and several Teutoniac knights, and once with a band of Hrowakas. Everybody except him had been uneasy on the moon, close to panic, and the vacations had been failures.

# XVII

IT HAD BEEN three years since he had gated through to the moon. Now he was back in circumstances he could never have fantasied. The Harpy and eagles were outside the room and he was trapped inside. Standoff. He could not get out, but they could not attack without serious, maybe total, loss. However, they had an advantage. They could get food and water. If they wanted to put in the time, they could wait until he was too weak from thirst and hunger to resist or until he could no longer fight off sleep. There was no reason why they should not take the time. Nobody was pressing them.

Of course, somebody soon could be. It seemed likely, or at least somewhat probable, the Bellers would be returning through other gates. And this time they would come in force.

If Podarge thought he'd stay in the room until he passed out, she was mistaken. He'd try a few tricks and, if these didn't work, he'd come out fighting. There was a slight chance that he might defeat them or get by them to the pits. It wasn't likely; the beaks and talons were swift and terrible. But then he wasn't to be sneered at, either.

He decided to make it even tougher for them.

He rolled the wheel-like door from the space between the walls until only a narrow opening was left. Through this, he shouted at Podarge.

"You may think you have me now! But even if you do, then what? Are you going to spend the rest of your life on this desolate place? There are no mountains worthy of the name here for your aeries! And the topography is depressingly flat! And your food won't be easy to get! All the animals that live in the open are monstrously big and savage fighters!

"As for you, Podarge, you won't be able to queen it over your hundreds of thousands! If your virgin eagles do lay their eggs so your subjects may increase, they'll have a hard time with the little egg-eating animals that abound here! Not to mention the great white apes, which love eggs! And flesh, including eagle flesh, I'm sure!

"Ah, yes, the great white apes! You haven't met up with them yet, have you?"

He waited a while for them to think about his words. Then he said, "You're stuck here until you die! Unless you make a truce with me! I can show you how to get back to the planet! I know where the gates are hidden!"

More silence. Then a subdued conversation among the eagles and the Harpy. Finally, Podarge said, "Your words were very tempting, Trickster! But they don't fool me! All we have to do is wait until you fall asleep or become too thirst-torn to stand it! Then we will take you alive, and we will torture you until you tell us what we need to know. Then we kill you. What do you think of that?"

"Not much," he muttered. He yelled, "I will kill myself first! Podarge, slut-queen of the big bird-brains, what do you think of that?"

Her scream and the flapping of huge wings told him that she thought as little of his words as he of hers.

"I know where the gates are! But you'll never be able to find them without me! Make up your so-called mind fast, Podarge! I'll give you half an hour! Then I act!"

He rolled the door entirely shut and sat down with his back against the red-brown, highly polished hardwood. They could not move it without giving him plenty of time to be up and ready for them. And he could rest for a while. The long hard battle in Talanac, the shock of being hurled onto the moon, and the subsequent chase had exhausted him. And he lusted for water.

He must have nodded off. Up out of black halfoily waters he surged. His mouth was dry, dripping dust. His eyes felt as if hot hard-boiled eggs had just been inserted in his sockets. Since the door was not moving, he did not know what had awakened him. Perhaps it was his sense of vigilance belatedly acting.

He let his head fall back against the door. Faintly, screams and roars vibrated through, and he knew what had cannoned him from sleep. He jumped up and rolled the door halfway back into the inner-wall space. With the thick barrier removed, the sounds of the battle in the corridor struck full force.

Podarge and the three eagles were facing three huge, tawny, catlike beasts with ten legs. Two were maned males; the third was a sleek-necked female. These were *banths*, the Martian lions described by Burroughs and created by Wolff in his biolab and set down on this moon. They preyed on *thoats* and *zitidar* calves and the great white apes and anything else they could catch. Normally, they were night hunters, but hunger must have sent them prowling the daytime city. Or they may have been roused by all the noise and attracted by the blood.

Whatever their reasons, they had cornered the cornerers. They had killed one eagle, probably in the first surprise attack, Kickaha surmised. A green eagle was a fighter formidable enough to run off a tiger or two without losing a feather. So far, though the *banths* had killed one and inflicted enough wounds on the others to cover them with blood, they were bleeding from cuts and gashed all over their bodies and heads.

Now, roaring, they had separated from their intended prey. They paced back and forth in the corridor and then one would hurl himself at an eagle. Sometimes the charges were bluffs and fell just short of the range of beaks as deadly as battle-axes. Other times, they struck one of the two remaining eagles with a huge scythe-clawed paw, and then there would be a flurry of saberish canines, yellow beaks, yellow or scarlet talons, patches of tawny hide flying or mane hairs torn out by the bunch, green feathers whirling through the air, distended eyeballs green or yellow or red, blood spurting, roars, screams. And then the lion would disengage and run back to his companions.

Podarge stayed behind the twin green towers of her eagles.

Kickaha watched and waited. And presently all three lions attacked simultaneously. A male and an eagle rolled into the door with a crash. Kickaha jumped back, then stepped forward and ran his sword forward into the mass. He did not care which he stabbed, lion or eagle, although he rather hoped it would be an eagle. They were more intelligent and capable of greater concentration and devotion to an end—principally his.

But the two rolled away and only the tip of his sword entered flesh. Both were making so much noise that he could not tell which was hurt by the sword.

For just a moment, he had a clear avenue of escape down the center of the corridor. Both eagles were engaged with the lions, the Podarge was backed against the wall, her talons keeping the enraged female at bay. The lioness was bleeding from both eyes and her nose, which was half torn off. Blinded by blood, she was hesitant about closing in on the Harpy.

Kickaha dashed down the aisle, then leaped over two bodies as they rolled over to close off his route. His foot came down hard on a tawny muscle-ridged back, and he soared into the air. Unfortunately, he had put so much effort in his leap that he banged his head against the marble ceiling, cutting his temple open on a large diamond set in the marble.

Half stunned, he staggered on. At that moment, he was vulnerable. If eagle or lion had fallen on him, it could have killed him as a wolf kills a sick rabbit. But they were too busy trying to kill each other, and soon he was out of the building. Within a few minutes, he was free of the city and making great leaps toward the hills.

He bounded past the torn body of the eagle crippled from the collision. Another body, ripped up, lay near it. This was a *banth*, which must have attacked the eagle with the expectation of an easy kill. But it had been mistaken and had paid for the mistake.

Then he was soaring over the body of Quotshaml—rather, parts of the body, because they were scattered. The head, legs, arms, entrails, lungs, and pieces thereof.

He leaped up the hill, which was so tall that it could almost be dignified with the name of mountain. Two-thirds of the way up, hidden behind a curving outcrop of quartz-shot granite, was the entrance to the cave. There seemed no reason why he could not make it; only a few minutes ago all luck seemed to have leaked out of him, and now it was trickling back.

A scream told him that good fortune might only have seemed to return. He looked over his shoulder. A quarter of a mile away, Podarge and the two eagles were flapping swiftly toward him. No *banths* were in sight. Evidently, they had not been able to keep Podarge and the eagles in a corner. Perhaps the great cats had been glad to let them escape. That way, the *banths* could keep on living for sure and could enjoy eating the one eagle they had killed.

Whatever had happened, he was in danger of being caught in the open again. His pursuers had learned how to fly effectively in the lesser gravity. As a result, they were traveling a third faster than they would have on the planet—or so it seemed to Kickaha. Actually, the fighting and the loss of blood they had endured had to slow them down.

Podarge and one eagle, at a second look, did seem to be crippled. Their wings had slowed down since the first look, and they were lagging behind the other eagle. This one, though covered with blood over the green feathers, did not seem to be as deeply hurt. She overtook Kickaha and came down like a hawk on a gopher.

The gopher, however, was armed with a sword and had determined what action he would take. Calculating in advance when her onslaught would coincide with his bound, he whirled around in mid-air. He came down facing backwards, and the eagle's outstretched talons were within reach of the blade. She screamed and spread her wings to brake her speed, but he slashed out. His sword did not have the force that his sure footing on the ground would have given it, and the stroke spun him further than he wanted to go and threw him off balance for the landing. Nevertheless, the blade chopped through one foot at the juncture of talons and leg and halfway through the other foot. Then Kickaha struck the earth and fell on his side, and the breath exploded from him.

He was up again sobbing and wheezing like a damaged bagpipe. He managed to pick up his sword where he had dropped it. The eagle was flopping on the ground now like a wounded chicken and did not even see him when he brought the sword down on her neck. The head fell off, and one black, scarlet-encircled eye glared at him and then became dull and cold.

He was still sucking in air when he bounded through the cave entrance twenty yards ahead of Podarge and the last eagle. He landed just inside the hole in the hillside and then leaped toward the end of the cave, a granite wall forty feet away.

He had interrupted a domestic scene: a family of great white apes. Papa, ten feet tall, four-armed, white and hairless except for an immense roach of white hair on top of his breadloaf-shaped skull, gorilla-faced, pink-eyed, was squatting against the wall to the right. He was tearing with his protruding canines and sharp teeth at the ripped-off leg of a small *thoat*. Mama was ripping the flesh of the head of the *thoat* and at the same time was suckling twin babies.

(Wolff and Kickaha had goofed in designing the great white apes. They had forgotten that the only mammals on Burroughs' Mars were a small creature and man. By the time they perceived their mistake, they agreed that it was too late. Several thousand of the apes had been placed on the moon, and it did not seem worthwhile to destroy the first projects of the biolabs and create a new nonmammalian species.)

The colossal simians were as surprised as he, but he had the advantage of being in motion. Still, there was the delaying business of rolling a small key boulder out of a socket of stone and then pushing in on a heavy section of the back wall. This resulted in part of the wall swinging out and part swinging in to reveal a chamber. This was a square about twenty feet across. There were seven crescents set into the granite floor near the back wall. To the right was a number of pegs at eye-level, on which were placed seven of the silvery metallic crescents. Each of these was to be matched to the appropriate crescent on the floor by comparing the similarity of hieroglyphs on the crescents.

When two crescents were joined at their ends to form a circle, they became a gate to a preset place on the planet. Two of the gates were traps. The unwary person who used them would find himself transmitted to an inescapable prison in Wolff's palace.

Kickaha scanned the hieroglyphs with a haste that he did not like but could not help. The light was dusky in the rear chamber, and he could barely make out the markings. He knew now that he should have stored a light device here when the cave was set up. It was too late even for regret—he had no time for anything but instant unconsidered reaction.

The cavern was as noisy as the inside of a kettledrum. The two adult apes had gotten to their bowed and comparatively short legs and were roaring at him while the two upper arms beat on their chests and the two intermediary arms slapped their stomachs. Before they could advance on him, they were almost knocked over by Podarge and the eagle, who blasted in like a charge from a double-barreled shotgun.

They had hoped to catch a cornered and relatively helpless Kickaha, although their experience with him should have taught them caution. Instead, they had exchanged three wounded and tiring, perhaps reluctant, *banths* for two monstrously large, refreshed, and enraged great white apes.

Kickaha would have liked to watch the battle and cheer the apes, but he did not want to chance wearing his luck through, since it had already given indications of going threadbare. So he threw the two "trap" crescents on the floor and picked the other five up. Four he put under his arm with the intention of taking them with him. If the Harpy did escape the apes and tried to use a crescent, she would end up in the palace prison.

Kickaha lingered when he knew better, delayed his up-and-going too long. Podarge suddenly broke loose—perhaps thrown was a more exact description of her method of departure from the ape—and she shot like a basketball across the cave. She came into the chamber so swiftly that he had to drop the crescents to bring up his sword for defense. She hit him with her talons first, and he was slammed against the wall with a liver-hurting, kidney-paining jolt. He could not bring the sword down because, one, she was too close and, two, he was too hurt at the moment to use the sword.

Then they were rolling over and over with her talons clenched in his thighs. The pain was agonizing, and she was beating him in the face, the head, the neck, and the shoulders with the forward edges of her wings.

Despite the pain and the shock of the wing-blows, he managed to hit her in the chin with a fist and then to bang the hilt of the sword against the side of her head.

Her eyes crossed and glazed. Blood flowed from her nose. She fell backward, her wings stretched like outflung arms. Her talons, however, remained sunk in his thighs; he had to pry them loose one by one. Blood ran down his legs and pooled out around his feet. Just as he pulled the last talon loose, the male ape charged on all sixes into the chamber. Kickaha picked up his sword with both hands and brought it down on an outstretched paw. The shock ran up his hand and arm and almost made him lose his grip. But the paw, severed at the wrist, fell on the floor. The stump shot blood all over him, momentarily blinding him. He wiped the blood off in time to see the ape flee shrieking on two feet and three of its paws. It ran headlong into the last eagle, which had just finished disemboweling the female ape with its beak and talons They locked and went over and over.

At that moment Podarge recovered her senses.

She soared from the floor with a shriek and a frantic beating of wings. Kickaga picked up a crescent from the floor, saw that the hieroglyph on its center matched the nearest one in the floor, and set the two end against end. Then he whirled and slashed at Podarge, who was dancing around, trying to frenzy herself enough to attack him. She dodged back and he stepped into the ring formed by the two crescents.

"Goodbye, Podarge!" he cried. "Stay here and rot!"

# XVIII

HE HAD GOTTEN no further than her name when the gate activated. He was out of the cave with no sense of passage—as always—and was in another place, standing inside another ring of two crescents. The contact of the two crescents in the cave, plus the entrance of his mass into the field radiated by the crescents, had activated the gate after a delay of three seconds. He and the loose crescent had been transferred to the crescent which matched the frequency of the crescent in the cave, at the other end of the undercontinuum.

He had escaped, although he would bleed to death soon if he did not find something to staunch the flow.

Then he saw what mistake he had made by acting so quickly because of pressure from Podarge. He had picked up the wrong crescent after dropping the five when attacked by the Harpy. During the struggle, one of the trap crescents must have been kicked out of its corner and among the others. And he had picked it up and used it to gate out.

He was in the prison cell of the palace of the Lord.

Once, he had bragged to Wolff that he could escape from the so-called escape-proof cell if he were ever in it. He did not think that any prison anywhere could hold a man who was clever and determined. The escape might take a long time, but it could be done.

He groaned now and wished he had not been so big-mouthed. Wolff had arranged the prison very well. It was set under eighty feet of solid stone and had no direct physical connection to the outside world. It was an entirely self-enclosed, self-sustaining system except for one thing: food and water for the prisoner were transmitted from the palace kitchen through a gate too small to admit anything larger than a tray.

There were gates in the prison through which the prisoner could be brought up to a prison cell in the palace. But this could be activated only by someone cognizant in the palace above.

The room was cylindrical and was about forty feet long. Light was seemingly sourceless and there were no shadows. The walls were painted by Wolff with scenes from the ancient ancestral planet of the Lords. Wolff had not expected any prisoners other than Lords and so had done these paintings for their benefit. There was some cruelty in the settings of the murals—all depicted the wide and beautiful outdoors and hence could not help reminding the prisoner of his narrow and enclosed space.

The furniture was magnificent and was in the style known among the Lords as Pre-Exodus Middle Thyamarzan. The doors of the great bureaus and cabinets housed many devices for the amusement and education of the prisoner. Originally, these had not been in the cells. But when Wolff had rewon the palace, he had placed these in the prison—he no longer believed in torturing his captives even with boredom. And he provided them with much because he was sometimes gone for long periods and would not be able to release them.

Until now, this room had held no prisoners. It was ironical and sourly amusing that its first prize should be the jailer's best friend and that the jailer knew nothing of it.

The Bellers in the palace would not know of him either, he hoped. Lights would be flashing in three places to indicate that the buried cell now housed someone: a light would be pulsing in Wolff's bedroom; a second, on an instrument panel in the great control room; a third, in the kitchen.

If the Black Bellers were observing any of these, they must be alarmed or, at the least, edgy and uncertain. They would have no way of knowing what the lights meant. The kitchen taloses would know, but even if they were asked, they could not reply. They heard orders but had mouths for tasting and eating only, not for talking.

Kickaha, thinking about this, looked for first aid devices in the cabinets. He soon came across antiseptics, local anesthetics, drugs, bandages, all he needed. After cleaning his wounds, he prepared films of pseudoflesh and applied them to stop the bleeding. They began their healing efforts immediately.

He got a drink of water then and also opened a bottle of cold beer. He took a long shower, dried off, and searched for and found a pill which would dull his overstimulated nerves so he could get a restful sleep. The pill would have to wait, however, until he had eaten and finished exploring this place.

It was true that he should not, perhaps, be thinking of rest. Time was vital. There was no telling what was happening in Talanac with Anana and the Red Beards. They might be under attack this very moment by a Beller flying machine with powerful beamers. And what was von Turbat doing now? After he had escaped Podarge, he and von Swindebarn must have gated back to the palace. Would they be content to hole up in it? Or would they, as seemed more likely to Kickaha, go back to the moon through another gate? They would suppose him to be marooned there and so out of action. But they also must have some doubts. It was probable that they would take at least one craft and a number of men to hunt him down.

He laughed. They would be up there, frantically trying to locate him, and all the time he would be underfoot, so to speak. There was, of course, the possibility that they would find the cave near Korad. In which case, they would test all the crescents left there, and one Beller at least would soon be in this cell. Perhaps he was making a mistake in sleeping. Maybe he ought to keep on going, get out of this cell as soon as possible.

Kickaha decided that he *had* to sleep. If he didn't, he would collapse or be slowed down so much he would be too vulnerable. Light-headed from a bottle of beer and three glasses of wine, he went to a little door in the wall, over which a topaz was flashing a yellow light. He opened the door and took a silver tray from the hollow in the wall. There were ten silver-colored, jewel-encrusted dishes on the tray, each holding excellent foods. He emptied every dish and then returned the tray and contents to the hollow. Nothing happened until he closed the little door. He raised it again a second later. The hollow was empty. The tray had been gated up to the kitchen, where a talos would wash and polish the dishes and the tray. Six hours from now, the talos would place another tray of food in the kitchen gate and so send it to the stone-buried cell.

Kickaha wanted to be up and ready when the tray came through the next time. Unfortunately, there were no clocks in the prison, so he would have to depend on his biological clock. That, in its present condition, was undependable.

He shrugged and told himself what the hell. He could only try. If he didn't make it this time, he would the next. He had to get sleep because he did not know what would be required of him if he ever got out of prison. Actually, this was the best place for him in the universe—if the Bellers did not find the cave of gates on the moon.

First, he had to explore the rest of the prison to make sure that all was right there and also to use anything he might find helpful. He went to a door in one end of the cell and opened it. He stepped into a small bare anteroom. He opened the door on its opposite wall and went into another cylindrical cell about forty feet long. This was luxuriously decorated and furnished in a different style. However, the furniture kept changing shape, and whenever he moved near to a divan, a chair, or table, it slid away from him. When he increased his pace, the piece of furniture increased its speed just enough to keep out of reach. And the other furniture slid out of its way if they veered toward it.

The room had been designed to amuse, puzzle, and perhaps eventually enrage the prisoner. It was supposed to help him keep his mind off his basic predicament.

Kickaha gave up trying to capture a divan and left the room at the door at the opposite end. It closed behind him as the others had done. He knew that the doors could not be opened from this side, but he kept trying, just in case Wolff had made a mistake. It refused to move, too. The door ahead swung open to a small anteroom. The room beyond it was an art studio. The next room was four times as large as the previous and was mainly a swimming pool. It had a steady supply of cool fresh water, gated through from the palace water supply above and also gated out. Inflow was through a barred hole in the center of the pool's floor. Kickaha studied the setup of the pool and then went on to the next room.

This was the size of the first. It contained gymnastic equipment and was in a gravitic field one-half that of the planet's, the field of which was equivalent to Earth's. Much of the equipment was exotic, even to a man who traveled as much as Kickaha. The only things to hold his interest were some ropes, which were strung from ceiling hooks or bars for climbing exercises.

He fashioned a lasso from one rope and coiled several more over his shoulder to take with him. In all, he passed through twenty-four chambers, each different from the others. Eventually, he was back in the original.

Any other prisoner would have supposed that the rooms were connected to form a circular chain. He knew that there was no physical connection between the rooms. Each was separated from the next by forty feet of granite.

Passage from one to the next was effected by gates set inside the doorways of the anterooms. When the door was swung open, the gate was activated and the prisoner was transmitted instantaneously to another anteroom which looked just like the one he thought he was entering.

Kickaha entered the original cell cautiously. He wanted to make sure that no Beller had been gated here from the cave on the moon while he was exploring. The room was empty, but he could not be sure that a Beller had not come here and gone investigating, as he had. He stacked three chairs on top of each other and, carrying them, walked through into the next room, the one with the shape-shifting elusive furniture. He picked out a divan and lassoed a grotesquely decorated projection on top of its back. The projection changed form, but it could metamorphose only within certain limits, and the lasso held snugly. The divan did move away when he walked toward it, but he lay down and then pulled himself along the lasso while the divan fled here and there. The thick rugs kept him from being skinned, although he did get rug-burns. Finally he clutched the divan and hauled himself up onto it. It stopped then, seemed to quiver, solidified, and became as quiescent and permanent as ordinary furniture. However, it would resume its peculiar properties if he left it.

Kickaha tied one end of the lasso to the projection. He then snared the top of a chair which had been innocently standing nearby. The chair did not move until Kickaha pulled it on the rope. Then it tried to get away. He jumped off the divan and went through a series of maneuvers to herd the divan and chair, still connected by the rope, near the entrance. With the other ropes and various objects used as weights, he rigged a Rube Goldberg device. The idea was that anyone coming through the entrance would step inside the noose laid on the floor. The nearby mass of the intruder would then send both divan and chair away in flight, and this would draw the noose tight around the intruder's ankle. One end of the noose was tied to the rope stretched between the divan and chair. Another rope connected the projection on the divan to a chandelier of gold set with emeralds and turquoises. Kickaha, standing on the topmost of the three chairs he'd carried, had performed a balancing act while withdrawing the kingpin that secured the chandelier to the ceiling fixture. He did not entirely remove the kingpin but left just enough to keep the chandelier from falling. When the divan and chair pulled away from the intruder, the strain on the rope tied to the kingpin would yank it the rest of the way out, he hoped. The chandelier would come crashing down onto the floor. And, if his calculations were correct, it would fall on whoever was being dragged along by the noose around his leg.

Actually, he did not expect it to work. He did not think anybody would be imperceptive enough not to see the noose. Still, there was a chance. This world and the next were full of fools and clumsy idiots.

He went to the next room, the art studio. Here he picked up a large ball of plastic. This was extremely malleable and could be fixed to retain a desired shape by shooting a chemical hypodermically into the stuff. He took the ball and needle syringe into the swimming pool room. He dived to the bottom of the pool and jammed the plastic down over the outlet. He molded the plastic into a disc which covered the hole and then fixed it with the hypo. After this, he rose to the surface and drew himself up onto the pool edge. The water level began to rise immediately. It was as he had hoped: there was no regulation or feedback between inflow and outflow, so water continued to pour in even when the outlet was blocked. Wolff had overlooked this. Of course, there was no reason why he should have been concerned about it. If a prisoner wanted to drown himself, he was free to do so.

Kickaha walked into the next room. Here he piled some furniture and statues against the door, dried himself, and lay down to sleep. He was confident that no one would enter the room without having had much difficulty getting there. And no one could enter without making a lot of noise.

He awoke with a jerk and a feeling that bells attached to his nerves were jingling. His heart was drumming like a grouse's wings on takeoff. Something had crashed into his dreams. No, into the room. He jumped up from behind the divan, the sword in his hand. He came up just in time to see a man strike the floor in a wave of water. Then the door automatically shut. The man was gasping as though he had been holding his breath for a long time.

He was a long-legged, powerfully built fellow with pale skin, large freckles, and dark hair that would be red-blond when it dried. He carried no hand-beamers. His only weapons seemed to be a dagger and a short sword. He was unarmored. He wore a short-sleeved red shirt, a big leather belt, and yellow tights striped along the seams.

Kickaha bounded out from behind the divan and ran up with his sword raised. The man, shocked and seeing that he could not get up in time to defend himself, and that Kickaha was giving him a chance to surrender, took the only course a wise man could. Kickaha spoke to him in Lordspeech. The man looked puzzled and answered in German. Kickaha repeated the order in German, then let him get up so he could sit down in a chair. The man was shivering from the cold water and possibly from the thought of what Kickaha might yet do to him.

The fact that the man spoke German fluently was enough to convince Kickaha that he could not be a Beller. His speech was that of a native of the Einhorner Mountains. Evidently, the Bellers had not wanted to expose themselves to the unknown dangers of the gates and so had sent in expendables.

Pal Do Shuptarp told Kickaha everything he knew. He was a baronet who was in command of the castle garrison of King von Turbat of Eggesheim. He had stayed behind while the invasion of Talanac was taking place. Suddenly, von Turbat and von Swindebarn had reappeared. They came from somewhere inside the castle. They ordered the garrison and a number of other troops to follow them into a "magic" room in the castle. Von Turbat had explained that their archenemy Kickaha was now on the moon and that it was necessary to go by sorcery—white magic, of course—to track him down. Von Turbat did not say anything of what had happened to the soldiers in Talanac.

"They're all dead," Kickaha said. "But how did von Turbat talk to you?"

"Through a priest, as he has done for some time," Do Shuptarp said.

"And you didn't think that was peculiar?"

Do Shuptarp shrugged and said, "So many peculiar things were happening all of a sudden that this was just one more. Besides, von Turbat claimed to have received a divine revelation from the Lord. He said he had been given the gift of being able to speak the holy tongue. And he was forbidden to speak anything else because the Lord wanted everyone to know that von Turbat was favored of the Lord."

"A pretty good rationalization and excuse," Kickaha said.

"A magical flying machine appeared above the castle," Do Shuptarp said. "It landed, and we helped take it apart and carried the pieces into the room where we were to be transported magically to the moon."

It was a terrifying experience to be transported instantaneously to the moon and to see the planet they had been on just a moment before now hanging in the sky, threatening to fall down on the moon and crush them all.

But a man could get used to almost anything.

The cave in the hillside had been discovered by the searchers when they came across the carcass of an eagle minus her feet and head. The cave held two dead adult apes, and another dead eagle. There were five loose crescents on the floor. Kickaha, hearing this, knew that Podarge had escaped via a gate.

Von Turbat had selected ten of his best knights to use the gates, two to a circle. He hoped that some would find and kill Kickaha.

"Two of you?"

"Karl voyn Rothadler came with me," Do Shuptarp said. "He's dead. He did not step into the noose, although he stormed into that room so fast he almost got caught in it. A great one for charging in, swinging a sword, and to hell with finding out first what's going on. He ran in and so that divan and chair moved away swiftly. I don't now how you bewitched them, but you must be a powerful magician. They pulled the kingpin loose and the chandelier fell on his head."

"So the trap worked, though not exactly as planned," Kickaha said. "How did you get through the room filled with water?"

"After Karl was killed, I tried to go back the way I'd come. The door wouldn't open. So I went on. When I came to the door to the water-filled room, I had to push with all my strength to open it. Water sprayed out of the opening. I quit pushing. But I couldn't go back; I had to go ahead. I pushed the door open again. The pressure of the water was very strong. I couldn't get the door open all the way, and the water spurting out almost knocked me down. But I managed to get through—I am very strong. The anteroom was almost full of water by the time I did get through, and the door closed as soon as I was inside the big room.

"The water was clear and the light was bright. Otherwise, I might have drowned before I found the other door. I swam to the ceiling, hoping there would be a space there with air, but there wasn't any. So I swam to the other end of the room. The water pressure had opened the door there and let some water into the next anteroom. But the door had closed itself again. In fact, it must have been doing this for some time. The anteroom was more than half full when I got into it.

"By then, the pressure was also opening the door into this room. I waited once while it closed. Then, when it began to open a little again, I shoved with my feet braced on the floor. And I came out like a marooned sailor cast up by a storm on a desert island, as you saw."

Kickaha did not comment for a minute. He was thinking of the predicament in which he had put himself—and this fellow—by causing the pool to overflow. Eventually, every room of the twenty-four would be flooded.

"Okay," he said. "If I can't figure a way to get out fast, we've had it!"

Do Shuptarp asked what he had said. Kickaha explained. Do Shuptarp got even paler. Kickaha then proceeded to outline much of what was behind the recent events. He went into some detail about the Black Bellers.

Do Shuptarp said, "Now I understand much of what was incomprehensible to me—to all of us—at the time. One day, life was proceeding normally. I was getting ready to lead a dragon-hunting expedition. Then von Turbat and von Swindebarn proclaimed a holy war. They said that the Lord, Herr Gutt, was directing us to attack the city on the level below us. And we were to find and kill the three heretics hiding there.

"Most of us had never heard of Talanac or the Tishquetmoac or of Kickaha. We had heard of the robber baron Horst von Horstmann, of course. Then von Turbat told us that the Lord had given us magical means to go from one level to the next. He explained why he used only the speech of the Lord.

"And now you tell me that the souls of my king and of von Swindebarn and a few others have been eaten up. And that their bodies are possessed by demons."

Kickaha saw that the soldier did not fully understand yet, but he did not try to disabuse him. If he wanted to think in superstitious modes, let him.

The important thing was that he knew that the two kings were now terrible perils in disguise.

"Can I trust you?" he said to Do Shuptarp. "Will you help me, now that you know the truth? Are you convinced that it is the truth? Of course, all this doesn't matter unless I can figure out a way to get us up into the palace before we drown."

"I will swear eternal fealty to you!"

Kickaha wasn't convinced, but he didn't want to kill him. And Do Shuptarp might be helpful. He told him to pick up his weapons and to lead the way back to the cell in which they had arrived. On getting back there, Kickaha looked for a recording device and found one. This was one of many machines with which a prisoner could entertain himself. Kickaha, however, had another purpose than amusement in mind. He took the glossy black cube, which was three inches across, pressed the red spot on its underside, and spoke a few words in Lord-speech at it. Then he pressed a white spot on its side, and his words were emitted back to him.

Kickaha waited for what seemed like hours until the topaz above the little door in the wall began flashing. He removed the tray, which contained enough food for two. Two lights were now flashing in the kitchen, and the talos, noting this, had made suitable provisions.

"Eat!" Kickaha said to Do Shuptarp. "Your next meal may be a long way off—if you ever get one!"

Do Shuptarp winced. Kickaha tried to eat slowly, but the sudden slight opening of the door and spurt of water caused him to gobble. The door shut but almost immediately opened a few inches again to spew in more water.

He put the dishes on the tray and set it in the

wallchamber. He hoped that the talos would not have something more pressing to do. If they delayed gating the tray back, it might be too late for the prisoners.

Also, the cube he had put on the tray had started replaying his instructions. It was set for sixty times by pressing the white spot three times, but the talos might not take in the tray until after the recordings were finished.

The topaz quit flashing. He lifted the door. The tray was gone. "If the talos does what I tell him to, we're okay," he said to the Teutoniac. "At least, we'll be out of here. If the talos doesn't obey me, then it's glub, glub, glub, and an end to our worries."

He told Do Shuptarp to follow him into the anteroom. There they stood for perhaps sixty seconds. Kickaha said, "If nothing happens soon, we might as well kiss our . . ."

## XIX

THEY WERE standing on a round plate of gray metal in a large room. The furniture was exotic, Early Rhadamanthean Period. The walls and floor were of rose-red and jet-veined stone. There were no doors or windows, although one wall seemed to be a window which gave a view of the outside.

"There'll be lights to indicate that we're now in this cell," Kickaha said. "Let's hope the Bellers won't figure out what they mean."

With all these unexplained lights on, the Bellers must be in a panic. Undoubtedly, they were prowling the palace to find out what—if anything—was wrong.

Presently, a section of the seemingly solid wall moved and disappeared into the wall itself. Kickaha led the way out. A talos, six and a half feet tall, armored like a knight, waited for them. It handed him the black-cube recorder.

Kickaha said, "Thank you," and then, "Observe us closely. I am your master. This man is my servant. Both of us are to be served by you unless this man, my servant, does something that might harm me. Then you are to stop him from trying to harm me.

"The other beings in this palace are my

enemies, and you are to attack and kill any as soon as you see one or more than one. First, though, you will take this cube, after I have spoken a message into it, and you will let the other taloses hear it. It will tell them to attack and kill my enemies. Do you understand fully?"

The talos saluted, indicating that he comprehended. Kickaha spoke into the cube, set it to repeat the message a thousand times, and gave it to the talos. The armored thing saluted again, turned, and marched off.

Kickaha said, "They carry out orders superbly, but the last one to get their ear is their master. Wolff knew this, but he didn't want to change their setup. He said that this characteristic might actually work out to his advantage someday, and it wasn't likely that any invader would know about it."

Kickaha next told Do Shuptarp how to handle a beamer if he should get his hands on one, then they set out for the armory of the palace. To get to it, they had to cross one entire floor of this wing and then descend six stories. Kickaha took the staircases, since the Bellers would be using the elevators.

Do Shuptarp was awed at the grandeur of the palace. The great size of the rooms and their furnishings, each containing treasure enough to have bought all the kingdoms in Dracheland, reduced him to a gasping, slavering, creeping creature. He wanted to stop so he could look and feel and, perhaps, fill his pockets. Then he became cowed, because the absolute quiet and the richness made him feel as if he were in an extremely sacred place.

"We could wander for days and never meet another soul," he said.

Kickaha said, "We could if I didn't know where I was going." He wondered how effective the fellow would be. He was probably a first-rate warrior under normal circumstances. His handling of himself in the water-filled chamber proved that he was courageous and adaptable. But to be in the palace of the Lord was for him as frightening, as numinous an experience, as it would be for a terrestrial Christian to be transported to the City of God—and to discover that devils had taken over.

Near the foot of the staircase, Kickaha smelled melted metal and plastic and burned protoplasm. Cautiously, he stuck his head around the corner. About a hundred feet down the hall, a talos lay sprawled on its front. An armored arm, burned off at the shoulder by a beamer, lay nearby.

Two Black Bellers, or so Kickaha presumed they were from the caskets attached to their backs by harnesses, lay dead. Their necks were twisted almost completely around. Two Bellers, each holding a hand-beamer, were talking excitedly. One held what was left of the black cube in his hand. Kickaha grinned on seeing it. It had been damaged by the beamer and so must have stopped its relay. Thus, the Bellers would not know why the talos had attacked them or what the message was in the cube.

"Twenty-nine down. Twenty-one to go," Kickaha said. He withdrew his head.

"They'll be on their guard now," he muttered. "The armory would've been unguarded, probably, if this hadn't happened. But now that they know something's stalking upwind, they'll guard it for sure. Well, we'll try another way. It could be dangerous, but then what isn't? Let's go back up the stairs."

He led Do Shuptarp to a room on the sixth story. This was about six hundred feet long and three hundred feet wide and contained stuffed animals, and some stuffed sentients, from many universes. They passed a transparent cube in which was embedded, like a dragonfly in amber, a creature that seemed to be half-insect, half-man. It had antennae and huge but quite human eyes, a narrow waist, skinny legs covered with a pinkish fuzz, four skinny arms, a great humped back, and four butterfly-like wings radiating from the hump.

Despite the urgency of action, Do Shuptarp stopped to look at the strangeling. Kickaha said, "That exhibit is ten thousand years old. That *kwiswas*, coleopter-man, is the product of Anana's biolabs, or so I was told, anyway. The Lord of this world made a raid on his sister's world and secured some specimens for his museum. This *kwiswas*, I understand, was Anana's lover at that time, but you can't believe everything you hear, especially if one Lord is telling it about another. And all that, of course, was some time ago."

The monstrously large eyes had been staring through the thick plastic for ten millennia, five thousand years before civilization had set in on Earth. Though Kickaha had seen it before, he still felt an awe, an uneasiness, and insignificance before it. How strongly and cleverly had this creature fought to preserve its life, just as Kickaha was now fighting for his? Perhaps as vigorously and wildly. And then it had died, as he must, too, and it had been stuffed and set up to observe with unseeing eyes the struggles of others. All passed . . .

He shook his head and blinked his eyes. To philosophize was fine, if you did so under appropriate circumstances. These were not appropriate. Besides, so death came to all, even to those who avoided it as ingeniously and powerfully as he! So what? One extra minute of life was worth scrapping for, provided that the minutes that had gone before had been worthy minutes.

"I wonder what this thing's story was?" Do Shuptarp muttered.

"Our story will come to a similar end if we don't get a move on," Kickaha said.

At the end wall of the room, he twisted a projection that looked as fixed as the rest of the decorations. He turned the projection to the right 160 degrees, then to the left left 160, and then spun it completely around twice to the right. A section of wall slid back. Kickaha breathed out tension of uncertainty. He had not been sure that he remembered the proper code. The possibility was strong that a wrong manipulation would have resulted in anything from a cloud of poisonous gas or vapor to a beam which would cut him in half.

He pulled in Do Shuptarp after him. The Teutoniac started to protest. Then he began to scream as both fell down a lightless shaft. Kickaha clapped his hand over Do Shuptarp's mouth and said, "Quiet! We won't be hurt!"

The wind of their descent snatched his words away. Do Shuptarp continued to struggle, but he subsided when they began to slow down in their fall. Presently, they seemed to be motionless. The walls suddenly lit up, and they could see that they were falling slowly. The shaft a few feet above them and a few feet below them was dark. The light accompanied them as they descended. Then they were at the bottom of the shaft. There was no dust, although the darkness above the silence felt as if the place had not seen a living creature for hundreds of years.

Angrily, the Teutoniac said, "I may have heart failure yet."

Kickaha said, "I had to do it that way. If you knew how you were going to fall, you'd never have gone through with it on your own. It would have been too much to ask you."

"You jumped," Do Shuptarp said.

"Sure. And I've practiced it a score of times. I didn't have the guts either until I'd seen Wolff—the Lord—do it several times."

He smiled. "Even so, this time, I wasn't sure that the field was on. The Bellers could have turned it off. Wouldn't that have been a good joke on us?"

Do Shuptarp did not seem to think it was funny. Kickaha turned from him to the business of getting out of the shaft. This demanded beating a code with his knuckles on the shaft wall. A section slid out, and they entered a whitewalled room about thirty feet square and well illuminated. It was bare except for a dozen crescents set in the stone floor and a dozen hanging on wall-pegs. The crescents were unmarked.

Kickaha put out a hand to restrain Do Shuptarp. "Not a step more! This room is dangerous unless you go through an undeviating ritual. And I'm not sure I remember it all!"

The Teutoniac was sweating, although the air was cool and moving slightly. "I was going to ask why we didn't come here in the first place," he said, "instead of walking through the corridors. Now, I see."

"Let's hope you continue to see," Kickaha said

ambiguously. He advanced three steps forward straight from the entrance. Then he walked sideways until he was even with the extreme right-end crescent on the wall. He turned around once and walked to the crescent, his right arm extended stiffly at right angles to the floor. As soon as his fingertips touched the crescent, he said, "Okay, soldier. You can walk about as you please now—I think."

But he lost his smile as he studied the crescents. He said, "One of these will gate us to inside the armory. But I can't remember which. The second from the right or the third?"

Do Shuptarp asked what would happen if the wrong crescent were chosen.

"One of these—I don't know which—would gate us into the control room," he said. "I'd choose that if I had a beamer or if I thought the Bellers hadn't rigged extra-mass-intrusion alarms in the control room. And if I knew which it was.

"One will gate us right back to the underground prison from which we just came. A third would gate us to the moon. A fifth, to the Atlantean level. I forget exactly what the others will do, except that one would put you into a universe that is, to say the least, undesirable."

Do Shuptarp shivered and said, "I am a brave man. I've proved that on the battlefield. But I feel like a baby lost in a forest full of wolves."

Kickaha didn't answer, although he approved of Do Shuptarp's frankness. He could not make up his mind about the second or third crescent. He had to pick one because there was no getting back up the shaft—like so many routes in the palace, it was one-way.

Finally, he said, "I'm fairly sure it's the third.

Wolff's mind favors threes or multiples thereof. But . . ."

He shrugged and said, "What the hell. We can't stand here forever."

He matched the third right-hand crescent with the third from the left on the floor. "I do remember that the loose crescents go with opposing fixed ones," he said. He carefully explained to Do Shuptarp the procedure for using a gate and what they might expect. Then the two stepped into the circle formed by the two crescents. They waited for about three seconds. There was no sensation of movement or flicker of passage before their eyes, but, abruptly, they were in a room about three hundred feet square. Familiar and exotic weapons and armor were in shelves on the walls or in racks and stands on the floor.

"We made it," Kickaha said. He stepped out of the circle and said, "We'll get some hand-beamers and power-packs, some rope, and a spy-missile guider and goggles. Oh, yes, some short-range neutron hand-grenades, too."

He also picked two well-balanced knives for throwing. Do Shuptarp tried out his beamer on a small target at the armory rear. The metal disc, which was six inches thick, melted away within five seconds. Kickaha strapped a metal box to his back in a harness. This contained several spy-missiles, power broadcasting-receiving apparatus for the missiles, and the video-audio goggles.

Kickaha hoped that the Bellers had not come across these yet. If they had guards who were looking around corners or prowling the corridors with the missiles, it was goodbye.

The door had been locked by Wolff, and, as nearly as Kickaha could determine, no one had unlocked it. It had many safeguards to prevent access by unauthorized persons from the outside, but there was nothing to prevent a person on the inside from leaving without hindrance. Kickaha was relieved. The Bellers had not been able to penetrate this, which meant they had no spy-missiles. Unless, that is, they had brought some in from the other universes. But since the crafts had used none, he did not think they had any.

He put on the goggles over his eyes and ears and, holding the control box in his hands, guided a missile out the open doors. The missile was about three inches long and was shaped like a schoolboy's folded-paper airplane. It was transparent, and the tiny colored parts could be seen in a strong light at certain angles. Its nose contained an "eye," through which Kickaha could get a peculiar and limited view and an "ear" through which he could hear noises, muted or amplified as he wished.

He turned the missile this way and that, saw that no one was in the hall, and shoved the goggles up on top of his head. When he left the armory, he closed the door, knowing that it would automatically lock and arm itself. He used his eyes to guide the missile on the straightaway, and when he wanted to look around corners, he slipped the goggles down.

Kickaha and Do Shuptarp, with the missile, covered about six miles of horizontal and vertical travel, leaving one wing and crossing another to get to the building containing the control room. The trip took longer than a mere hike because of their caution.

Once, they passed by a colossal window close to the edge of the monolith on which the palace sat.

Do Shuptarp almost fainted when he saw the sun. It was *below* him. He had to look downward to see it. Seeing the level of Atlantis spread out flatly for a five hundred mile radius, and then a piece of the level below that, and a shard of still a lower one, made him turn white.

Kickaha pulled him away from the window and tried to explain the tower structure of the planet and the rotation of the tiny sun about it. Since the palace was on top of the highest monolith of the planet, it was actually above the sun, which was at the level of the middle monolith.

The Teutoniac said he understood this. But he had never seen the sun except from his native level. And, of course, from the moon. But both times the sun had seemed high.

"If you think that was a frightening experience," Kickaha said, "you should look over the edge of the world sometime from the bottom level, the Garden level."

They entered the central massif of the building, which housed the control room. Here they proceeded even more slowly. They walked down a Brobdingnagian hall lined with mirrors which gave, not the outer physical reflection, but the inner physical reflection. Rather, as Kickaha explained, each mirror detected the waves of a different area of the brain and then synthesized these with music and colors and subsonics and gave them back as visual images. Some were hideous and some beautiful and some outrageously obscene and some almost numinously threatening.

"They don't mean anything," Kickaha said, "unless the viewer wants to interpret what they mean to him. They have no objective meaning."

Do Shuptarp was glad to get on. Then Kickaha took a staircase broad enough for ten platoons of soldiers almost to march up. This wound up and up and seemed never to end, as if it were the staircase to Heaven itself.

## XX

FINALLY, the Teutoniac begged for a rest; Kickaha consented. He sent the spy-missile up for another look. There were no Bellers on the floor below that on which the control room was. There were the burned and melted bodies of ten taloses, all on the first six steps of the staircase. Apparently, they had been marching up to attack the Bellers in the control room, and they had been beamed down. The device which may have done this was crouching at the top of the stairs. It was a small black box on wheels with a long thin neck of gray metal. At its end was a tiny bulb. This bulb could detect and beam a moving mass at a maximum distance of forty feet.

It moved the long neck back and forth to sweep the staircase. It did not notice the missile as it sped overhead, which meant that the snake-neck, as Kickaha termed it, was set to detect only larger masses. Kickaha turned the missile and sent it down the hall toward the double doors of the control room. These were closed. He did see, through the missile's "eye," that there were many small discs stuck on the walls all along the corridor—mass-detectors. Their fields were limited, however. A narrow aisle would be left down the center of the corridor so that the warned might walk in it without setting off alarms. And there must be visual devices of some sort out here, too, since the Bellers would not neglect these. He moved the missile very slowly along the ceiling because he did not want it seen. And then he spotted devices. They were hidden in the hollowed-out heads of two busts on tops of pedestals. The hollowing-out had been done by the Bellers.

Kickaha brought the missile back carefully and took off the goggles, then led Do Shuptarp up the staircase. They had not gone far before they smelled the burned protoplasm and plastic. When they were on the floor with the carnage, Kickaha stopped the Teutoniac.

"As near as I can figure out," he said, "they're all holed up now in the control room. It's up to us to smoke them out or rush them before they get us. I want you to watch our rear at all times. Keep looking! There are many gates in the control room which transmit you to other places in the palace. If the Bellers have figured them out, they'll be using them. So watch it!"

He was just out of range of the vision and beamer of the snake-neck at the top of the steps. He sat down and frayed out the fibers at one end of his thinnest rope and tied these around the missile. Then he put the goggles back on and directed the missile up the steps. It moved slowly because of the weight of the rope. The snake-neck continued to sweep the field before it, but did not send a beam at the missile or rope. Though this meant that it was set to react to greater masses, it did not mean that it wasn't transmitting a picture to the Bellers in the control room. If they saw the missile and the rope, they might come charging out and shoot down over the railing. Kickaha told Do Shuptarp to watch above, too, and shoot if anything moved.

The missile slid by the snake-neck and then around it, drawing the rope with it. It then came back down the steps. Kickaha removed the goggles, untied the rope, seized the ends of the rope, pulled to make sure he had a snug fit, and yanked. The snake-neck came forward and tumbled halfway down the steps. It lay on its side, its neck-and-eye moving back and forth but turned away from the right side of the staircase. Kickaha approached it from the back and turned it off by twisting a dial at its rear.

He carried the machine back up under one arm while he held a beamer ready in his right hand. Near the top, he got down against the steps and slid the machine onto the floor. Here he turned it so it faced the bust at the end of the hall past the control room doors. He set the dials and then watched it roll out of sight. Presently, there was a loud crash. He dropped the goggles down and sent the missile to take a look. As he had hoped, the snake-neck had gone down the hall until the mass of the pedestal and its bust had set it off. Its beamer had burned through the hollow stone pedestal until it fell over. The bust was lying on its side with the transmitter camera looking at the wall. The snake-neck had turned its beam on the fallen bust.

He went back down the staircase and down the hall until he was out of sight of anyone who might come to the top of the steps or look down the side of the well. He replaced the goggles and took the missile to a position above the double doors. The missile, flat against the wall, was standing on its nose and looking straight down.

He waited. Minutes went by. He wanted to take the goggles off so he could make sure that Do Shuptarp was watching everywhere. He restrained the impulse—he had to be ready if the doors opened.

Presently, they did open. A periscopic tube was stuck out and turned in both directions. Then it withdrew and a blond head slowly emerged. The body followed it soon. The Beller ran over to the snake-head and turned it off. Kickaha was disappointed because he had hoped the machine would beam the Beller. However, it scanned and reacted only to objects in front of it.

The bust was completely melted. The Beller looked at it for a while, then picked up the snake-neck and took it into the control room. Kickaha sent the missile in through the upper part of the doorway and up into the high parts of the room, which was large enough to contain an aircraft carrier of 1945 vintage. He shot the missile across the ceiling and down the opposite wall and low to the floor to a place behind a control console. The vision and audio became fuzzy and limited then, which made him think that the doors had been shut. Although the missile could transmit through material objects within a limited range, it lost much of its effectiveness.

Zymathol was telling Arswurd of the strange behavior of the snake-neck. He had replaced it with another, which he hoped would not also malfunction. He had not replaced the camera. The other at the opposite end of the hall could do what was needed. Zymathol regretted that they had been so busy trying to get laser-beam or radio contact with von Turbat on the moon. Otherwise, they might have been watching the monitor screens and seen what had happened.

Kickaha wanted to continue listening, but he had to keep his campaign going. He switched off the missile in the control room and tied the end of the rope to another missile. This he sent up and around the new snake-neck and pulled it down. It tumbled much farther, bringing up short against the pile of talos bodies at the staircase foot. It was pointed up in the air. Kickaha crawled up to it, reached over the bodies, and turned it off. He took it back up the steps and sent it against the pedestal and bust at the other end of the hall. He was down the steps and had his goggles on and another missile on its way before the crash sounded. The crash came to his ears via the missile.

Its eye showed him that the same thing had happened. He turned it to watch the door, but nothing happened for a long time. Finally, he switched to the missile in the control room. Zymathol was arguing that the malfunctioning of the second machine was too coincidental. There was something suspicious happening, something therefore dangerous. He did not want to go outside again to investigate.

Arswurd said that, like it or not, they couldn't stay here and let an invader prowl around. He had to be killed—and the invader was probably Kickaha. Who else could have gotten inside the palace when all the defenses were set up to make it impregnable?

Zymathol said that it couldn't be Kickaha. Would von Turbat and von Swindebarn be up on the moon looking for him if he weren't there?

This puzzled Kickaha. What was von Turbat

doing there when he must know that his enemy had escaped via the gate in the cave-chamber? Or was von Turbat so suspicious of his archenemy's wiliness that he thought Kickaha might have gated something through to make it look as if he were no longer on the moon? If so, what could make him think that there was anything on the moon to keep Kickaha there?

He became upset and a trifle frightened then. Could Anana have gated up there after him? Was she being chased by the Bellers? It was a possibility, and it made him anxious.

Zymathol said that only Kickaha could have turned the taloses against them. Arswurd replied that that was all the more reason for getting rid of such a danger. Zymathol asked how.

"Not by cowering in here," Arswurd said.

"Then you go look for him," Zymathol said.

"I will," Arswurd answered.

Kickaha found it interesting that the conversation was so human. The Bellers might be born of metal complexes, but they were not like machines off an assembly line. They had all the differences of personality of humans.

Arswurd started to go to the door, but Zymathol called him back. Zymathol said that their duty demanded they not take unnecessary chances. There were so few of them now that the death of even one greatly lessened their hope of conquest. In fact, instead of aiming for conquest now, they were fighting for survival. Who would have thought that a mere *leblabbiy* could have killed them so ingeniously and relentlessly? Why, Kickaha was not even a Lord—he was only a human being.

Zymathol said they must wait until their two

leaders returned. They could not be contacted; something was interfering with attempts to communicate. Kickaha could have told them why their efforts were useless. The structure of the space-time fabric of this universe made a peculiar deformation which would prevent the undistorted transmission of radio or laser. If an aircraft, for instance, were to try to fly between planet and moon, it would break up in a narrow zone partway between the two bodies. The only way to travel from one to the other was by a gate.

The two Bellers talked nervously of many things. Twenty-nine of the original Bellers were dead. There were two here, two in Nimstowl's universe, two in Anana's, two in Judubra's. Zymathol thought that these ought to be recalled to help. Or, better, that the Bellers in this universe should leave and seal off all gates. There were plenty of other universes; why not cut this one off forever? If Kickaha wanted it, he could have it. Meanwhile, in a safe place, they could make millions of new Bellers. In ten years, they would be ready to sweep out the Lords everywhere.

But von Turbat, whom they called Graumgrass, was extraordinarily stubborn. He would refuse to quit. Both agreed on that.

It became evident to Kickaha that Arswurd, despite his insistence on the necessity of leaving the room to find the invader, really did not want to and, in fact, had no intention of doing so. He did need, however, to sound brave to himself.

The two did not seem the unhuman, cold, strictly logical, utterly emotionless beings described to him by Anana. If certain elements were removed from their conversation, they could have been just two soliders of any nation or universe talking.

For a moment, he wondered if the Bellers could not be reasoned with, if they could be content to take a place in this world as other sentients did.

That feeling passed quickly. The Bellers preferred to take over bodies of human beings; they would not remain enclosed in their metal bells. The delights and advantages of flesh were too tempting. No, they would not be satisfied to remain in the bells; they would keep on stripping human brains and moving into the dispossessed somas.

The war would have to be to the end, that is, until all Bellers or Kickaha died.

At that moment, he felt as if the entire world were a burden on him alone. If they killed him, they could move ahead as they wished, because only a few knew their identities and purposes, and these few would also die. This was his world, as he had bragged, and he was the luckiest man in two worlds, because he alone of Earthmen had been able to get through the wall between the worlds. This, to him, was a world far superior to Earth and he had made it his in a way that even Wolff, the Lord, had not been able to do.

Now, the delights and rewards were gone, replaced by a responsibility so tremendous that he had not thought about it because he could not endure to do so.

For a man with such responsibility, he had acted recklessly.

That was, however, why he had survived so long. If he had proceeded with great caution because he was so important, he probably would have been caught and killed by now. Or he would have escaped but would be totally ineffective, because he would be afraid to take any action. Reckless or not, he would proceed now as he had in the past. If he misjudged, he became part of the past, and the Bellers took over the present and future. So be it.

He switched back to a third missile and placed it against the wall just above the doors. Then he laid the control box and goggles beside him. He told Do Shuptarp what he meant to do next. The Teutoniac thought it was a crazy idea, but he agreed. He didn't have any ideas of his own. They picked up a talos and dragged the body, which possibly weighed five hundred pounds, up the steps. They pulled it down the hall in the aisle between the detector fields and propped it up in front of the doors. Then they retreated hastily but carefully to the floor below.

After taking a quick look, Kickaha replaced the goggles. He lowered the missile above the door, positioned it to one side of the sitting talos, and hurled the missile aginst the helmet-head of the talos. The impact ruined the missile so that he could not observe its effect. But he quickly sent another up and stationed this above the doors. The talos had fallen as he had wished. Its head and shoulders were within the detector field. The alarms must be ringing wildly inside the control room.

Nothing happened. The doors did not open. He waited until he could endure the suspense no longer. Though it was essential that he keep the missile posted above the doors, he sent it to the floor and then switched back to the missile inside the control room. He could see nothing except the rear of the control console, and he could hear nothing. There were no alarms whooping, so these must have been turned off. The Bellers were not talking or making a sound of any kind, even though he turned the audio amplification up.

He switched back to the missile outside the doors. The doors were closed, so he returned to the device in the room. There was still no noise.

What was going on?

Were they playing a game of Who's-Got-The-Coolest-Nerves? Did they want him to come charging on in?

He returned to the missile in the room and sent it back along the floor to the wall. It went slowly up the wall, the area just ahead of it clear for a foot and then fuzzy beyond that . He intended to put it against the ceiling and then lower it with the hopes that he would see the Bellers before they saw the missile. The missile could be used to kill as a bullet kills, but his range of vision was so limited that he had to be very close. If a Beller yelled, he would betray his position by sound and Kickaha might be able to send the missile at him before the Beller burned the missile down. It was a long chance which he was willing to take now.

He had brought the device down approximately where the control console it had hidden behind should be. The missile came straight down to the floor without seeing or hearing anything. It then rose and circled the area without detecting the Bellers. He expanded the territory of search. The Bellers, of course, could be aware of the missile and could be retreating beyond its range or hiding. This did not make sense unless they wanted to keep the operator of the missile busy while one or more left the room to search for him. They probably did not know exactly how the missile worked, but they must realize that its transmission was limited and that the operator had to be comparatively close.

Kickaha told Do Shuptarp to be especially alert for the appearance of Bellers at the top of the staircase—and to remember to use the neutron grenades if he got a chance. He had no sooner finished saying this than Do Shuptarp yelled. Kickaha was so startled that he threw his hands up. The control box went flying. So did Kickaha. Yanking off the goggles, he rolled over and over at the same time, to spoil the aim of anybody who might be trying to shoot at him. He had no idea of what had made the Teutoniac shout, nor was he going to sit still while he looked around for the source of the alarm.

A beam scorched the rug as it shot on by him. It came from an unexpected place, the far end of the hall. A head and a hand holding a beamer were projecting from a corner. Luckily, Do Shuptarp had fired as soon as he saw the Beller, so the Beller could only get off a wild beam. Then he dodged back. At this distance, a beamer's effectiveness was considerably reduced. At short range it could melt through twelve inches of steel and cook a man through to the gizzard in a second. At this distance it could only give him a third degree burn on his skin or blind him if it struck the eyes.

Do Shuptarp had retreated to the first few bottom steps of the staircase where he was lodged behind the pile of talos bodies. Kickaha ran down the hall away from the opposite end, wary of what might pop out from the near side. One or both of the Bellers in the control room had gated to another part of the palace and had made a flank attack. Or one or both had gated elsewhere to get help from other Bellers.

Kickaha cursed, wheeled, and ran back toward the abandoned goggles and control box. The Beller at the far end popped his head out close to the floor and fired. Do Shuptarp, at a wider angle to the Beller because he was on the staircase, replied with his beam. Kickaha shot, too. The Beller withdrew before the rays, advancing along the rug, could intersect at the corner. The non-flammable rug melted where the beams had made tracks.

The three grenades were too far away to risk time to go for them. Kickaha scooped up the box and goggles, whirled, and dashed back along the corridor. He expected somebody to appear at the near end, so he was ready to pop into the nearest doorway. When he was two doorways from the end, he saw a head coming around a corner. He triggered off a beam, played it along the molding, and then up the corner. The head, however, jerked back before the ray could hit it. Kickaha crouched against the wall and fired past the corner, hoping that some energy would bounce off and perhaps warm up the person or persons hidden around the corner. A yell told him that he had scared or perhaps scorched someone.

He grinned and went back into the doorway before the Bellers would try the same trick on him. This was no grinning business, but he could not help being savagely amused when he put one over on his enemies.

## XXI

THE ROOM in which he had retreated was comparatively small. It was like hundreds of others in the palace, its main purpose being to store art treasures. These were tastefully arranged, however, as if the room were lived in or at least much visited.

He looked swiftly around for evidence of gates, since there were so many hidden in the palace that he could not remember more than a fraction of them. He saw nothing suspicious. This itself meant nothing, but at this time he had to take things on evidence. Otherwise, he would not be able to act.

He slipped on the goggles, hating to do so because it left him blind and deaf to events in the hall. He switched to the missile in the control room. It was still in the air, circling in obedience to the last order. No Bellers came within its range. He then transferred to the missile outside the doors and brought it down the staircase and along the corridor. The closer it came to him, the stronger its transmission of sight and sound was. And the better his control.

Do Shuptarp was keeping the Beller at the far end from coming out. Whoever was at the near end was the immediate danger. He sent the missile close to the ceiling and around the corner. There were three Bellers there, each with hand-beamers. The face of one was slightly reddish, as if sunburned. At a distance were two coming down the hall and pushing a gravsled before them. This bore a huge beamer, the equivalent of a cannon. Its ray could be sent past the corner to splash off the wall and keep Kickaha at a distance while the others fired with the hand-beamers. And then, under the covering fire, the big projector would be pushed around the corner and its full effect hurled along the length of the hall. It would burn or melt anything in its path.

Kickaha did not hesitate. He sent the missile at full speed toward the right-hand man pushing the sled. His vision was blurred with the sudden increase of velocity, then the scene went black. The missile had buried itself in the flesh of the Beller or had hit something else so hard it had wrecked itself. He took another missile from the box, which he had unharnessed from his back and laid beside him, and he sent it up out of the room and along the ceiling. Abruptly, a Beller, yelling to disconcert anyone who might be in the hall, sprang out from around the corner. He saw the missile and raised his beamer. Kickaha sent it toward him, pressing the full-speed button on the control box. The scene went black. It was deep in the target's flesh, or ruined against the hard floor or wall, or melted by the beamer.

He did not dare to take the time to send another missile out to look. If the Beller had escaped it, he would be looking into the doorways now for the operator of the missile. And he probably had called the others out to help him.

Kickaha snatched off the goggles and, beamer in one hand and goggles in the other, strode to the door. He had left the door open for better control and vision of the missile. In a way, this was a good thing because the Beller would look in the rooms with closed doors first. But, as he neared the doorway, he confronted a Beller. Kickaha was holding his beamer in front of his chest; he squeezed the trigger as the man's shoulder came in sight. The Beller turned black, smoke rose from skin frying and shredding away in layers, the whites of the eyes became a deep brown and then the aqueous humor in the balls shot out boiling, the hair went up in a stinking flame, the white teeth became black, the lips swelled and then disappeared in layers, the ears became ragged and ran together in rolls of gristle. The clothes, fireproof, melted away.

All this took place in four seconds. Kickaha kicked the door shut and pressed the plate to lock it. Then he was across the room and pushing the plate which turned off the energy field across the window. He threw the missile box out so it could not be used by the Bellers. He tied one end of the rope to a post on a bureau and he crawled out the window. Below was a hundred thousand feet of air. This part of the palace projected over the edge of the monolith; if he cared to, he could sweep almost half its area with a turn of his head. At this moment, he did not want to think about the long, long fall. He kept his eyes on the little ledge about six feet below the end of the rope. He slid down the rope until he was near the end, then he swung out a little and let loose as he swung back in. He dropped with both feet firmly on the ledge and both hands braced against the sides of the window.

His knees, bent slightly forward, were perilously close to the invisible force field.

Keeping one hand against the side of the window, he removed his shirt, wrapped a hand in it and then took a knife out. Slowly he moved the knife in the shirt-wrapped hand forward. His head was turned away and his eyes were shut. The force field, activated by the knife, would burn it, and the energy would probably lash out and burn the cloth and the hand beneath. The energy might even hurl the knife away with such violence that it would jerk his arm and him along with it on out the window.

He did have hopes, however, that the field would not be on. This did not seem likely, since Wolff surely would have set all guards and traps before leaving—if he had time. And the Bellers certainly would have done so if Wolff had failed.

A light burned even through his shut eyelids. A flame licked at his face and his bare shoulders and ribs and legs. The knife bucked in his hand, but he kept it within range of the field even when the cloth smoldered and burst into flames and his hand felt as if it had been thrust in an oven.

Then he plunged on through the window and onto the floor. There was a two-second pause between recharge of the field after activation, and he had jumped to coincide with it, he hoped. That he was still alive, though hurt, was proof that he had timed himself correctly. The knife was a twist of red-hot metal on the floor. The shirt was charred off, and his hand was blackened and beginning to blister. At another time, he would have been concerned with this. Now, he had no truck with anything except major crippling injuries. Or with death.

At that moment, the rope fell by the window, its end smoking. The projector had burned through the door and burned off the rope. In a moment, the Bellers would be coming downstairs after him. As for poor Do Shuptarp, he had better look out for himself and fast. The big projector would undoubtedly be used on him first to clear him out of the way. If only he had sense enough to get up the staircase and away, he could cause the Bellers to split their forces.

Kickaha looked out the doorway, saw no one, and fled down the corridor. On coming to the foot of the staircase, he looked upward before crossing in front of it. No Bellers were in sight yet. He ran on down the hall and then down the unusually long staircase and on across the corridor and past the hall of retropsychical mirrors. He had passed several elevators but did not enter them because they might be booby-trapped or at least have monitoring devices. His goal was a room which contained a secret gate he had not wished to use before this. Nor would he use it now unless he was forced to do so. But he wanted to be near it in case he was cornered.

In the room, he disassembled a chair that looked solid and pulled out a crescent from a recess under the seat.

Another crescent came from under the base of a thick pedestal for a statue. Both, though they looked as if each weighed half a ton, were light and easy to move. He stuck the two crescents into the back of his belt and tightened the belt to hold them. They were awkward but were insurance, worth the inconvenience.

There were thousands of such hidden gate-halves all over the palace and other thousands unmarked, in open places. The latter could be used by anybody, but the user would not know what waited for him at the other end of the passage. Even Wolff could not remember where all were hidden or the destinations of all the unconcealed ones. He had them all listed in a code-recorder but the recorder was itself disguised and in the control room.

Kickaha had run fast and gone far but not swiftly enough. A Beller appeared at the far end of the corridor as he stepped out of the room. Another looked around the corner of the corridor at the opposite end. They must have caught sight of him as he ran and had come this way with the hope of catching him. One at least had been intelligent enough to run on past where he was and come down the staircase to intercept him.

Kickaha retreated, deactivated the force field, and looked out the window. There was a ledge about fifty feet below, but he had nothing with which to lower himself. And he did not want to test another field unless he absolutely had to do so. He went back to the door and stuck the beamer out without putting his head out first, and fired in both directions. There were yells, but they were so far away that he was sure he had not hit anyone. The door of the room across from his was closed. He could dash across the hall and into it on the chance that it might offer a better route of escape. But if the door was locked, and it could easily be, then he would be exposed to fire from both sides, and they would have a better chance to catch him during the recrossing.

It was too late for regrets now. If he had not stopped to get the gate, he could have still been ahead of them. Again he was cornered, and though he had a way out, he did not want to use it. Getting back into the palace would be far more difficult a second time. And Do Shuptarp would be left on his own. Kickaha felt as if he were deserting him, but he could not help it.

He put the two crescents together to form a circle. He straightened up just as a grenade struck the inside of the doorway and ricocheted inside the room. It rolled about five feet and stopped, spinning on its axis. It was about thirty feet from him, which meant that he was out of range of the neutrons. But there would be others tossed in, the two he had left behind, and perhaps the Bellers had more. In any event, they would be bringing up the big projector. No use putting off the inevitable until it was too late to do even that.

# XXII

HE STEPPED into the gate. And he was in the temple-chamber of Talanac. Anana and the Red Beards and a number of Tishquetmoac were there. They were standing to one side and talking. They saw him and jumped or yelled or just looked startled. He started to step forward and then they were gone. The sky was starless, but a small glowing object raced across the sky from west to east and a slower one plodded along to the west. The leaning Tower of Pisa mass of the planet hung bright in the heavens. At a distance, the marble buildings of Korad gleamed whitely in the planet-light. A hundred yards away, a platoon of Drachelander soldiers were becoming aware that someone had appeared in the gate. And over a hill a dark object was rising. The Beller aircraft.

Then all was gone. He was in a cave about ten feet across and eight feet high. The sun shone brightly against the entrance. A giant, crazily angled tree with huge azure hexagram-shaped leaves stood in the distance. Beyond it were some scarlet bushes and green vines that rose seemingly without support, like a rope rising into the air at the music of a Hindu sorcerer. Beyond those were a thin blue line and a white thread and a thin black line. The sea, surf, and a black sand beach.

He had been here several times before. This was one of the gates he used to get to the lowest level, the Garden level, on his "vacations."

Though numbed, he knew that he had been caught in a resonant circuit. Somewhere, somebody had set up a device which would trap a person who stepped into any of the gates in the circuit. The caught one could not step out because the activation time was too short. That is, he could but he would be cut in half, one part left behind, the other gated on to the next circle.

The cave disappeared, and he was on top of a high narrow peak set among other peaks. Far to one side, visible through a pass, was what looked like the Great Plains. Certainly, that must be an immense herd of buffalo which covered the brown-green prairie like a black sea. A hawk soared by, screaming at him. It had an emerald-green head and spiraling feathers down its legs. As far as he knew, this hawk was confined to the Amerind level.

Then that was gone, and he was in a cave again. This was larger than the Garden cave and darker. There were wires clipped to the crescents of the gate; these ran across the dirt floor and behind a huge boulder about twenty feet away. Somewhere, an alarm was ringing. There was a cabinet with open doors by the far wall. The shelves contained weapons and devices of various kinds. He recognized this cave and also knew that here must be where the reasonance originated. But the trapper was not in sight, though he soon would be, if he were within earshot of the alarms.

Then that was gone, and he was in a chamber of stone slabs which were leaning in one direction as if they had been pushed by a giant hand, and part of the roof was fallen in. The sky was a bright green. The monolith of which he could see part was thin and black and soaring, so he knew by this that he was in an Atlantean chamber and that the shaft of stone was that which supported the palace of the Lord, a hundred thousand feet up.

Then that was gone, and he was where he had started his hopscotch willy-nilly journey. He was standing in the crescents in the room in the palace. Two Bellers were goggling at him, and then they were raising their beamers. He shot first, because he expected to have to use his weapon, bringing the ray across the chests of both.

Thirty-four down. Sixteen to go.

That was gone. Anana and the Thyuda were standing by the gate now. He shouted to her, "Resonant circuit! Trapped!" and he was back on the moon. The aircraft was a little closer now, coming down the hillside. Probably the occupants had not seen him yet, but they would on the next go-around or the one after that. And all they had to do then was a keep a ray across the gate, and he would be cut down as soon as he appeared.

The Drachelander soldiers were running toward him now; several were standing still but were winding up the wires of their crossbows. Kickaha, not wishing to attract the attention of the Bellers in the craft, refrained from discouraging the soldiers with his beamer.

Followed the Garden cave. And then he was upon the top of the peak in the Amerind level and very startled because the hawk flew into the area of the gate just as he appeared. The hawk was as startled as he. It screamed and landed on his chest and sank its talons in. Kickaha placed one hand before his face to protect it, felt agony as the hawk's beak sank into the hand which was burned, and he shoved outward. The hawk was torn loose by the push, but it took gobbets of flesh of chest and hand with it. It was propelled out of the circle but was not cut in half. The feathers of one wing-tip were sheared off, and that was all. Its movement coincided with the border of the field as the gate action commenced. And it passed over the border in the cave on the Dracheland level, and into the chamber itself.

It was unplanned split-second timing.

The enormously fat man who had just entered the cave was holding a dead, half-charred rabbit in one hand and a beamer in the other. He had expected a man or woman to appear though he could not, of course, know just when. But he had not expected a shrieking fury of talons and beak in his face.

Kickaha got a chance to see Judubra drop the rabbit and beamer and throw his hands up in front of his face. Then he was in the ruins of the Atlantean chamber. He squatted down and leaped upward as high and as straight as he could so no part of him would be outside the limits of the circle. He was at the height of his leap, with his legs pulled up, when he appeared in the palace room. His leap, designed to take him above a ray which might be shot across the circle to cut him in half, was unnecessary. The two Bellers lay on the floor, blackened, their clothes burned off. The odor of deeply burned flesh choked the room. He did not know what had happened, but the next time around, there should be Bellers in this room. They would not, he hoped, know any more than he did about what was happening. They would be mystified, but they would have to be stupid not to know that the killer had popped back into the gate and then popped out again. They would be waiting.

He was in the gate of the temple in Talanac. Anana was gone. The priest, Withrus, shouted at him, "She jumped in! She's caught, too, and she . . ."

He was on the moon. The craft was closer but had not increased its speed. And then a beam of light shot out from its nose and centered full on him. The Bellers in the craft had suddenly noticed the excitement of the troops running toward the gate and the crossbowmen aiming at it. They had turned on the light to find out the cause of the uproar.

There was a twang as the crossbowmen released their darts. And he was in the cave on the Garden level. Next stop, the little flat area on top of the peak. He looked down at his chest, which was dripping blood, and at his hand, which was also bloody. He hurt but not as much as he would later. He was still numb to lesser pains; the big pain was his situation and the inevitable end. Either the fat man in the cave would get him or the Bellers would. The fat man, after ridding himself of the hawk, could hide behind the boulder and beam him as he appeared. Of course, there was the hope that the fat man wanted to capture him.

He was in the cave. The hawk and the fat man lay dead, blackened, and the odor of fried feathers and flesh jammed his nostrils. There was only one explanation: Anana, riding ahead of him in the circuit, had beamed both of them. The fat man must still have been struggling with the hawk and so Anana had caught him.

If he had doubted that she loved him, he now had proof that she did—she had been willing to sacrifice her life in an effort to save him. She had done so with almost no thought; there had been very little time for her to see what was happening, but she had done it quickly and even more quickly she had hurled herself into the gate. She must have known that only if she went through exactly after activation would she get through unsevered. And she had no way of telling the exact moment to jump; she had seen him appear and disappear and then taken the chance.

She loved him for sure, he thought.

And if she could get in without being hurt, then he could get out.

The Atlantean ruins materialized like a gigantic pop-up, and he leaped outward. He landed on the floor of the room in the palace, but not untouched. His heel hurt as if a rat had gashed it. A sliver of skin at the edge of the heel had been taken off by the deactivating field.

Then something appeared. Anana. She said, "Objects! Throw them in . . ." and was gone.

He did not have to stop to think what she meant because he had hoped before that she would take these means to stop the resonant circuit. Aside from turning off the activating device, the only way to stop the circuit was to put objects with enough mass into an empty gate. Eventually, when all the gates were occupied, the ciruit would stop.

The obvious method of separating the crescents of a gate would not work in this case. A resonant circuit set up a magnetic attraction between the crescents of the gates that could not be broken except by some devices in the palace. And these would be locked up in the armory.

Keeping his eye on the door, and with the beamer ready, he dragged the body of a Beller by one hand to the crescent. He was counting the seconds in an effort to figure the approximate time when she would next appear here. And while he was counting, he saw out of the side of his eye, five objects come into being in the gates and go out of being. There was a barrel, the torso of a Drachelander soldier severed at the belly, half a large silver coffer with jewels spilling out of it, a large statue of jade, and the headless, legless, almost wingless body of a green eagle.

He was in a frenzy of anxiety. The Thyuda in Talanac must be obeying her orders, given just before she leaped into the gate. They were throwing objects into the gate as fast as possible. But the circuit might stop now when she was on the moon, and if it did, she would assuredly be caught or killed.

And then as he was about to topple the body of the Beller into the gate, Anana appeared. And she did not vanish again.

Kickaha was so delighted that he almost forgot to watch the doorway: "Luck's holding out!" he cried and then, realizing that he might be heard outside the room, said softly, "The chances for the circuit stopping while you were here were almost nothing! I . . ."

"It wasn't chance," she said. She stepped out of the gate and put her arms around him and kissed him. He would have been delighted at any other time. Now he said, "Later, Anana. The Bellers!"

She stepped away and said, "Nimstowl will be here in a second. Don't shoot."

The little man was there all of a sudden. He held

a beamer in one hand and a beamer in his belt. He also wore a knife and carried a rope coiled around one shoulder. Kickaha had turned his beamer away from the door and held it on Nimstowl. The Lord said, "No need for that. I'm your ally."

"Until . . . ?" Kickaha said.

"All I want to do is to get back to my own world," Nimstowl said. "I've had more than enough of this killing and almost being killed. In the name of Shambarimen, isn't one world enough for one man?"

Kickaha did not believe him, but he decided that Nimstowl could be trusted until the last of the Bellers was dead. He said, "I don't know what's going on out there. I had expected an attack, but it would have been launched before now. They had a large beamer out there; they could have shot it in here by now and cooked us out."

He asked Anana what had happened, though he could guess part of it. She replied that Nimstowl had come into the cave to find his partner dead, caught by the one he had trapped. Nimstowl had decided that he was tired of hiding out in this cave. He wanted a chance to get back to his own world and, of course, as every Lord should, to wipe out the Bellers. He had turned the resonating device off when Anana had appeared again. It had taken only a few seconds after that to set the resonator so it would deliver two people, at safe intervals, into the palace where Anana had seen Kickaha.

He said, "What do you mean? I had to jump out! I got out but lost the skin off my heel."

"Of course, you had no way of knowing," she said. "But if you had not jumped, you could have stepped out quite safely a moment later."

"Anyway, you came after me," he said. "That's what counts."

She was looking at him with concern. He was burned and bleeding, still dripping blood on the floor. But she said nothing. There was nothing to do for him until they found some aid. And that could be close enough, if they could get out of this room.

Somebody had to stick his head out of the room. Nimstowl wasn't going to volunteer and Kickaha did not want Anana to do it. So he looked out. Instead of the beam he expected, he saw a deserted corridor. He motioned for them to come after him and led the way to a room about a quarter of a mile down the corridor. Here he sterilized his wounds and burns, put pseudoflesh over them, and drank potions to unshock him and to accelerate blood replenishment. They also ate and drank while they discussed what to do.

There wasn't much to talk about. The only thing to do was to explore until they found out what was going on.

# XXIII

NOT UNTIL they came to the great staircase which led up to the floor of the control room did they find anything. There was a dead Beller, his legs almost entirely burned off. And behind a charred divan lay another Beller. This one was burned on the side, but the degree of burn indicated that the beam's energy had been partially absorbed before striking him. He was still alive.

Kickaha approached him cautiously and, after making sure he wasn't playing possum, Kickaha knelt down by him. He intended to use rough methods to bring him to consciousness so he could question him. But the Beller opened his eyes when his head was raised.

"Luvah!" Anana cried. "It's Luvah! My brother! One of my brothers! But what's he doing here? How. . . ?"

She was holding an object which she must have picked up from behind the divan or some other piece of furniture. It was about two and a half feet long, was of some silvery material, and was curved and shaped much like the horn of an African buffalo. It did flare out widely at the mouth, however, and the tip was fitted with a mouthpiece of some soft golden material. Seven little buttons sat on top of the horn in a row.

He recognized the Horn of Shambarimen. Hope lifted him to his feet with a surge. He said, "Wolff is back!"

"Wolff?" Anana said. "Oh, Jadawin! Yes, perhaps. But what is Luvah doing here?"

Luvah had a face that, under normal circumstances, would have been appealing. He was a Lord, but he could easily have passed for a certain type of Irishman with his snub nose and broad upper lip and freckles and pale blue eyes.

Kickaha said, "You talk to him. Maybe he'll . . ."

She got to her knees by Luvah and spoke to him. He seemed to recognize her, but his expression could have meant anything. She said, "He may not remember me in his condition. Or he may be frightened. He could think I'm going to kill him. I am a Lord, remember."

Kickaha ran down the hall and into a room where he could get water. He brought a pitcher of it back and Luvah drank eagerly. Luvah then whispered his story to Anana. She rose a few minutes later and said, "He was caught in a trap set by Urizen, our father. Or so he thought at the time, though actually it was Vala, our sister. He and Jadawin—Wolff—became friends. Wolff and his woman Chryseis were trapped with others, another brother and some cousins. He says it's too long a story to tell now.* But only Luvah and Wolff and Chryseis survived. They returned by using the

**The Gates of Creation,* Philip José Farmer, ACE.

Horn; it can match the resonance of any gate, you know, unless that gate is set for intermittent resonance at random.

"They were gated back into a secret compartment of the control room. Wolff then took a look into the control room via a monitor. No one was in it. He tapped in on other videos and saw a number of dead men and taloses. Of course, he didn't know that the men were Black Bellers, at first; then he saw the caskets. He still didn't get the connection—after all, it's been, what, ten thousand years? But he gated into the control room with Chryseis. Just to have additional insurance, he gated Luvah into a room on a lower floor. If somebody attacked them in the control room, Luvah could slip up behind them."

"Wolff's cagey," said Kickaha. He had wondered why Wolff didn't see the live Bellers, but remembered that the palace was so huge that Wolff could have spent days looking into every room. He was probably so eager to get some rest after his undoubtedly harrowing adventures and so glad to be home that he had rushed things somewhat. Besides, the control room and the surrounding area were unoccupied.

"Luvah said he came up the staircase and was going to enter the control room to tell Wolff all was clear. At that very moment, two men appeared in an especially big gate that had been set up by the dead men. By the Bellers, of course. There were pieces of a diassembled craft with them and a big projector."

"Von Turbat and von Swindebarn!" Kickaha said.

"It must have been," Anana said. "They knew

something was wrong, what with your appearance and disappearance in the gate on the moon and then mine. They gave up their search, and—''

"Tell me the rest while I'm carrying Luvah,'' he said. "We'll get him to a room where we can treat his burns.''

With Nimstowl covering their rear and Anana their front, he lugged the unconscious Lord to the room where he had treated himself a short while ago. Here he applied antishock medicines, blood replenishers, and pseudoflesh to Luvah.

Anana meanwhile finished Luvah's story. The two chief Bellers, it seemed, had expected trouble and were ready. They fired their big projector and forced Wolff and Chryseis to take refuge among the many titanic consoles and machines. Luvah had dived for cover behind a console near the doorway. The two Bellers had kept up a covering fire while a number of troops came through. And with them was a creature that seemed strange to Luvah but Anana recognized the description as that of Podarge. From the glimpse Luvah got of her, she seemed to be unconscious. She was being carried by several soldiers.

"Podarge! But I thought she had used one of the gates in the cave to get off the moon,'' Kickaha said. "I wonder. . . . Do you suppose?''

Despite the seriousness of the situation, he couldn't help chuckling. One of the gates would have taken her to a cave in a mountain on the Atlantean level. There would have been six or seven gates there, all marked to indicate the level to which they would transport the user. But all lied, and only Kickaha, Wolff, and Chryseis knew the code. So she had used a crescent which would presumably take her to the Amerind level, where she would be comparatively close to her home.

But she found herself back on the moon, in the very same cave.

Why, then, were there only four crescents, when her return should have made the number five?

Podarge was crafty, too. She must have gated out something to leave only four crescents. And since Do Shuptarp had not mentioned finding great white ape cubs in the cave, she must have gated them out. Why didn't she try some of the other crescents? Perhaps because she was suspicious and thought that Kickaha had used the only good one. Who knows what motives that mad bird-woman had? In any event, she had elected to remain on the moon. And the Bellers may have been hunting her in the ruins of Korad when Kickaha saw them while he was in the resonant circuit.

Luvah had been forced out of the control room by the soldiers, some of whom had beamers. This surprised Kickaha. The Bellers must have been very desperate to give the Drachelanders these weapons.

So Luvah had had to retreat, but he had killed a number of his pursuers while doing so. Then he had been badly burned but even so had managed to burn down those left. Six of the killed were wearing caskets on their backs.

"Wolff! Chryseis!" Kickaha said. "We have to get up there right now! They may need us!"

Despite his frenzy, he managed to check himself and to proceed cautiously as they neared the control room. They passed charred bodies along the way, evidences of Luvah's good fight.

Kickaha led the others at a pace faster than caution demanded, but he felt that Wolff might be needing him at the moment. The path to the control room was marked with charred corpses and damage to the furniture and walls. The stink of crisped flesh became stronger the closer they got to their goal. He dreaded to enter the room. It would be tragic indeed, and heart-twisting, if Wolff and Chryseis survived so much only to be killed as they came home.

He steeled himself, but, when he ran crouching into the room, the vast place was as silent as a worm in a corpse. There were dead everywhere, including four more Black Bellers, but neither Wolff nor Chryseis were there.

Kickaha was relieved that they had escaped—but to where? A search revealed where they had taken a last stand. It was in a corner of the back wall and behind a huge bank of video monitors. The screens were shattered from the beamer rays, and the metal of the cabinet was cut or melted. Bodies lay here and there behind consoles—Drachelander troops caught by Wolff's or Chryseis' beams.

Von Turbat (Graumgrass) and von Swindebarn were dead, too. They lay by the big projector, which had continued to radiate until its power pack had run down. The wall it was aimed at had a twelve foot hole in its metal and a still-hot lava puddle at its base. Von Turbat had been cut almost in half; Von Swindebarn was fried from the hips up. Their caskets were still strapped to their backs.

"There's only one Beller unaccounted for," Kickaha said. He returned to the corner where

Wolff and Chryseis had fought. A large gray metal disc was attached to the metal floor here. It had to be a new gate which Wolff had placed here since Kickaha's last visit to the palace.

He said, "Anana, maybe we can find out where this gate goes to, if Wolff recorded it in his code book. He must have left a message for me, if he had time. But the Bellers may have destroyed it.

"First, we have to locate that one Beller. If he got out of here, gated back to your universe or Nimstowl's or Judubra's, then we have a real problem."

Anana said, "It's so frightening! Why don't the Lords quit fighting among themselves and unite to get rid of the Beller?"

She edged away. Her anxiety and near-panic at the tolling in her brain, generated by her nearness to the Bellers' caskets, was evident.

"I have to get out of here," she said. "Or at least some distance away."

"I'll look over the corpses again," he said. "You go—hold it! Where's Nimstowl?"

"He was here," she said. "I thought that . . . no, I don't know when he disappeared!"

Kichaha was irked because she had not been keeping her eye on the little Lord. But he did not comment, since nothing was to be gained by expressing anger. Besides, the recent events were enough to sidetrack anyone, and the tolling in her mind had distracted her.

She left the room in a hurry. He went through the room, checking every body, looking everywhere.

"Wolff and Chryseis sure gave a good account of themselves," he muttered. "They really banked their shots to get so many behind the consoles. In fact, they gave too good an account. I don't believe it."

And Podarge?

He went to the doorway, where Anana crouched on sentry duty.

"I can't figure it out," he said. "If Wolff killed all his attackers, a very unlikely thing, why did he and Chryseis have to gate on out? And how the hell did Wolff manage to beam the two Bellers when they should have fried him at the first shot with that projector? And where is Podarge? And the missing Beller?"

"Perhaps she gated out, too, during the fight," Anana said. "Or flew out of the control room."

"Yeah, and where is Nimstowl? Come on. Let's start looking."

Anana groaned. He did not blame her. Both were drained of energy, but they could not stop now. He urged her up and soon they were examining the bodies in the corridors outside the control room on the staircase. He verified that he had killed two Bellers with the spy-missiles. While they were looking at a burned man rayed during the fight with Luvah, they heard a moan.

Beamers ready, they approached an overturned bureau from two directions. They found Nimstowl behind the furniture, sitting with his back against the wall. He was holding his right side while blood dripped through his fingers. Near him lay a man with a casket strapped to his back.

This was the missing Beller. He had a knife up to the hilt in his belly.

Nimstowl said, "He had a beamer, but the charge must have been depleted. He tried to sneak up and kill me with a knife. Me! With a knife!"

Kickaha examined Nimstowl's wound. Though the blood was flowing freely, the wound wasn't deep. He helped the little Lord to his feet, then he made sure that Nimstowl had no weapons concealed on him. He half-carried him to the room where Luvah lay sleeping, put pseudoflesh on Nimstowl's wound and gave him some blood replenishers.

Nimstowl said, "He might have gotten me at that, he jumped at me so quickly. But this"—he held up a hand with a large ring just like Anana's—"warned me in time."

"All the Bellers are dead," Anana said.

"It's hard to believe!" he replied. "At last! And I killed the last one!"

Kickaha smiled at that but did not comment. He said, "All right, Nimstowl, on your feet. And don't try anything. I'm locking you up for a while."

Again, he frisked Nimstowl. The little Lord was indignant. He yelled, "Why are you doing this to me?"

"I don't believe in taking chances. I want to check you out. Come on. There's a room down the hall where I can lock you up until I'm sure about you."

Nimstowl protested all the way. Kickaha, before shutting the door on him, said, "What were you doing so far from the control room? You were supposed to be with us. You weren't running out on us, were you?"

"So what if I was?" Nimstowl said. "The fight was won, or at least I thought it was. I meant to get back to my universe before the bitch Anana tried to kill me, now that she didn't need me. I couldn't trust you to control her. Anyway, it's a good thing I did leave you. If I hadn't, that Beller might have gotten away or managed to ambush you."

"You may be right," Kickaha said. "But you stay here for a while, anyway." He shut the door and locked it by pressing a button on the wall.

# XXIV

AFTER THAT, he and Anana continued the long search. They could have cut down the room-to-room legwork if they had been able to use the video monitors in the control room, since many rooms and corridors could be seen through these. But Wolff had deactivated these when he left the palace, knowing that Kickaha was able to turn them on if he revisited the palace. The Bellers had not been able to locate the source of control, and they had not had time or enough hands to disassemble the control console and rewire it. Now Kickaha could not use them because the fight had put them out of commission.

They looked through hundreds of rooms and dozens of corridors and scores of staircases and yet had covered only a small part of the one building. And they had many wings to go.

They decided they had to get food and sleep. They checked in on Luvah, who was sleeping comfortably, and they ordered a meal from the kitchen. There were several taloses there, the only taloses not involved in the attack on the Bellers. These gated a meal through to the two. After eating, Kickaha decided to go up to the control room to make sure nothing important had happened. He had some hopes that Wolff might come back, though this did not seem likely. The chances were high that the gate was one-way unless the Horn of Shambarimen were used, and Luvah had had that.

They trudged back up the staircases, Kickaha did not dare use the elevators until he was certain they were not booby-trapped. Just before they went into the control room, he stopped.

"Did you hear something?"

She shook her head. He gestured to her to cover him and he leaped through the doorway and rolled onto the floor and up behind a control console. Listening, he lay there for a while. Presently, he heard a low moan. Silence followed. Then another moan. He snaked across the floor from console to console, following the sounds. He was surprised, though not shocked, when he found the Harpy, Podarge, slumped against a console. Her feathers were blackened and stinking; her legs were charred so deeply that some of the toes had fallen off. Her breasts were brown-red meat. A half-melted beamer lay near her, a talon clutched around its butt.

She had come into the room while he and Anana were gone, and somebody had beamed her. Still on his belly, he investigated and within a minute found the responsible person. This was the soldier, Do Shuptarp, whom he had supposed was slain by the Bellers. But, now that he thought back, he had not been able to identify any corpse as his. This was not unexpected, since many were too burned to be recognizable.

Do Shuptarp, then, had escaped the Bellers and probably fled to the upper stories. He had returned to find out what was happening. Podarge had also returned after her flight from the room during the battle between the Bellers and Wolff. And the two, who really had no cause for conflict, had fatally burned each other.

Kickaha spoke to the Teutoniac, who muttered something. Kickaha bent close to him. The words were almost unintelligible, but he caught some of them. They were not in German. They were in Lord-speech!

Kichaha retured to Podarge. Her eyes were open and dulling, as if layer upon layer of thin veils were slowly being laid over them. Kickaha said, "Podarge! What happened?"

The Harpy moaned and then said something, and Kickaha was startled again. She spoke, not in Mycenaean, but in Lord-speech!

And after that she died.

He called Anana in. While she stood guard, he tried to question Do Shuptarp. The Teutoniac was in deep shock and dying swiftly. But he seemed to recognize Kickaha for just a moment. Perhaps the lust to live surged up just enough for him to make a plea which would have saved him—if Kickaha had had mercy.

"My bell . . . over there . . . put it . . . my head . . . I'll be . . ."

His lips twitched; something gurgled in his throat. Kickaha said, "You took over Do Shuptarp, didn't you, instead of killing him? Who were you?"

"Ten thousand years," the Beller murmured. "And then . . . you."

The eyes became as if dust had sifted into the brain. The jaw dropped like a drawbridge to release the soul—if a Beller had a soul. And why not, if anyone did? The Bellers were deadly enemies, peculiarly horrible because of their method of possession. But in actuality they were no more vicious or deadly than any human enemy, and though possession seemed especially horrible, it was not so to the victim, whose mind was dead before the Beller moved into the body.

Kickaha said, "A third Beller usurped Do Shuptarp's brain. He must have taken off for the upper stories then, figuring that if his buddies didn't get me, he would later. He thought I'd accept him as Do Shuptarp.

"Now, there's Podarge. I would have said a Beller had transferred to her on the moon, but that couldn't be. There were only two Bellers, von Tubat and von Swindebarn, on the moon. And Luvah said he saw them gate into the control room. So the transference must have taken place after Wolff and Chryseis had gotten away. One of those two Bellers took over Podarge, but not until the two had rayed down the Drachelander troops with them to make it look as if everybody had been killed by Wolff and Chryseis.

"Then they switched to Pordarge and one soldier they must have spared for this purpose. And the Beller in that soldier was the one who jumped Nimstowl. So now von Turbat and von Swindebarn are dead, despite their trickery! And the Beller in Podarge's body was to pretend that she had given up the attempt to get me, I'll bet. She was to plead friendship, act as if she'd really repented. And when my guard was down, powie! It's real funny, you know. Neither the Podarge-Beller nor the Do Shuptarp-Beller knew the other was a Beller in disguise. So they killed each other!"

He whooped with laughter. But, suddenly, he became thoughtful.

"Wolff and Chryseis are marooned somewhere. Let's go to his library and look up the code book. If he's logged that gate, then we can know how to operate it and where they are."

They walked toward the door. Kickaha hung back a little because the sight of Podarge saddened him. She had Anana's face, and that alone was enough to make him downcast, because she looked like Anana dead. Moreover, the madness of the Harpy, the torment she had endured for 3,200 years, weighed him down. She could have been put into a woman's body again, if she had accepted Wolff's offer. But she was too deep in her madness; she wanted to suffer and also wanted to get a horrible revenge on the man who had placed her in the Harpy's body.

Anana stopped so suddenly that he almost bumped into her.

"That tolling!" she said. "It's started again!"

She screamed and at the same time brought her beamer up. Kickaha had already fired. He directed his ray perilously close to her, at the doorway, even before anyone appeared in it. It was on full-power now, raised from burning effect to cutting effect. It sliced off a piece of Nimstowl's left shoulder.

Then Nimstowl jumped back.

Kickaha ran to the doorway but did not go through.

"He's von Turbat or von Swindebarn!" Kickaha yelled. He was thinking furiously. One of the two chiefs had possessed Podarge; the other had switched to a soldier. Then they had burned their former bodies and left the control room, each to go his own way with the hopes of killing their enemies.

The one in the soldier's body had attacked Nimstowl. Perhaps he had actually wounded Nimstowl. He had, however, managed to switch to the Lord.

No, that could not be, since it required two Bellers to make a switch. One had to handle the bell-shape for the transfer of the other.

Then Podarge—rather, the Beller in her body—must have been with the one in the soldier's body. She must have performed the transference and then left. The Beller in Nimstowl's body had put a knife in the belly of the soldier, who must have been knocked out before the switch.

The change to Nimstowl might have worked, if Kickaha had not operated on his usual basis of suspicion. Somehow, the Nimstowl-Beller had gotten out of the locked room. With what? A small low-power beamer hidden in a body cavity?

The Nimstowl-Beller had come back hoping to catch Kickaha and Anana unaware. If he had been successful, he would have been able to fulfill the Beller's plans of conquest. But he had not been able to resist taking his bell with him and so Anana had detected its presence just in time.

Podarge may have been the one to help effect the transference for the soldier-Beller into Nimstowl. But if she were not the one, then there was an extra Beller to be identified, located, and killed.

First, the business of the Nimstowl-Beller.

Kickaha had waited long enough. If the Beller were running away, then he could have gotten far enough so that Kickaha could leave the control room safely. If the Beller were lying out in the corridor bleeding to death—or bled to death—then Kickaha could go into the corridor. If the

Beller were not too badly wounded, he might be waiting for Kickaha to come out.

Whatever the situation, Kickaha could not wait any longer.

He motioned to Anana to stand aside. He backed up a few paces, then ran forward and leaped through the doorway. He turned as he soared, his beamer already on, its ray flashing along the wall and digging a two inch deep trough in the marble, striking out blindly but ready to move down or outward to catch the Beller.

The Beller was crumpled against the base of the wall with blood pooling from around his shoulder. His beamer lay at his feet, his head was thrown back, and his jaw sagged. His skin was bluish.

Kickaha landed, shut the beamer off, and slowly approached the Beller. Convinced that he was harmless, Kickaha bent over him. Nimstowl looked at him with eyes in which the life was not yet withdrawn.

"We're a doomed people," the Beller croaked. "We had everything in our favor, and yet we've been defeated by one man."

"Who are you?" Kickaha said. "Graumgrass or the one calling himself von Swindebarn?"

"Graumgrass. The king of the Bellers. I was in von Turbat's body and then that soldier's."

"Who helped you transfer to Nimstowl—to this body?" Kickaha said.

The Beller looked surprised. "You don't know?" he said faintly. "Then there is still hope for us."

Anana unsnapped the casket from the Beller's harness. She opened it and, grimacing, removed the big black bell-shape. She said, "You may think you will die without telling us who that Beller is and what he is going to do. But you won't."

She said, "Kickaha, hold his head! I'm going to put the bell on it!"

Grumgrass tried to struggle but was too weak to do anything except writhe a little. Finally, he said, "What are you going to do?"

"Your mind contents will automatically be transferred to the bell," she said. "As you well know. This body will die, but we'll find you a healthy body. And we'll put your mind in it. And when we do, we'll torture you until you tell us what we wish to know."

Graumgrass said, "No! No!" and he tried again to get away. Kickaha held him easily while Anana placed the bell on his head. After a while, Graumgrass's eyes glazed, and death shook a castenet in his throat. Kickaha looked at the bottom of the bell as Anana held it up for his inspection. The two tiny needles were withdrawn into the case.

"I think his mind was taken in before the body died," he said. "But, Anana, I won't let you strip a man's brain just to put this thing in his body so we can get some information. No matter how important that information is."

"I know it," she said. "And I wouldn't do it, either. I've regained some of my lost humanity because of you. Furthermore, there aren't any living bodies available to use."

She paused. He said, "Don't look at me. I haven't the guts."

"I don't blame you," she said. "And I wouldn't want you to do it, anyway. I will do it."

"But . . . !" He stopped. It had to be done, and he supposed that if she had not volunteered, he would have done so, though very reluctantly. He felt a little shame that he was allowing her to be the subject, but not enough to make him insist that he do this. He had more than one share of courage; he would be the first to say so. But this act required more than he had at this moment or was likely to have, as long as someone else would act. The utter helplessness it would produce made a coward of him. He could not stand that feeling.

He said, "There are drugs here which can get the truth, or what the subject thinks is the truth, anyway. It won't be hard to get the facts out of you—out of the Beller, I mean, but do you really think this is necessary?"

He knew that it was. He just could not accept the idea of her submitting to the bell either.

"You know what a horror I have of the bell," she said. "But I'll put my mind into one and let one of those things into my body if it'll track down the last Beller, the last one, for once and all."

He wanted to protest that nothing was worth this, but he kept his mouth shut. It had to be done. And though he called himself a coward because he could not do it, and his flesh rippled with dread for her, he would allow her to use the bell.

Anana clung to him and kissed him fiercely before she submitted. She said, "I love you. I don't want to do this! It seems as if I'm putting myself in a grave, just when I could look forward to loving you."

"We could just make a search of the palace instead," he said. "We'd be bound to flush out the Beller."

"If he got away, we'd know who to look for," she said. "No. Go ahead! Do it! Quickly! I feel as if I'm dying now!"

She was lying on a divan. She closed her eyes while he fitted the bell over her head. He held her then while it did its work. Her breathing, which had been quick and shallow with anxiety, slowed and deepened after a while. Her eyes fluttered open. They looked as if the light in them had become transfixed in time, frozen in some weird polarity.

After waiting some extra minutes to make sure the bell was finished, he gently lifted it off her head. He placed it in a casket on the floor, after which he tied her hands and feet together and then strapped her down tightly. He set the bell containing the mind of Graumgrass on her head. When twenty minutes had passed, he was sure that the transference was complete. Her face worked; the eyes had become as wild as a trapped hawk's. The voice was the lovely voice of Anana but the inflections were different.

"I can tell that I am in a woman's body," she—it—said.

Kickaha nodded and then shot the drug into her arm. He waited sixty seconds before beginning to dredge the information he needed. It took less time to get the facts than it had for the drug to take effect.

The Lords had been mistaken about the exact number of missing Bellers. There had been fifty-one, not fifty, and the Bellers, of course, had not enlightened their enemies. The "extra" one was Thabuuz. He had been down in the palace biolabs most of the time, where he was engaged in creating new Bellers. When the alarm was raised about Kickaha, he had come up from the labs. He did not get a chance to do much, but he was able to help Graumgrass knock out Nimstowl and then transfer him.

Graumgrass, as the little Lord, was to make one

more attempt to kill the two remaining enemies of the Bellers. In case he did not succeed, Thabuuz was to gate to Earth with his bell and his knowledge. There, on Earth, that limbo among the universes, hidden in in the swarms of mankind, he was to make new Bellers for another attempt at conquest.

"What gate did he use?" Kickaha asked.

"The gate that Wolff and Chryseis used," Graumgrass-Anana said. "It leads to Earth."

"And how do you know it does?"

"We found the code book and cracked the code, and so found that the gate was to Earth. Thabuuz had orders to take it if an emergency required that he get out of the palace to a place where he could hide."

Kickaha was shocked, but, on reflection, he was pleased. Now he had two reasons to go to Earth. One, and the most vital, was to find Thabuuz and kill him before he got his project started. Two, he must find Wolff and Chryseis and tell them they could return home. That is, they could if they wished. Undoubtedly, Wolff would want to help him and Anana hunt down the Beller.

He replaced the bell on Anana's head. In fifteen minutes, the withdrawal of Graumgrass' mind into the bell was completed. Then he put the bell containing Anana's mind on her head. In about twenty minutes, she opened her eyes and cried out his name. She wept for a while as she held him. Being in the bell, she said, was as if her brain had been cut out of her head and placed in a dark void. She kept thinking that something might happen to Kickaha and then she would be locked up forever in that bell. She knew she would go mad, and the idea of being insane forever made her even more frenzied.

Kickaha comforted her, and when she seemed to be calmed, he told her what he had learned. Anana said they must go to Earth. But first, they should dispose of Graumgrass.

"That'll be easy," he said. "I'll embed the bell in a plastic cube and put it in the museum. Later, when I have time—that is, when I come back from Earth—I'll gate him to Talanac. He can be discharged into a condemned criminal and then killed. Meantime, let's get ready for Earth."

He checked the code book for information that the Beller had not given him. The gate transmitted to an ancient gate in southern California, the exact area unspecified. Kickaha said, "I've had some twinges of nostalgia for Earth now and then, but I got over them. This is my world, this world of tiers, of green skies and fabled beasts. Earth seems like a big gray nightmare to me when I think about having to live there permanently. But still, I get just a little homesick now and then."

He paused and then said, "We may be there for some time. We'll need money. I wonder if Wolff has some stored somewhere?"

The memory bank of an underground machine told him where to locate a storage room of terrestrial currency. Kickaha returned from the room with a peculiar grin and a bag in his hand. He dumped the contents on the table. "Lots of U.S. dollar bills," he said. "Many hundred dollar bills and a dozen thousand dollar bills. But the latest was issued in 1875!"

He laughed and said, "We'll take it along, anyway. We might be able to sell it to collectors. And we'll take along some jewels, too."

He set the machines to turn out clothes for himself and Anana. They were designed as he remembered the latest American styles circa 1945. "They'll do until we can buy some new."

While they were getting ready, they moved Luvah to a bigger and more comfortable room and assigned the kitchen taloses to look after him. Kickaha left Anana to talk to her brother while he busied himself collecting the necessities for the Earth trip. He got some medicines, drugs, beamers, charges for the beamers, a throwing knife, and a little stiletto for her with poison in the hollow hilt. The Horn of Shambarimen was in a case.

He carried the case into the room where the two were. "I look like a musician," he said. "I ought to get a haircut as soon as I get a chance after we get there. My hair's so long I look like Tarzan—I don't want to attract attention. Oh, yes, you might as well start calling me Paul from now on. Kickaha is out. It's Paul J. Finnegan again."

They made their farewell with Luvah, who said that he would be the palace guardian while they were gone. He would make sure that the taloses put all the bodies in the incinerators, and he would set the defenses of the palace for marauding Lords. He was ecstatic that Anana had been reunited with him, even if only briefly. He was not, it was obvious, the customary Lord.

Despite which, once they were out of his room, Kickaha said, "Did you talk about old times, as I told you?"

"Yes," she said, "and there were many things he just could not remember."

Kickaha stopped and said, "You think. . . ?"

She shook her head and laughed. "No. There

were also many things he did remember, things which a Beller could not possibly know. And he reminded me of some things I had forgotten. He is my brother all the way through; he is not a Beller, as you suspected, my suspicious lover."

He grinned and said, "You thought of the idea the same time as myself, remember?"

He kissed her. Just before they stepped onto the gate, which would be activated by a code-sentence, he said, "You speak English?"

"I spent most of my three years on Earth in Paris and London," she answered. "But I've forgotten all my French and English."

"You'll pick it up again. Meanwhile, let me do the talking."

He paused, as if he hated to begin the journey.

"One thing about going to Earth. We have to track down that Beller. But we won't have to worry about running foul of any Lords."

Anana looked surprised.

"Didn't Wolff tell you? Red Orc is the secret Lord of Earth!"

130